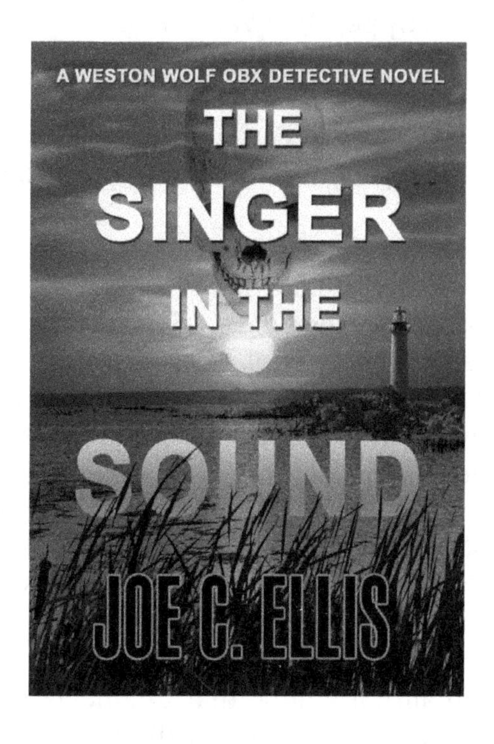

The Singer in the Sound

A Weston Wolf Outer Banks Detective Novel

A novel by

Joe C. Ellis

Weston Wolf- Outer Banks Detective Series

Upper Ohio Valley Books
Joe C. Ellis
71299 Skyview Drive
Martins Ferry, Ohio 43935
Email: **JoeCEllisNovels@comcast.net**

PUBLISHER'S NOTE

Although this novel, *The Singer in the Sound*, is set in actual locations on the Outer Banks of North Carolina, it is a work of fiction. The characters' names are the products of the author's imagination. Any resemblance of these characters to real people is entirely coincidental. Many of the places mentioned in the novel—the Island Bookstore in Corolla, the Whalehead Club in Corolla; the Jolly Rodger Restaurant in Kill Devil Hills, the Currituck Beach Lighthouse, the Bodie Island Lighthouse and other places mentioned in the novel—are real locations. However, their involvement in the plot of the story is purely fictional. It is the author's hope that this novel generates great interest in this wonderful regions of the U.S.A., and, as a result, many people will plan a vacation at these locations and experience the beauty of these settings firsthand.

CATALOGING INFORMATION
Ellis, Joe C., 1956-
The Singer in the Sound
A Weston Wolf Outer Banks Detective Novel
by Joe C. Ellis
ISBN 978-0-9796655-5-4
1.Outer Banks—Fiction. 2. Nags Head—Fiction
3. Mystery—Fiction 4. Suspense—Fiction
5. Kill Devil Hills—Fiction 6. , Kitty Hawk--Fiction
7. Noir Detective—Fiction 8. Detective—Fiction

Books by Joe C. Ellis
Click on the links below to go to the Amazon Kindle page.

Weston Wolf Outer Banks Detective Series

These are stand-alone novels and can be read in any order.

Book 1 – Roanoke Island Murders

Book 2 – The Singer in the Sound

Book 3 – Kitty Hawk Confidential (August 2021)

Outer Banks Murder Series

These are stand-alone novels and can be read in any order.

The Healing Place (Prequel to Murder at Whalehead)
Book 1 – Murder at Whalehead
Book 2 – Murder at Hatteras
Book 3 – Murder on the Outer Banks
Book 4 – Murder at Ocracoke
Book 5 – The Treasure of Portstmouth Island
Outer Banks Murder Series 5-Book Set

OUTER BANKS MURDER SERIES by Joe C. Ellis

Prequel - The Healing Place

Murder at Whalehead

Murder at Hatteras

Murder on the Outer Banks

Murder at Ocracoke

The Treasure of Portsmouth Island

The Singer in the Sound
A Weston Wolf Outer Banks Detective Novel
Joe C. Ellis

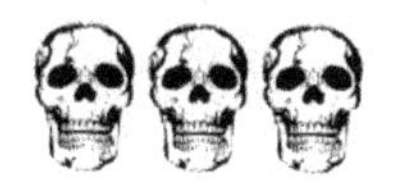

Chapter 1

The sea cast its spell. Weston Wolf often found himself under its trance. In the mid-morning sunshine, he stood on his back deck with a cup of coffee and stared at the horizon. The waves rhythmically pounded the shore, the rush and rumble of the water a familiar and soothing refrain. The minutes slipped by without cognition or memory. He transfixed his eyes on the line where the sky touched the sea. The view absorbed him like a Rothko painting. *Calm and stability.*

He needed calm and stability in his line of work. Just this morning a father called about his missing daughter. She'd been gone for ten days, and the police had no idea what happened to her. About noon he and his partner would head up to Corolla to talk to the man. In all likelihood she ran away with a boyfriend and would show up sooner or later. They would take the case and do their best to find her, hopefully, still breathing.

For now, though, he submitted to the sea's therapy. No shrink could match its mastery. Living on the ocean's edge offered advantages to people who had to deal with the world's ugliness day after day. Whether calm and tranquil or rough and raging, the sea was always beautiful.

Wolf caught a glimpse of a person several hundred yards out beyond the breakers. He leaned on the rail and focused. The person swam toward shore. *Is that a woman?* She sank into the depths. Wolf blinked several times to clear his vision. No sign of anyone on the surface. *Did a riptide get her? Am I seeing things? Maybe it was a dolphin.* A minute passed, and panic pulsated deep inside. A head bobbed. She didn't appear to be struggling, just treading water. Now she was floating on her back. Her body flipped over and entered the water, her calves and tips of her toes disappearing. *Gone again. Is she diving down to the seabed?* Two minutes passed, and the panic triggered again. He set his cup on the railing, rushed toward the steps and pulled off his orange t-shirt. Stopping at the top of the steps, he glanced out to sea one more time. She broke the surface.

He faced the horizon, breathing deeply to slow his heartrate. *Who is that woman? Aquagirl?* The September sun felt warm on his bare chest as he walked back to the middle of the deck and leaned on the railing. Now she was swimming toward shore again. She definitely knew how to swim. It didn't take long for her to get to the breakers. She body surfed a wave into the shallows and stood. She held a large white object in her hands and examined it as the waves splashed around her calves. From sixty yards away, Wolf noticed she had an exquisite body, long, lean and well-shaped in all the right places. Her long ash blonde hair hung over her face. He wondered if her face matched her body.

She high stepped through the water to shore, ascended the bank, turned and faced the sea. She wore a black bikini, a more modest one than Wolf preferred. He wanted to get a better look at her. He guessed she was in her early thirties and vacationing with her husband and two kids. *That would be my luck.* She bent over, placed the object on the sand, picked up a white robe and slipped into it. Then she reached behind and pulled a hood over her head. *Damn. That'll make it harder to see her face.* She picked up the object, turned and walked in his direction. Wolf's heartrate ramped up again. Halfway across the stretch of sand she angled to the right toward the rental cottage next to his beach bungalow.

As she neared, Wolf could see the object more clearly—a large seashell. Paying no attention to him, she mounted the steps to the small deck on the back of the cottage. She pulled back the hood, lifted the shell to her ear and listened.

"Hear anything?" Wolf called.

She turned slightly in his direction and lowered the shell, her long ashen hair matted against her face. "Of course. Every shell has a story to tell."

"What's that one saying?"

"It's telling me that you're a nosy neighbor."

Wolf laughed. "I'm just trying to be friendly."

She raised the shell to her ear again and nodded. "The shell says to mind your own business." She set the shell down on a small wooden table.

Wolf crossed the deck and leaned on the railing facing her. *Is she kidding around?* "I take offense to the shell's comment." He placed his hand on his hairy chest. "The shell really doesn't know me. When you disappeared under the water, I was about ready to dive in and rescue you."

"Oh really?"

Wolf raised his other hand which held the orange t-shirt. "This is proof. I took it off a few minutes ago, ready to spring into action, but then you resurfaced."

She crossed the deck to the railing which faced the ocean. The wind loosened the wet grip her hair held on her face, blowing the long strands across her shoulder. "I'm not on the waiting list for a white knight."

Wolf admired her profile. She had the Nordic-woman look—blonde hair, blue eyes, straight nose, full lips and slightly tanned. His guess at her age was accurate, the telltale lines around her mouth and eyes just beginning to show. But even without makeup she dazzled him. "I'm not applying for the job. I just stepped out on my deck to commune with the ocean, and there you were."

"I guess we have one thing in common."

"What's that?"

She continued to gaze at the sea. "We both like to commune with the ocean."

That's a step in the right direction. Wolf scoured his mind to come up with a good line. "They say the sea has no memory."

"Where did you come up with that one? Some quote from a movie?"

Wolf chuckled. "You guessed it—*The Shawshank Redemption*, one of my favorite flicks."

"I thought so." She smiled. "We have two things in common. That's one of my favorite movies, too."

Another step in the right direction. "Seriously, though, I come out here every morning to get a better perspective on the world and . . . myself."

She nodded. "I get lost in the sea."

"Lost?"

"A good lost, like when you get lost in a book or a hobby."

"I get what you mean. I like taking long walks at Jockey's Ridge State Park. On a hot day it's like walking across the desert. Trudging through the sand and heat can be smothering, but I appreciate what it does to me."

"What does it do to you?"

Wolf wished she would turn in his direction. He wanted to make eye contact. "It causes me to suffer."

"And you like to suffer?"

"Sure. Suffering is good for the soul."

She raked her fingers through her hair as the wind dried it, winnowing those ashen locks behind her. "Suffering should not be the goal."

"Oh yeah? What's the goal?"

"Finding meaning in the suffering."

"That's not an easy task."

"Not easy but necessary if you want to endure. What do you do for a living?"

"I'm a private detective."

She gave a quick snort. "That makes sense."

"You don't like detectives?"

"I don't like or dislike them. Your occupation explains your need to suffer."

"How so?"

"Yours is a job that demands immersion in the seamy and sordid swamps of this world: cheating spouses, child custody battles, investigating fraud, missing persons, that sort of thing."

Wolf took a deep breath and blew it out. "Yeah, you swatted the fly on that window. I'm investigating a missing persons case this afternoon."

"Uh huh." Her lips tightened, and the lines around her mouth deepened. "You've seen some ugly things in life. They've left an imprint on the canvas of your memory. Suffering helps to smudge them, turn them into softer shadows."

Her words struck a chord of concurrence with him. His memories were filled with fading shadows: abused children, treacherous conmen, the faces of dead victims and the hollow eyes of their loved ones. Maybe walking in the heat of the day across hot sand helped to soften the sharp edges. "How did you become such a sage?"

"I've done my share of suffering."

Wolf rubbed his chin. Her appeal was deepening. Her words carried weight. Unfortunately, she didn't seem too impressed with him. No time to give up, though. "Have your memories become shadows?"

"Some of them but not all."

"Why not all?"

"There are some things that suffering cannot smooth over. When I wake up every morning, I have to face myself in the mirror."

"And you don't like what you see?"

"No."

What in the world did she do? Cheat on her income taxes? Commit a murder? "What do you do for a living?"

"I'm in between jobs."

"I thought maybe you were a mermaid. I've never seen someone stay under water as long as you did."

A smile lit her face again. "Maybe I am. It took years of diving for shells to turn myself into a mermaid. I can hold my breath under water for three minutes. Do you know anything about mermaids?"

"I saw the movie *Splash*."

"That doesn't count."

"Enlighten me."

She slid her hands over her head, grasped the long trail of her hair, twisted it several times and drooped it across the front of her shoulder. It lay appealingly over her right breast. "The goddess Atargatis accidentally killed her lover. Out of shame, she turned herself into a mermaid. Confined to the sea, she caused storms, shipwrecks and drownings."

"If you're a mermaid, then you've come to the right place. The Outer Banks is known for its shipwrecks."

"Right now I'm focused on finding shells."

"Oh well . . . the shipwrecks and drownings can wait. Find another shell, and you'll have another story to tell."

She shook her head. "Keep your day job. You'll never make it as a poet."

"That's what my partner always tells me: 'Lay off the rhymes.' What did you do before you were a mermaid?"

"Believe it not, I was a singer and an aspiring actress."

"Why wouldn't I believe that? You're a very beautiful woman."

She laughed. "I'd never put you on the judges panel for the Miss America pageant."

"You're wrong about that. I think I'd make a great judge." *Alright, time to swing for the fences.* "Give me a chance to convince you. Let me take you out to dinner tonight."

She lowered her focus to her hands which were clasped on the deck railing. "Believe me, you don't want to be seen with me at one of these local restaurants where everybody knows you."

"Why not? Are you married?"

"Yes."

"Oh . . . I'm sorry. Sometimes I leap before I look."

"Being married isn't the reason." She raised her head and stared at the sea. "If I only had a brain, I would have never fallen in love with my husband. He and I have been separated for more than two years."

"Do you want to get back together with him?"

"No. "

"Well then, why not go out with me?"

"Because you truly have leapt before looking."

"What do you mean?"

She turned toward him. Pinkish and white scars scored the left side of her face. The skin lacked elasticity. Wrinkles and lumps created swirling dips and valleys. Her left lower eyelid sagged slightly, the tight skin pulling it downward.

He gasped and straightened.

She glared at him and stepped closer. "Make sure you get a good look before the next time you leap."

Chapter 2

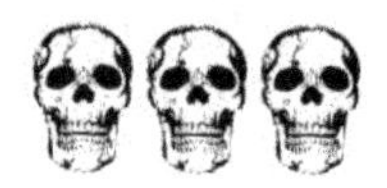

Wolf gazed in the bathroom mirror. *I'm not so perfect myself.* He drew his hand across his left cheek and jaw. He hadn't shaved for two days, and the stubble felt like sandpaper. He needed a haircut. His sandy brown hair never obeyed his wishes. It curled and flowed in whatever direction it wanted to go. The best he could do was comb it behind his ears and flatten it with his hands. Ten minutes later strands would pop out like springs from an old mattress. He didn't have time to trim his bushy eyebrows.

I've got nice eyes. I'll give myself that much credit. And my body's not bad. He didn't overeat that often, and his morning regimen of one hundred pushups and five minutes of leg lifts kept his thirty-seven-year-old frame in fair shape. He had been a decent defensive back in his day and battled the sands of time with stubborn resolve.

He entered his bedroom and sorted out his clothes for the day. He liked the new logo on his gray Polo shirt: *Wolf and Stallone Detective Agency*. The words *Wolf and Stallone* were centered in the lens of a magnifying glass with *Detective* and *Agency* on each side of the handle. His new partner, Angie Stallone, added a fresh face to the business. Although she was young and inexperienced, Wolf admired her dedication and spunk. Insightful and smart, she cut a facet into the investigation field that he lacked: the willingness to spend hours researching, reading and studying details that could make a difference in a case. Wolf had good instincts. Angie had a sharp mind. They made a great team.

He strapped on his shoulder holster, his Sig Sauer semi-automatic pistol snug against his side. The loose-fitting

Polo shirt did an adequate job of covering the gun. He decided to go with well-worn Levi's today. The man they were meeting, an old fisherman, lived near the Currituck Sound just north of the Whalehead Club. He figured an informal appearance would raise the comfort level with this guy.

Slipping into his loafers, he closed his eyes and envisioned the face of the blonde mermaid, wonderfully attractive and alarmingly repulsive at the same time. *What happened to her?* He felt embarrassed over his initial reaction. Somehow he had gathered himself and stood up to her confrontational posture. Did she view him as some smooth operator who only perceived beauty on the surface? He used to lean in that direction, but time had tempered his testosterone. At thirty-seven years old he wanted more from a relationship than physical appeal. He enjoyed talking with her and felt comfortable in her presence once the shock had worn off. In truth, he felt oddly attracted to her.

He sauntered down the hall and into the front office. Turning half of his little beach house into offices kept costs down. Angie Stallone sat at the desk gazing at the computer screen. She was a boyish looking girl, sleek and athletic. She had baby blonde hair recently cut in the undercut pixie style. She wore a gray Polo shirt that matched his and ragged jeans, the kind costing sixty bucks a pair with pre-worn patches and holes.

Wolf leaned over her shoulder. "What are you doing, Angel, cruising the internet for prom dresses?"

She gave him a perturbed frown. "When are we going to hire a receptionist?"

"Might be a while. It'll be hard to replace my former secretary. She was top notch."

"Thanks for the compliment, but don't expect me to do both jobs. I'm no longer your front office girl. I'm your partner."

"I know. Give me time. We'll find a replacement. What are you reading?"

"The articles from area newspapers on the missing girl."

"Anything interesting?"

"She's a real looker."

Wolf examined the picture on the screen. The girl appeared to be about eighteen years old with long golden-brown hair, the kind that flowed over her shoulders in loose curls. The photo looked like a high school yearbook picture. She had full lips, a pixie nose, dark eyes and thick but neatly trimmed burgundy eyebrows. She reminded him of Brooke Shields in her younger days. The name Jennifer Cobb was printed below the photo.

"I agree," Wolf said. "Let's hope she's still alive and lovely."

Angie nodded. "Says here she won a local *American Idol* contest and qualified for the regionals. Must have a good set of pipes."

"A good set of pipes? You've been watching those old film noir movies again, haven't you?"

Angie chuckled. "Yeah."

"She might be a favorite at the karaoke bars around here."

"That's something we could check out."

"Anything else in the papers worth noting?"

Angie scrolled down. "She worked at the Island Bookstore in Corolla. I'm guessing she's a creative person."

"Why do you say that?"

"Most people who work in bookstores love to read. Obviously, she's an excellent vocalist. I looked up her yearbook online. She went to Manteo High and belonged to the Drama Club, Chorus and Pep Band."

"I see," Wolf said. "The artsy-fartsy type, like you."

"Yeah," Angie chuckled. "I draw portraits like Picrappo and sing like a wounded wildebeest. You're more the artsy-fartsy type with your lame impromptu poems."

Wolf straightened, gazed at the ceiling and extended his arms. "My poetry is swell, and I sing like Adele, but we must be on our way, because it's almost noonday."

"Oh, jeeez!" Angie rolled backwards on the office chair. "Gimme a break, would ya." She stood, pushed Wolf out of the way and headed for the door. "Let's go."

* * *

Mile posts dotted the drive from Nags Head to Kitty Hawk. Wolf's agency on East Hunter Street in Nags Head was a few hundred yards north of Mile Post 19. The Outer Banks had been a hidden gem of a vacation destination since the 1950s, and this stretch along Highway 158 had been the popular place to get away from the weary world. Two lanes headed north and two headed south through the middle of Nags Head, Kill Devil Hills and Kitty Hawk. The highway was lined with plenty of regular stores, souvenir shops, motels, restaurants, miniature golf courses, shopping plazas, gas stations and tourist sites.

Nags Head's Jockey Ridge State Park drew crowds throughout the in-season months. It boasted the tallest sand dune system in the eastern United States. Kill Devil Hills heralded the Wright Brothers Memorial, a sixty-foot-tall granite monument atop a sacred hill commemorating the first powered flight back in December of 1903. Kitty Hawk got credit as the town of the Wright Brothers' first flight because Kill Devil Hills hadn't been established as a settlement until years later.

Driving his '69 Cougar through the three towns, Wolf mulled over his encounter with the blonde mermaid. Their conversation lingered, the words repeating in his mind. She had depth and discernment, unlike a lot of the women he dated. Was their relationship about to take flight? She never gave him an answer about his offer to take her out to dinner, and he didn't push for a response. *Why was I so startled? My reaction must have disappointed her. Wolf, you are such a sorry sonuvabitch. You didn't even ask for her name or introduce yourself.* He took a frustrated breath and blew it out the side of his mouth. *If she'd go out with me, I'd do better with a second chance. Somehow I'd get this relationship off the ground.*

He peeled off into the right lane to head north on Route 12 toward Duck. Traffic always backed up at this intersection where vacationers who just crossed over the Currituck Sound on the Wright Memorial Bridge could head north or south along the narrow strip of barrier islands. The northern end and the southern end of the Outer Banks were much different than the middle. The southern end offered long stretches of natural seashore with a few small towns like Rodanthe, Salvo, Waves and Avon sprinkled along the way. The rustic setting offered visitors a raw and natural flavor, an escape from the turbulent, depressing world.

The northern end bustled with new growth. Whenever Wolf drove north, he noticed a multitude of recent beach house construction and resort community development. All this flurry of sticks and stones that turned into beautiful homes popped up in the last thirty years. The tourist industry was booming here. Back in the eighties, the northern end was just as rustic as the southern end.

They had been sitting at the stoplight in traffic for a couple of minutes when Angie said, "You're awful quiet today. Got something on your mind?"

"The wheels are always turning up there, Angel."

"Yeah, the hamster's working overtime."

"A good gumshoe has an active thought life."

"Gumshoe?" she laughed. "You watch those old movies too."

"I've learned a few things while observing Sam Spade and Phillip Marlowe chase down the bad guys."

"Like how to get the girl? I bet you're thinking about a woman."

Geesh, that young sass-mouth knows me like an oft-repeated Viagra commercial. "You must think I have a one-track mind."

"Nailed it, didn't I?"

The traffic moved, and Wolf turned onto Route 12. "Okay, I confess. I was thinking about an unusual lady I had recently met."

"What's her name?"

"I don't know. I forgot to ask."

"She must have really thrown you off your game. Don't you always come away with a name and a number?"

"Not this time. Have you met our new neighbor?"

"Freyja?"

"Who?"

"Freyja Beck. She's renting the cottage next to the office."

"Yeah. That's the one. How do you know her?"

Angie unfolded her hands toward the dashboard. "Like any good neighbor, I introduced myself."

"Oh. That makes me an insensitive jackass, I guess."

"I can see why she flustered you. Once you got a good look at her, you lost it."

"I didn't go into shock or anything. I saw her from the sideview. She was gazing at the ocean. I wasn't expecting . . . you know . . ."

"Admit it. You were disappointed when you saw the scarred side of her face."

Wolf regripped the steering wheel as he negotiated an S curve. "Maybe a little, but once I regained my composure, I became more and more intrigued with her."

"Really?"

"We had a long talk. I even asked her out."

Angie chuckled. "I'm impressed."

"You must think I'm some kinda skin-deep Don Juan."

"The jury is still out on that judgment. Where're you taking her?"

"I'm not, since you asked."

"Ha! She turned you down."

"Noooo." Wolf cleared his throat. "She never got around to answering me. The topic changed."

"Denied! Did that make you feel dumb?"

"I told you the topic changed. There's a dummy in this car, alright."

"Who me? You told me when you hired me that you didn't hire stupid people?"

"Yeah. So what?"

"That leaves you. Case closed."

"You're another Sarah Silverman. Wait and see. I haven't given up on Miss Beck yet."

Angie sat quietly for a few moments and then reached and patted Wolf's forearm. "I hope you do go out with Freyja. I can tell she's a good person. If you had a heart, you'd fall in love with a lady like her."

"If I only had a heart."

"Do you want me to put in a good word for you?"

"Can I list you as a reference on my romance resume? That should tip the scales in my direction."

Angie grinned like a kid with a Magic 8-Ball. "Well, duh!"

* * *

The twenty-mile stretch from Southern Shores to Corolla offered nice views along a two-lane, newly paved road. After driving through the busy town of Duck, traffic thinned, and Wolf picked up the pace to fifty mph. They flew by the *Entering Currituck County* sign. To the left, dense shrub thickets grew about ten feet high, blocking the view of the wetlands and Currituck Sound. A long row of newly constructed, three-story beach houses rose up on the right.

Vacationers prized these ocean front rentals during the summer and fall months and paid top dollar for them.

They passed a Hampton Inn, one of the few chain hotels on the northern end of the Outer Banks. An occasional biker or runner appeared on the sidewalk to the right of the road along with young couples walking with their kids. The narrow barrier island had become a favorite family destination. That pleased Wolf. He preferred more laid-back surroundings to the commercialized South Carolina and Florida beaches which drew loads of college students to party and raise havoc during the spring and summer breaks.

Wolf slowed down to thirty-five mph as they entered the town of Corolla. The local boys in blue handed out tickets liberally to unsuspecting drivers who failed to notice the reduced speed signs. Back in the old days Corolla thrived as a fishing and hunting village. The redbrick Currituck Beach Lighthouse had loomed over the place since the 1870s, providing a light for ships in the gap between Bodie Island and Cape Henry to the north. Now everything in the area seemed to shine like a restored Model A Ford.

The old structures, the Whalehead Club and Light Keeper's House, beamed with new paint. The local historical society had raised funds to painstakingly restore these buildings to their original glory. They became tourist attractions along with the lighthouse and drew tons of visitors to the town. Exquisite beach homes, most of them rentals, lined the streets of the newly established communities all the way to the end of the road. And the road ended literally a mile north of town. To go any farther one needed a four-wheel-drive vehicle to manage the shifting sands along the beach all the way up to the Virginia state line.

As they passed the towering lighthouse, Wolf asked, "How close are we, Angel?"

"Not far. Mr. Cobb lives somewhere along Lost Lake Lane, about a half mile from here."

"When I was your age, I'd drive up here all the time to see the wild horses."

"That must have been decades ago."

"No so fast with your sass. More like fifteen years ago. I'm not that much older than you. Back in the nineties the horses wandered the neighborhoods. Unfortunately, they kept getting hit by cars because of the increased tourist traffic."

"So that's why they keep them fenced out beyond town."

"The price of progress. They still have plenty of room to roam. Sometimes I'd come up here and walk two miles along the beach and see nary a one."

Angie shook her head. "Would you please speak English. Sometimes you sound like Grandpa Jones sitting on the steps of the General Store."

"You need to learn to appreciate the colorful tapestry of my expressive dialect."

Angie raised her phone and studied the screen. "Lost Lake Lane is on the left about another hundred yards or so."

Wolf turned onto the sandy-gravel road. Scraggly weeds and bushes grew unconstrained on each side. They passed a graveyard of a dozen rusted cars and beat-up pickup trucks. The road narrowed to one lane and entered a tunnel of overhanging trees and thick underbrush. Branches scratched at the sides of the car, and the shadows deepened with only a few spots of sunlight breaking through and glowing in the darkness like forlorn spirits.

"Jeeez," Angie said. "This must be the underbelly of Corolla."

"Not the shiny, welcome-to-paradise appearance we're used to seeing on this end of the island."

Angie snorted. "Not at all."

They rounded a turn, and light streamed through a break in the trees. Up ahead in the clearing, a ramshackle house sat on the edge of a small lake. He pulled up next to an old Ford pickup and cut the engine. The truck was dark red, but Wolf couldn't tell if that was the actual color, or it had rusted that way. A red Ford Focus sat in the shade of live oak across the grass-and-dirt patched yard.

"This must be the place," Wolf said.

Moss grew on the roof, and a few of the bricks of the chimney were missing. The house sat on posts about three feet off the ground. Bare pine siding broke through in patches where gray paint peeled away from the surface. The front porch sagged in the middle, and someone had stacked cement blocks in a couple rows to form steps. Off to the side an old fishing boat rested on a broken-down trailer.

"I hate to admit this," Angie said, "but I'm glad you're with me."

"Yeah. This place is a little creepy."

The front door creaked open and a large man with a pot belly filled the entire doorframe. Wearing a dirty, white tank-top, too small for his bulk, he raised his arm and pointed a revolver at them.

"What are you doing on my property?" the man growled

Chapter 3

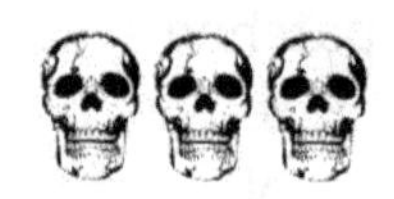

Wolf raised his hands. "Whoa!"

"Sir," Angie said, "you made an appointment to meet with us."

"Are you the detectives?"

"Yes sir. I'm Angie Stallone, and this is my partner, Weston Wolf."

He lowered the gun. "Sorry. I didn't think detectives would ride up in an old Cougar. I've been living on a ragged edge ever since my daughter disappeared."

Wolf spread his hands. "May we come in?"

The man nodded and stepped back from the door. He had a do-it-yourself buzzcut, the kind old guys give themselves with electric clippers purchased from Walmart. With small ears, a bulbous nose and large jowls covered with a three-day stubble of whiskers, he reminded Wolf of an old pro wrestler sent out to pasture.

They entered the darkened front room of the cabin. Almost everything was made of wood except for the stone fireplace on the far wall and a tattered oval rug that covered the middle of the floor. Two rocking chairs sat near the fireplace, and a beat-up leather lounge chair faced a floor model console television from the 1980s. Several framed photographs hung on the wood-planked wall above the television. One was a family photo of a thinner Mr. Cobb, his redheaded wife and young daughter. Wolf assumed the youngster was Jennifer. The picture to the right was definitely Jennifer, the same photograph Wolf had seen on the computer screen. The third photo showed Mr. Cobb standing on a dock next to his boat. Several men stood beside him hefting large tunas with both arms.

Mr. Cobb dragged a wooden armchair away from a rolltop desk and turned it toward the two rocking chairs. "Have a seat," he said and waved toward the rockers. Wolf angled the chairs in Mr. Cobb's direction, and he and Angie settled onto the seats, rocking slightly. Angie withdrew a small notepad and pen from her shoulder bag.

The old man gazed at them with red-rimmed eyes. "Thanks for coming. I haven't given up hope yet."

Wolf nodded. "How long has your daughter been missing, Mr. Cobb?"

"Ten days. The cops haven't found a clue. In the last three days they had nothing to report. They think she took off with some boy to get away from this place. I don't believe that for one minute."

"Why not?" Wolf asked.

"She didn't have a steady boyfriend, and they found her car in the Food Lion parking lot at the south end of town. She just bought that car two months ago with the money she made at the bookstore."

Angie thumbed over her shoulder. "Was that the red Ford Focus we saw out front?"

He nodded. "I had an extra set of keys, so I drove it home after the cops were done looking it over."

Angie glanced around the room and then refocused on the man. "What do you think, sir? Did she want to get away from here?"

He shrugged and gazed at an empty corner of the room. "I wish I knew. She didn't hate it here. We got along good. She had her singing and work and church. One morning she went to work and never came home."

"She works at the Island Bookstore in Corolla, correct?" Angie said.

"That's right. She loved her job. Been there about two years."

"Did anyone at the store have anything to say about her disappearance?"
Wolf asked.

"The cops interviewed the employees. As far as I know, they didn't have much to say."

Wolf leaned forward on the rocker. "We'll make sure we stop by and talk to them. You never know. We might be able to dig something up."

"I hope you do."

Angie cleared her throat. "From what I have gathered, Jennifer was an incredibly talented singer."

The old man bobbed his head slowly. "She sang like an angel. Almost made it to the big time on that TV show."

"American Idol?" Angie said.

"That's right."

Angie jotted some notes on a yellow pad and then glanced up. "Did she ever sing at the local karaoke bars?"

He rubbed the stubble on his chin. "She wasn't a drinker, but she did go to the bars to sing. Her friends persuaded her. I guess she was a favorite of the customers. They would even make requests. That's what her buddies told me, anyway."

Wolf said, "We'll get a list of all of her friends' names and try to interview them." You mentioned her church. Was she active in a local congregation?"

He bowed his head and blinked several times. "She belongs to the Methodist Church in Duck. Jennifer and her mom were very religious. I didn't go that often with them, maybe Christmas and Easter. They never missed a Sunday until . . . until . . ." His voice cracked, and eyes watered. "until . . . Dorothy passed away. Then Jenny went by herself."

"Was Dorothy your wife?" Angie asked.

A tear slipped down his rough cheek. "She died of pneumonia about a year ago last Christmas." He breathed haltingly and swallowed. "You've got to find Jenny," he sobbed. "She's the only person I got left in this world."

Angie reached into her shoulder bag and pulled out a tissue. "Here, Mr. Cobb."

He extended his thick arm, took the tissue and wiped his eyes and cheeks. Sniffling, he took a deep breath and steadied himself. "I'm sorry. I'm blubbering like a baby."

"We understand, sir," Wolf said, "and we'll do our best to find her." He gripped the arms of the rocking chair. "Did your daughter keep a diary or anything like that?"

He shook his head. "I don't think so." His eyes clouded over, and he sat oddly still for several seconds. "Wait a second now. I do remember seeing her writing something." He snapped his fingers and nodded. "That's right! I saw her writing in her Bible one morning not long ago."

"A lot of people make notes in their Bibles," Angie said.

"That's right." Mr. Cobb focused on a doorway to the right of the fireplace. It led down a hallway. "I walked past her room and saw her lying on her bed. From where I stood, I could see her writing something on the side of the page."

Wolf straightened. "Along the margin?"

"That's right. The Bible was spread open on the bed, and I could see it."

Angie tucked her notepad into her shoulder bag. "Do you mind if we take a look in her bedroom, Mr. Cobb?"

"Not at all. Follow me."

Pushing off the arms of the chair, he lifted his mass and rose. He lumbered toward the hallway and clicked on a light switch. An amber glow cut through the doorway into the darkness of the front room. Wolf and Angie followed him halfway down the hallway where he opened a door. He stepped aside and allowed them to enter first.

A pastel yellow coat of paint brightened the wood-paneled walls. The window to the left, adorned with flower-patterned curtains, flooded the room with light. A twin bed sat in the middle of the room neatly made with a colorful patched quilt. Wolf walked to the wall opposite the window and examined two posters taped there. One showed a mountain range with a rainbow hanging over it. The rainbow reflected in the lake below with the words: *Little girls who dream big become women with vision*. The other one displayed a child with a long shadow standing in a schoolyard. The caption on the bottom stated: *Don't tell me my goals are too big. One day I'll grow into my goals*. Wolf heard the strum of guitar strings and spun around.

Angie stood in the corner next to an acoustic guitar that leaned against its case. "Wow. Your daughter played the guitar too," Angie said. "She was very musical."

Mr. Cobb offered a faint smile. "She got all that talent from her mother. My job was to teach her to fish and swim and ride her bike. She could do anything she put her mind to."

"I believe you." Wolf motioned toward the posters. "Obviously, she was the kind of person who wanted to achieve big things."

The old man nodded. "She's an innocent kid with big dreams. She'd stand right up in front of a crowd and belt out a song without hesitation. Singing solos in the church choir gave her confidence. Everyone told her she had a voice like Mariah whatshername."

Angie picked a book up from the nightstand next to the bed. "Is this her Bible?"

"That's it."

"May I look through it."

"Sure."

Angie thumbed through the book, stopping here and there through the pages. "She made a lot of notes."

"Like I said, she was a religious girl, always praising the Lord and praying for people."

"May I take this with me to look it over."

"Just make sure I get it back."

Wolf drifted over to a bookshelf against the wall by the guitar. The books were neatly ordered, Tolkein's *The Lord of the Rings Trilogy,* C.S. Lewis's *The Chronicles of Narnia,* and a plethora of Amish romances. Several stacks of CDs of various popular artists and gospel music crowded another shelf. "I can see she liked to read," Wolf said.

The old man rubbed the top of his head. "She saw new horizons in those books, faraway places. I knew I couldn't hold her here forever. You can't cage a songbird like Jenny. But I swear we didn't fight about it. She could live here with me the rest of her life if she wanted. But I knew she had dreams. Maybe I made her feel guilty now and again about leaving me all alone, but I was just popping off. She knew I would support her whcn she was ready to go."

"So you're sure," Angie said, "that she didn't take off just to get away from here."

"Like I said, she was free to go whenever she was ready. There's no need to run away when you're free."

Wolf placed his hand on the old man's shoulder. "We'll do our best to find her."

Mr. Cobb hung his head. "I've saved up some money. I've got a couple thousand I can spare."

"That may do it." Wolf said. "If we pick up on a good trail and need more time, we can work something out."

He smiled. "Good enough. I trust you'll do your best."

Wolf covered a few more details with the old man: Jennifer's age, a list of friends, her hangouts, the name and location of her church, a description of the clothing she wore on the day she disappeared, etc. He gave him his cell phone number just in case Mr. Cobb came up with anything else that might help with the investigation. When Wolf had finished asking questions, Angie led the way into the front room. Both she and Wolf shook hands with him and promised they would update him regularly.

As they headed out the door, Mr. Cobb said, "Hey, I want to apologize again."

Angie and Wolf turned around on the sagging porch, and Wolf said, "For what?"

"For pointing my Colt .45 at you when you got here. It's just an old army pistol. Not loaded. I'm so damn jumpy nowadays I flinch at my own shadow."

"Don't worry about it, Mr. Cobb." Angie gave him a big smile. "We're used to it."

* * *

The drive to Island Bookstore only took about three minutes. You could walk it in less than ten if you kept up a good pace. It was located on Corolla Village Road about a quarter mile north of the Currituck Beach Lighthouse. Independent bookstores thrived on the Outer Banks. It seemed like there was one in every town. Wolf figured the big chain stores didn't want to bully their way in and take over because the number of vacationers dropped way down from October through April. To the big boys, that kind of drop-off meant commercial suicide. One had to be an indomitable business manager to survive the lean months. Wolf had met several of the local bookstore owners during past investigations. They were strong people.

As Wolf turned right onto Corolla Village Road, Angie said, "How do you think the interview went?"

"A few things surprised me."

"Like what?"

"I expected to hear about some kind of rift between them, something that would provoke a young girl to want to get out of there."

"I agree." Angie braced her elbow on the door's armrest as they went around a turn. "He convinced me that her homelife wasn't bad at all."

"Yeah, and I found something else very convincing along those lines."

"What?"

"Her room." Wolf slowed the car as they passed a family of five on bicycles. "It wasn't the room of a depressed teenager with a wardrobe full of black clothes and goth-rock CDs lining the shelf."

"No. I would describe it as bright and hopeful."

"Maybe too hopeful."

Angie shifted her gaze to Wolf. "Why do you say that?"

"With those go-for-your-dream posters on the wall, the Bible on the nightstand and the guitar in the corner, I see her as the naive type: too trusting and unaware of the dangers in the world. A good sense of fear can be a life preserver."

Angie patted the Bible on her lap. "Though I walk through the valley of the shadow of death, I will fear no evil."

"Exactly." Wolf slowed to make a right turn into the bookstore parking lot. "Let's hope we don't find her in that valley."

Three vehicles lined the right side of the building in the gravel lot, a white Chevy pickup and two sedans, a Honda and a Buick. Wolf parked next to the silver Buick LeSabre. The two-story building, sided with grayish-brown wooden shingles, had large windows with white trim. The front of the building welcomed visitors with a nice sized porch displaying a variety of books to whet a reader's appetite before entering the store. To the left of the porch, a bike rack secured the front wheels of two beach cruiser bikes, the old-fashioned kind with the thicker tires and old school handlebars.

Angie led the way onto the porch and held the door open for Wolf to enter. "Go ahead, old man, age before youth."

Wolf gave her a sideways glance. "Age is only a number."

"Is that right?"

Wolf entered, and Angie followed him into the front of the store. Rows of tall bookshelves lined the place all the way to the back. A staircase in the middle of the large room led to the second floor. A few customers lingered between the rows, and a young brunette, probably in her mid-thirties stood behind the counter on the left next to the cash register.

Wolf turned and faced Angie. "That's right. When I was a young cop, I arrested a seventy-year-old man who had the body of a twenty-five-year-old."

"Impressive."

"Unfortunately for him, he kept the body in a freezer in his basement."

Angie laughed. "That's one way to keep your body well preserved."

"May I help you?" The woman at the register smiled. She was a pretty girl, light complected and wearing a blue-violet sleeveless shirt. She had swirled her caramel-colored hair into a medium-sized bun.

"Yes, Ma'am," Wolf said. "We're detectives investigating the Jennifer Cobb case. Is the store owner around?"

Her smile faded. "Mr. Richards is in the office. I'll go get him." She quickly cut around the counter and hurried down the aisle toward the back of the store.

Angie glanced here and there across the spacious room. "This is a nice place. I've shopped at their other store in Duck. I can get lost in a good bookstore."

"Me, too."

"You'd get lost in the poetry aisle looking for a murder mystery."

Wolf placed his hand on his chest. "'If you prick me, do I not bleed.' That's from Macbeth in case you're wondering."

"Gimme a break. You think McBeth is the latest McDonalds burger."

A man approached them followed by the brunette. He strode confidently, wearing a green button-down shirt with white stripes and white casual pants. He had a round, friendly face, bright eyes, warm smile and receding brown hair with a few gray streaks. He stopped a few feet from them and said, "Good afternoon. I'm Bernie Richards. I'm the owner."

The brunette angled to the right and returned to her place behind the counter.

Angie extended her hand, and he shook it. "My name's Angie Stallone, and this is my partner, Weston Wolf. You've got a very nice shop, sir."

"Thank you. We've been selling books here a long time."

Wolf shook his hand. "We've just met with Mr. Cobb, Jennifer's father. He informed us that she worked here."

"That's correct." His smile dimed, and his eyes saddened. "We love Jenny. She's been a great addition to our staff for the last two years." He took a long breath and blew it out slowly. "I hope . . . I hope someone finds her soon."

Wolf said, "Mr. Cobb has hired us to investigate his daughter's disappearance. We'll need any help we can get, though."

Mr. Richards shook his head. "I'm not sure how much more I can add to the story. I told the police everything I know. Jenny showed up for work that day, on time as usual. It was a normal day. No problems. No hassles from any customers. She did her job well, and at the end of the day she left. That was the last we saw her."

"She didn't say anything out of the ordinary that day?" Wolf asked.

He shook his head.

Angie cleared her throat. "Mr. Richards, did the police interview all of your employees who were scheduled to work with her that day?"

"As far as I know, yes."

"Bernie, that's not quite right," the brunette behind the counter said.

The three of them turned and faced her.

Mr. Richards waved in her direction. "This is Maddie Bosley, one of my managers."

The girl swallowed and took a breath. "I was here that day, but then I left for a trip up north to visit some friends. When I got back a week later, the police had finished their investigation."

Wolf stepped in her direction. "Do you have anything to add?"

"Not really. Jenny was always upbeat and friendly. The few things she said to me that day weren't unusual."

Angie extracted her pad and pen from her shoulder bag. "Anything may help us, Maddie. Can you remember what she said?"

"Well . . ." She stared at the ceiling for a few seconds and refocused on them. "She said something good was about to happen, but she was always saying stuff like that. She had high hopes of hitting it big with her singing career."

"Anything else?" Wolf asked. "Did she mention any person's name that may have stirred this kind of wishful statement?"

"No. It was as if she felt she couldn't divulge any more about this notion because she didn't want to somehow spoil it. I didn't press her."

"Hmmm." Angie stopped writing on her pad. "Maybe there was something else you noticed, not necessarily words she said but perhaps an unusual mannerism."

Maddie's eyes lit up. "Now that you mention it, she kept rubbing this beautiful scarf she had tied around her neck. It matched her yellow sundress."

Angie scribbled a few words on the pad. "Can you describe the scarf?"

"It had a spattering of pastel colors, pinks, blues and yellows, like an abstract flower garden. There were lines and shapes that intertwined the flowers. I didn't get a close enough look to identify the shapes. I assumed they were some kind of pattern."

"Thanks, Maddie." Angie stuffed the pad and pen back into her shoulder bag. "Knowing a particular unusual accessory could be very helpful to us as we proceed with our investigation."

A far-off siren sounded and grew louder.

Wolf shifted his eyes to the front door. "Sounds like the E-squad."

Angie nodded. "Could be a beach emergency."

Another siren joined in. Wolf turned and faced Bernie Richards. "Thanks for answering our questions. We'll get back with you if anything else comes up."

"We'll be here." His friendly smile returned. "Please keep us updated on your progress."

"Will do," Wolf said.

"Thanks, Maddie," Angie said. "It was nice meeting both of you."

Maddie placed her hands flat on the counter. "I'm glad I could contribute."

Wolf led the way out the front door and onto the porch. Angie shut the door behind her and stepped next to him.

The sirens continued to scream. He pointed down the road to his right. "Sounds like a big calamity. I'd guess it's down by the Whalehead Club, not far from here."

Angie laid her hand on his shoulder. "We're heading in that direction. Let's go check it out."

Chapter 4

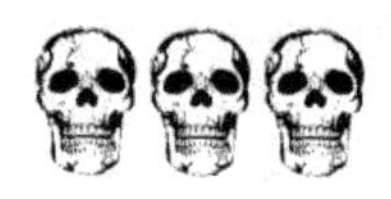

Wolf swerved onto Corolla Village Road, heading south. The narrow lane had no yellow lines to separate two-way traffic. Pines and live oaks lined both sides with an occasional driveway snaking off to the right or left. Wolf wanted to get to the scene of the emergency quickly, but he kept his speed under control, watching for tourists and bikers. To the left above the trees, he glimpsed the top of the lighthouse where several people stood on the parapet, gazing toward the old hunting club. The blare of sirens increased as he turned onto Village Lane, the road that circled the Historic Corolla Park and led to the Whalehead Club. As he neared the north entrance of the park, two Currituck County Sheriff's vehicles, a white Ford sedan and a Ford Bronco, flew by on the road just ahead, their lights swirling and sirens howling.

Angie pointed across the open field to the right. "I see two E-squads parked in front of the Whalehead Club. Something happened near the old bridge. That's where the crowd is forming. The sheriff's boys just pulled up next to it."

A hundred years ago the bright yellow mansion served as an exclusive hunting club. Five tall chimneys, spaced evenly across the length of the building, jutted from the peak of the steep roof. Nine dormers fronted the lower part of the roof, giving the three-story edifice a unique aspect. It had become one of the town's top tourist attractions since being fully restored to its roaring twenties glory a couple of decades ago. Wolf turned left into a small parking lot on the near side of the mansion and brought the Cougar to a skidding stop. He and Angie bolted out of the car, slamming their doors behind them, and trotted past the ambulances.

A throng of people had gathered on the wooden pedestrian bridge that crossed the narrow channel which led to the Currituck Sound. The channel fed a pond where the public could dock small boats. The bridge formed a wide triangle over the water, slanting up and then sharply down the other side. Lining the bridge's railing, the crowd stared into the water. Wooden posts formed retaining walls along both sides of the channel, creating a three-foot drop off to the water. EMTs carried a plastic stretcher to the edge of the channel near the bridge. To Wolf it appeared as if they were getting ready to enter the water. They slowed their pace as they neared the bridge.

"Somebody must have drowned," Wolf said.

They came to a stop, and Angie elbowed his ribs. "Let's cross to the middle of the bridge and see if we can get a better look."

Wolf led the way up the wooden-planked slope. At the top he and Angie squeezed between several onlookers and leaned against the railing. Two deputies and three EMTs motioned toward the water, excitedly talking. A bloated body bobbed facedown near the surface. Was it a woman? Although the corpse was half naked, it was hard to tell. The pale-gray flesh had been gnawed away in places with chunks floating here and there. The smell nauseated Wolf. He glanced at Angie and noticed she had turned away.

Two of the EMTs dropped into the water, and the deputies handed down the plastic stretcher. As they maneuvered it under the body and lifted, the crowd groaned, and someone near the end of the bridge spewed their lunch. The EMT on shore bent over the edge of the posts and clasped the end of the stretcher. The three of them lifted the body, and the two deputies helped from the sides once the stretcher was halfway out of the water. An arm dropped off the edge and dangled. About half the flesh had been eaten away it. Wolf feared it might even break off at the elbow and plop onto the ground.

He turned his back on the spectacle and nudged Angie's arm. "Are you alright?"

Her normally tanned face had turned a lighter shade of pale "I'll be fine. Just give me a few minutes for my stomach to settle."

"I'm going down to get a closer look."

"Make sure you take some pictures with your phone. You never know. It might be Jennifer Cobb."

"I intended to do just that. You probably should head back to the car. Get away from here."

"No. Once I steady myself, I'm going to walk along the edge of the water. Maybe I'll find something."

"That's a good idea." He gripped the back of her neck and squeezed. "Hang in there, Angel. It took me years to be able to stomach a scene like this."

She nodded. "I can see why."

"Give me about fifteen more minutes, and we'll get the hell outta here."

She reached behind his waist and gave him a sideways hug. "Thanks for being patient with me, Wes. I'll be alright in a few minutes. Take as much time as you need."

Wolf scampered down the incline and headed toward the body. They had placed the stretcher on the ground about ten feet from the edge of the channel in the shade of a live oak. One of the EMTs turned and hustled toward the closest ambulance. The others stood around the corpse quietly talking and pointing, their faces fraught with dismay.

As Wolf approached, one of the deputies, a young woman with burgundy-brown hair in a ponytail, pivoted and raised her hand. "Hold up there, sir. We don't want anybody getting too close." Her dark gray shirt displayed the county's law enforcement patch: a redbrick lighthouse with a duck flying across a pond. She wore black pants, secured with a wide belt that held a holster encasing a large handgun.

Wolf halted. "My name's Weston Wolf. I'm a private investigator working on the Jennifer Cobb case."

The other deputy stepped forward, a tall, broad-shouldered fellow with short black hair. "I know you. We met a few years ago when I worked for Dare County. My name's Rob Duncan." Similar to the woman, he was dressed in a gray and black uniform but wore a black ballcap with the same logo. Wolf recognized his deformed ear, which had become cauliflowered. Wolf guessed he had wrestled in high school.

"Good to see you again, Rob," Wolf said. "That was another missing persons case. A husband hired me to find his estranged wife."

"Right. Her lover had murdered her, hauled her down to Buxton and dumped her body in the woods. Her husband was the prime suspect until you turned up evidence against her boyfriend."

"You've got a good memory. The killer was an artist from Frisco, famous for his violent nudes. I suspected him from the start."

"Guess you could say he was a little sketchy."

Wolf couldn't keep from chuckling. "You could say that. Mind if I take a closer look and snap a few photographs."

The deputy glanced at the others and shrugged. "Why not?" He leaned his head in the direction of the corpse. "She might be the one you're looking for."

"Thanks."

Wolf slid his cellphone out of his back pocket and approached the body. Slowing his breathing, he tried to avoid the odor. The victim wore a bra and panties, but the body had swollen so much that the skin threatened to burst through the undergarments. She lay on her stomach on the stretcher. Her head had shifted sideways when they had lifted her out of the water. She had golden brown hair, the same color and length pictured in Jennifer Cobb's photograph. Her thick walnut eyebrows matched too. However, her face resembled a horrific zombie from *The Day of the Dead*. Wolf zoomed in with his phone's camera, tapping out several pictures. The gray surface of her skin was riddled with raw rips and gashes. Blobs of gelatinous goo seeped from the holes. Her left eye had been half-eaten away. *That's not the face of the girl in the photo above Mr. Cobb's old television. Not the way it looks now, anyway.* He circled the corpse and took more photographs.

The tall deputy stepped next to him. "What do you think? Maybe a week in the water?"

"More like ten days. With this much damage, it'll be hard to identify her unless there're dental records."

"As far as I know, Jennifer Cobb is the only person missing in the county right now. Are you going to show those images to her father?"

Wolf slipped his phone into his back pocket, stretched his back, feeling some stiffness, and blew out a frustrated breath. "I have no choice. That's why he hired me. He might see something that could lead to a positive ID."

The young deputy shook his head. "If that were my child, I wouldn't want to look at those pictures. I'd want to remember her the way she was, not the way she is."

Lights flashing, the ambulance headed their way, turned toward the pond and then backed in the direction of the body. Wolf scampered out of the way and watched the female deputy motion the vehicle to keep on coming until it got to within ten feet. *Not much more I can do here.* Wolf panned the edge of the waterline, searching for Angie. He caught a glimpse of her about fifty yards away by the docks where a boat ramp sloped into the Currituck Sound. He hurried in that direction.

As he approached, he watched as she removed her Adidas slip-ons, rolled up her jeans and waded into the water down the ramp.

"What are you doing?" he called.

She bent over and reached for something in the sound. Lifting it, she stood still, allowing the water to drip off. She shook it, and it wavered in the wind like a small flag.

Wolf noticed it was quite colorful. "Is that a handkerchief?"

She shook her head no and splashed through the water toward him. "It's a scarf." She handed it to Wolf and shimmied her feet back into her shoes.

Wolf examined the silky cloth. It matched Maddie Bosley's description of the scarf Jennifer wore the day she disappeared: an abstract flower print in blues, pinks and yellows. The lines of a musical staff weaved in and out of the shapes with half notes, quarter notes and eighth notes patterning the spaces.

Angie met his gaze and thumbed toward the bridge. "Should we hand it over to the deputies?"

"Hell no." Wolf glanced over his shoulder as the EMTs loaded the body into the back of the ambulance. The two deputies ambled in the direction of their vehicles. "They gave up on the investigation. We're just getting started." He folded the scarf and tucked it into the breast pocket of his Polo shirt. "Let's head back over to the bookstore and let Maddie take a look at it. If it's the one Jennifer was wearing, we need to show it to her father along with the photographs. If not, the sheriff's office is on our way home. We can drop it off. We'll tell them we found it after they left."

"You don't mind telling a lie now and again, do you?"

Wolf grinned. "If someone tells you that I'm a compulsive liar, don't believe them."

Angie punched his shoulder and walked in the direction of the Cougar. "Come on, Pinocchio, before you decide to quit the detective business and become a politician."

Chapter 5

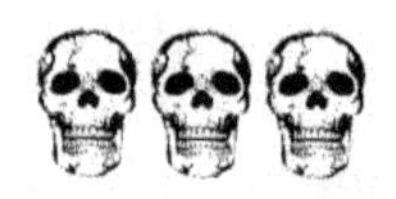

Wolf spread the scarf across the dashboard so the sun's rays would help to dry it. He pulled out of the Whalehead Club parking lot and onto the road. Checking the rearview mirror, he glimpsed the ambulance rumbling away from the bridge across the grass and onto the asphalt. Wolf figured the E-squad would turn right at the main entrance and head south to the Outer Banks Hospital in Nags Head. There a pathologist would perform a complete autopsy. Wolf turned left before the entrance and followed the same route by which he had arrived—around the park and then north on Corolla Village Road.

He glanced at Angie. The color had returned to her face. "Feeling any better?"

"Much. Sorry about the way I lost it back there."

"No need to apologize. You're human."

"You hired me because you believed I could handle whatever I encountered in the line of duty. I feel like a coward."

"You'll get used to it. Besides, you've got the smarts of a good investigator. You had the clarity of mind to check the shoreline for clues. Without you, we wouldn't have that scarf."

She reached and straightened the thin fabric. "It may have nothing to do with this case, just a random item that washed up."

"I'm betting it does. It matches Maddie's description. Anyway, we'll find out in a few minutes."

"What if it is Jennifer's scarf? What's the next step?"

Wolf grimaced, took a deep breath and blew it out. "We'll drive out to Mr. Cobb's house and show it to him along with the photographs I took."

"Jeeeze." She ran her fingers over the scarf. "That may be more difficult for me than watching them lift that bloated body out of the channel."

"It has to be done."

"I know."

"This may be the fastest missing persons case we'll ever solve."

"Yeah. Case closed in less than an hour."

"At least that'll save the old man a lot of money."

Angie sighed. "But not a lot of heartache."

Within a few minutes they reached the bookstore, and Wolf parked in the same space on the side of the building. Angie pinched the corner of the scarf and lifted it. It had become somewhat dryer but still slightly darkened because of the moisture. After shaking it out, she carefully folded it.

"Here." Wolf opened the divider compartment and drew out a plastic bag with a zip-type seal on it. "Put it in the bag for now."

Angie placed the scarf into the bag and sealed it.

They got out of the car and plodded into the store. Bernie Richards and Maddie Bosley stood next to each other behind the counter.

"Back already?" Bernie Richards said.

Wolf nodded. "We found something that might be relevant to the case."

Maddie placed her hands on the counter and leaned forward. "What were the sirens all about?"

Angie said, "A body washed into shore over by the Whalehead Club."

Maddie gasped. "Was it Jennifer?"

"We don't know for sure," Wolf said. "That's why we're here."

"Take a look at this." Angie raised the plastic bag and laid it on the counter in front of Maddie.

Maddie's eyes widened.

Angie unzipped the bag, withdrew the scarf and spread it on the counter. "Does it look like the scarf Jennifer was wearing on the day she disappeared?"

Maddie nodded, her eyes still wide. "Was . . . was it around . . . around her neck?"

Angie shook her head. "No. It washed up about forty or fifty yards away from where the body was floating."

Wolf cleared his throat. "You said she wore a yellow sundress that day."

"Yes. It was sleeveless and came down to just above her knees."

"The current must have stripped off the dress and the scarf. All she had on was panties and a bra. We didn't see the dress anywhere along the shore. It must still be out in the sound. It may wash up sooner or later."

Angie folded the scarf and slipped it back into the plastic bag. "We appreciate your help with identifying her scarf. With the body so badly decomposed, it might be difficult to get a positive ID."

"Hopefully, there'll be dental records," Wolf said, "but you can't count on that. The scarf might be the only solid evidence we have to give Mr. Cobb some closure."

"I wish . . . I wish . . ." Maddie breathed haltingly and started to cry. "I wish we would have talked more that day. We were . . . we were such good friends." She wiped her tears away with the backs of her hands. "Please excuse me." She turned and hurried down the aisle toward the office.

Bernie Richards bit his lip and blinked. "I better go check on her."

Angie slipped the plastic bag back into her shoulder bag. "We're sorry about the traumatic context of this investigation, Mr. Richards, but we have to do our job."

"I understand. I appreciate your efforts."

"We'll be on our way," Wolf said. "You better go see about Maddie."

He took a breath and swallowed. "Yes. This has been a difficult day for all of us."

* * *

On the way back to Mr. Cobb's house, Angie didn't say much.

"Are you having second thoughts?" Wolf asked.

"Second thoughts about what?"

"About wanting to be my partner instead of my office receptionist and secretary."

"No."

"Okay. I'm just checking."

Angie breathed audibly for several seconds. "My father taught me to face up to the difficult things in life. When I was ten, we had a mutt that got hit by a car. The poor thing was still alive, but its backend was crushed. It didn't have long to live and kept yelping and crying. Dad explained that he had to put it out of its misery. I understood. He walked over to the neighbor's house to borrow a rifle. I went up to my room and watched from the window. The dog lay in the grass next to the garage, crying out in pain. Dad came back with the rifle. I didn't want to look, but I knew this was one of those difficult things Dad always harped on. I made myself watch. He pulled the trigger, and the dog's suffering ended."

"Geeesh," Wolf sighed. "How'd that make you feel?"

"Not good but in a strange way better. I hurt on the inside, but I grew as a person. Facing the hard truth made me stronger. It was a terrible thing to witness as a ten-year-old, but I didn't run away from it."

"Seeing a bloated corpse ravaged by nine days in the sound is a terrible thing to see."

"Yes." Angie patted the shoulder bag on her lap. "Especially knowing the possible identity of the deceased. I could only look for a few seconds. My stomach started to turn."

"But you didn't run away. You kept working the case. You should feel good about that."

"I do, but I'll feel better if you let me do something."

"What?"

"I dread breaking the news to Mr. Cobb. That's what I need to face."

Wolf rubbed the stubble on his chin. "Do you want to do the talking?"

"Yes."

"Okay, partner. I'll let you handle it."

Wolf turned left onto Lost Lake Lane and left again on the narrow drive that tunneled through the overhanging trees and thick shrubs to the opening by the lake. He parked next to the rusty Ford pickup.

Mr. Cobb sat on the concrete blocks that served as steps for the sagging porch. As they exited the Cougar, the old man waved, his eyes anxious. "Did you forget something?"

"No sir," Angie said, "we found something."

The hefty man struggled to his feet. "Something that belonged to Jenny?"

They stopped a few feet away and faced him. Angie held the evidence bag at her side. "Did you notice what Jennifer was wearing on the morning she left for work?"

"I told Detective Wolf that she had on a yellow dress. I wasn't paying a lot of attention that morning."

"You don't remember any unusual accessory, something new that she might have recently purchased?" Angie asked.

He rubbed the stubble on his wide jowls. "I'm trying to picture the way she looked that day."

Angie unzipped the bag, extracted the scarf and shook it out. "Does this look familiar?"

"Yeah." He bobbed his head slowly. "She brought that home a couple days before she disappeared."

"Was she wearing it that morning?"

"She might have been." He closed his eyes. "Now that I think about it, I remember seeing it when she bent over to kiss me goodbye."

"Do you know where she got it?"

"I have no idea." He reached, took the scarf and rubbed it gently between his stubby fingers. "It's a little wet. Where did you find this?"

Angie coughed and cleared her throat. "Mr. Cobb, it washed up near the Whalehead Club boat launch ramp. Her co-worker identified it as the one she wore that day."

He wobbled his head. "What was it doing in the Currituck Sound?"

Angie glanced at Wolf and then eyed Mr. Cobb. "A body floated into the channel by the docks not far from where I found the scarf."

Mr. Cobb let out a deep groan. His knees grew weak, and he lowered himself onto the concrete blocks. He huffed in several breaths and said, "Was it Jenny?"

Angie bit her lower lip for a few seconds. "We think so, but we're not absolutely sure. The body was badly decomposed. Detective Wolf took photographs. The pathologist at the Outer Banks Hospital will perform an autopsy. Hopefully, with dental records, he can make a positive identification."

The old man shook his head. "She went to the dentist a couple of times but never had a cavity. I ran my own fishing charter business. We couldn't afford dental insurance. Paid cash for everything."

Wolf eyed Angie. "That'll definitely make the ID process more challenging."

"Let me see the pictures," Mr. Cobb bellowed. "I need to know."

Wolf slipped his phone out of his back pocket. "Prepare yourself, Mr. Cobb. These images are very graphic. Have you ever seen a body that's been in the water for days?"

He gazed up at them. "I'm a Gulf War veteran. I've seen some bad things in my life. I'll know if it's her. Show me the pictures."

Wolf tapped the access button on the iPhone, brought up the camera app, and scrolled through the photographs until he came to the closeup of the victim's face. "Remember, Mr. Cobb, brackish water, fish and natural decomposition can cause major damage to a body in just a short time." He handed Mr. Cobb the phone.

He adjusted the distance by extending his arm and focusing. His eyes tensed, and his lower lip trembled. "The face isn't human, but that's her hair and eyebrows." He examined the scarf again, holding it up with his other hand. "My poor Jenny!" he wailed. He dropped the scarf onto the ground and bent over as if he had been punched in the gut. Loud sobs escaped with every heaving of his lungs.

Angie blinked several times as tears trickled down her cheeks. She crouched and picked up the scarf. "We're so sorry, Mr. Cobb." She stood and placed her hand on his shoulder.

Wolf reached and tugged his iPhone out of the sobbing man's hand.

They waited patiently for many minutes until his crying diminished to a whimper. Finally, he sat up and stared blankly at the red Ford Focus parked under the tree across the clearing. "She's gone. Gone forever, and there's nothing I can do about it." He shifted his gaze to Angie. "Can I have the scarf?"

"I'm sorry, Mr. Cobb, but we have to turn this into the Currituck County Sheriff's Department. They'll be in contact with you later today."

"I understand." His breathing became shaky again, and tears flowed, tracing varied paths over his rough cheeks.

Wolf said, "Once their investigation is completed, they'll return the scarf to you."

Mr. Cobb buried his face in his hands and sniffled.

Angie folded the scarf and tucked it back into the plastic bag. "Again, we're sorry to bring this bad news to you."

He raised up and wiped his eyes. "It's not your fault. I appreciate your efforts. How much do I owe you?"

"Don't worry about that right now," Wolf said. "We'll send the bill in a few days. We'll be very fair with you." Wolf reached and placed his hand on Angie's shoulder. "We better get going."

They turned away, approached Wolf's car, opened the doors and slid into the seats. Wolf started the engine and backed out. As he drove away, he took one last look at Mr. Cobb. The old man sat on the concrete blocks, his head buried in his hands.

* * *

The Currituck County Municipal Offices for the Outer Banks section of the county was located along Route 12, a block or so north of the redbrick lighthouse. The large one-story building housed the sheriff's office, magistrate's office and the Corolla Public Library. Wolf turned left into the parking lot, found an empty space by the library entrance and cut the engine.

"Want me to run the scarf in?" Wolf asked.

"No." Angie opened the car door.

"Why not?"

"I don't want your nose to grow any longer than it is, Pinocchio."

"What are you going to tell them?"

"The truth."

"That's no good. What if they question the fact that you didn't turn it in to them at the scene?"

"Give me some credit, would you? I know how to choose my words." She stepped out of the car and flung the door closed. Carrying the evidence bag at her side, she scurried around a Chevy Tahoe parked next to Wolf's Cougar and headed for the sheriff's office on the left side of the building.

Wolf laid his head back against the headrest. *What a day.* It seemed like everything happened at once within a square mile. *How did she die? Why did she end up in the Currituck Sound?* They may have solved a missing persons case, but they didn't provide any real answers. *Poor Mr. Cobb. Once he suffers through a time of grief, he'll want some answers. Oh well, he hired us to find his daughter, and we accomplished that task. Maybe the Currituck County people will offer him an explanation concerning her death. We may have to keep the book open on Jennifer Cobb just in case her father isn't happy with the answers they give him.*

Wolf's thoughts drifted to Freyja Beck. He wanted to talk to her again. *Should I go up and knock on her door? She'd probably tell me to get lost or worse – to go to hell.* He hated the feeling of being misunderstood by a woman. He often came off as a chauvinistic pig. *I'm really not. I don't think I am anyway. Okay, maybe I am.* He wondered if a relationship with a woman like Freyja could help him become a more sensitive man. *Quit fooling yourself, you idiot. She's not going to give you a second chance. No way.* He had his chance at bat this morning on the back deck and struck out. *What's the saying? You don't get two chances to make a second impression. Or is it, you better make a good impression the first time because you don't get . . . No. That's not it. Ah crap! Forget it.*

Wolf caught sight of Angie heading his way and started the car. He gunned the engine a couple time as she climbed in.

"Very impressive," she said.

Wolf backed out and rumbled onto Route 12 heading south. "Well, what's the verdict?'

"No verdict. I went into the office, handed the evidence bag to one of the deputies, told him where I found it and about our interviews with Maddie and Mr. Cobb."

"And?"

"And what?"

"Did he give you the snake-eye?

"No. He thanked me."

"You're kidding?"

"I gave him my card and told him to call if they had any questions."

"Why did you do that?"

Angie twisted in her seat and faced him. "What is wrong with you? They just may want to know more details about what we discovered during our investigation."

Wolf protruded his lower lip. "I don't get it. If I would have delivered that evidence bag, he would have given me the third degree."

"Maybe there's something about you that people in authority don't trust."

"Could be." Wolf drummed his fingers on top of the steering wheel. "Maybe I know too much."

"No. I think it's your face."

"My face? People always tell me I've got a good face."

"Do you know what that's called?"

"What?"

"Sarcasm."

Wolf laughed. He felt glad that Angie was feeling better. She did have a way with people in authority. He definitely lacked that skill set. This partnership may be the best thing that happened to his agency for a while. His last partner, George Bain, had been murdered while out on a case. Wolf considered going it alone, but Angie kept insisting she could be the perfect partner to take George's place. The more time they spent working on cases, the more he realized she was right.

They avoided the subject of Jennifer Cobb's death, keeping the conversation light. When they drove through Duck, Angie noticed a yellow dress on display outside of a store called The Farmer's Daughter.

"I forgot to tell the deputy about the yellow dress," Angie said.

"They did their investigation. I'm sure they know she was wearing a yellow dress that day."

She raked her fingers through her short hair. "I know that. I'm talking about the possibility of the dress washing to shore. I should have told them to keep their eye out for it."

"Hopefully, they'll think of that."

"I can always call them when we get back to the office."

"Why do you want to be so helpful?"

She glared at him. "What's wrong with being helpful in an effort to ascertain a positive identification of a missing girl?"

Wolf shrugged. "Nothing. You're right. I guess my relationship with local law enforcement has been tainted by bad experiences. They seem to always accuse me of keeping information from them and stirring up trouble."

"Of course, you're always right, and they're always wrong."

"Not always. A cop came up to me once and asked if I wanted to buy tickets to the policemen's ball. I wasn't fond of the guy. I told him I didn't know he had balls." Wolf grinned and took a quick peek at Angie. "That was the wrong thing to say."

Angie laughed. "No kidding."

"Oh, I was kidding, but he didn't appreciate my sense of humor."

"You didn't really tell that to a cop. You said that just to make me smile, didn't you?"

"It worked, didn't it?"

"Yeah, but you don't need to treat me like Zuzu's petals. I'm not a fragile flower."

"Not at all. You're more like a cactus."

Angie smirked. "That's better." She arched her back and shifted in her seat. "I've been thinking about Jennifer Cobb's death."

"Me, too."

"How did she drown? We have no idea. Did she go out kayaking to Monkey Island and get caught by a rogue wave? Maybe she had one of those stand-up paddle boards and took it a mile out into the sound and tumbled into the water."

"I don't think so," Wolf said. "Remember, they found her car in the Food Lion parking lot."

"That's what I'm talking about. How did her body end up in the Currituck Sound? It doesn't make sense. We should have asked Mr. Cobb if she owned a kayak, or a jet ski or whatever."

"We may get the chance. If the Currituck County investigators can't come up with a satisfying answer, he may call on us again."

Angie nodded. "I hope he does. I forgot to give her Bible back."

As they entered Nags Head, the sky clouded over, and color drained from the storefronts, hotels and souvenir shops that lined Croatan Highway. Wolf checked his watch: 2:15. He had no pressing business back at the office. There were some background checks that needed to be completed for clients involved in questionable business relationships. Angie was better at that sort of thing. An infidelity investigation was ongoing, but the client's husband didn't get off work until five. Wolf had a few hours to kill. Maybe he'd head to Jockey's Ridge State Park and go for a walk. He needed to clear his mind and get some exercise. He couldn't shake his encounter with Freyja Beck from his thoughts. A good walk might help.

"Can you believe it's Thursday already?" Angie muttered. "One more day, and the weekend is here."

"Time goes by. Do you have a big date lined up with Deputy Joel tonight?"

"Nothing too exciting." She clasped her hands behind her head. "He's coming over to my place. We'll put on a movie and pop some popcorn. How about you?"

"Nothing planned."

"No more attempts at asking our new neighbor out for dinner?"

Wolf chuckled. "Mighty Casey has struck out."

"Since when do you give up so easily?"

"I've had time to think it over. She's not interested in me. She probably thinks I'm some kind of chauvinist pig. Of course, she doesn't know the real me."

"Right. You are the epitome of feminist conscientiousness and political correctness."

Wolf grunted.

"You're welcome to join Joel and me. We'll probably watch an old Bogart and Becall movie, maybe *The Big Sleep*. I'd hate to see you spend a lonely night in that back bedroom of yours, getting drunk on cheap wine."

"You don't need to treat me like Zuzu's petals. I'm not a fragile flower."

Angie laughed. "No. You're a blackberry bush, a few good berries but lots of thorns."

"That's better."

Wolf turned left onto East Hunter Street, drove down the lane and parked in front of his beach bungalow next to Angie's Honda Civic. Angie exited the car and trotted up the steps to the office door. Wolf lingered behind, glancing at the cottage to the left, the one Freyja Beck had rented. An olive-green Jeep Renegade, a 1980s model, sat in her driveway. *Hmmmm. She likes old cars, too.* When he got to the steps, he noticed Angie reading a note that had been taped to the frosted glass.

She reached, tugged the note away from the glass, turned and faced him, smiling like a gambler who just hit the nickel slot machine.

"What do you got there?" Wolf asked.

"Do you want me to read it?"

"Go ahead."

"Dear Detective Wolf. I never got back to you concerning your dinner date offer. I'd like to go to the Jolly Rodger in Kill Devil Hills. Pick me up at 7. Signed, Freyja Beck."

"Let me see that." Wolf swiped the note from Angie's hand and read it. He raised his eyebrows and grinned. "I'm back in the game."

Angie punched his shoulder. "Don't strike out this time."

Chapter 6

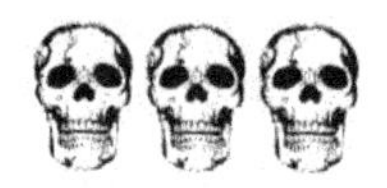

Wolf couldn't contain his excitement. While Angie situated herself in front of the computer in the front office to start working on background checks, he headed to his bedroom to change into his jogging clothes. His little beach house didn't offer much privacy. The front office and his office took up more than half of the space. In the back, his bedroom, bathroom and kitchen filled out the rest. He entered his bedroom, stripped off his Polo shirt, stepped out of his jeans and kicked them into the corner. He unhitched his shoulder holster and slung it over his bedpost. He hadn't gone for a jog in almost a week. Now that he was about to turn thirty-eight, keeping in shape wasn't as easy as it used to be. Getting into shape was even harder.

He decided to go shirtless with Nike running shorts. He really liked his new shoes, super-cushioned Hokas that reduced the shock to his hips and knees. After double knotting them, he slipped on his black-framed Oakleys and scampered out the back door and onto the deck. Leaning on the railing, he stretched his calves and checked out the back of Freyja Beck's cottage, hoping she might be hanging out there. *Nope. She's probably a mile out in the ocean diving for shells.* He rambled down the steps onto the soft sand and made a beeline for the shoreline where he could run on the firmer wet sand. The clouds had cleared, and the late afternoon sun felt warm on his back.

As he plugged along heading south, he wondered what changed Freyja's mind. Maybe she didn't change her mind. Perhaps she liked him but wanted to play mind games. That was probably it: put him on the defense so that he wouldn't feel so confident. Her take-control attitude made her even more attractive to him. He loved a challenge, especially with women. *For a while there I thought I lost my touch. I may not be twenty-five anymore, but I still got everything I had back then. It just takes a few more Advils and prune juice to get things going.*

After about a mile and a half, he had to stop. A cramp in his side and the afternoon heat put a kibosh on his expectations of running six miles. He bent over, hands on his knees, and gazed southward along the shore. A few sunbathers dotted the stretch of sand along with kids building sandcastles and teenagers splashing in the waves with their body boards. He walked another half mile to where the vacation rentals thinned, leaving an empty beach, dunes and the thundering of the surf as it tumbled and rushed up the bank. *Ahhhh. This is more like it.*

He planned on walking another mile, turning around and jogging back home or at least make the attempt. In the distance he saw an odd shape. He kept his eyes fixed on it. The form moved rhythmically and grew larger: a horse and rider. The animal, tan with a white flowing mane, tromped through the up-rushing water. Muscles rippling, it galloped with dynamic ease. Now that the horse had drawn nearer, Wolf focused on the rider, a woman with long ash blonde hair winnowed by the wind. She wore faded jeans and a plaid shirt with cutoff sleeves. She reined the stallion to a stop about thirty yards away. Wolf squinted to clear his vision. The woman was Freyja Beck!

He approached slowly and waved. "I know you."

She appraised him skeptically from her high position on the horse. "You think you know me."

"I hope to know you better."

"Maybe you will."

"I appreciate the opportunity. I got your note."

"We'll see how well you handle your opportunity tonight."

Geeesh! She's playing the hard-to-get princess to a T. "I'll give it my best." He spread his hands. "I never expected to see you on a deserted beach riding a horse today."

The horse whinnied and turned toward the sea. She reined it back around. "I never expected to see you without a shirt again."

Wolf laughed and glanced down at his tanned torso. "I hope I didn't shock you."

"Not any more than I shocked you this morning."

Wolf grimaced. "I apologize for my reaction. Sometimes I turn into a jackass without warning."

She leaned and patted the horse's neck. "I prefer handsome steeds over jackasses."

"That probably leaves me out."

She eyed his well-defined chest and abs. "I haven't passed on you yet." Finally, a hint of a smile creased her face. "I'll have to check your teeth before I make a decision."

Wolf gave a toothy grin. "Just don't ride me hard and put me away wet."

She laughed. "Now that was naughty! Shame on you."

"There I go, turning into a jackass again."

She shook her head. "You made me laugh. I'll give you credit for that. I need to get Freedom back to the stables." She turned the horse and glanced over her shoulder. "They let me ride him without a guide since I know what I'm doing. See you at seven."

Wolf waved and laughed to himself. *Freyja Beck, you do know what you're doing.* He turned and jogged back in the direction of his bungalow. Feeling incredibly alive, he picked up his pace to a trot. He hadn't looked forward to a date this much in years. Somehow he had cracked her outer shell and broke through to a softer place in her disposition. His mind filled with the possibilities of their date. *Don't get too excited, Casanova. She may not even let you touch her, let alone hold her hand.* Then again, he remembered that look she gave him. Could he steal a kiss? *Better not try. She might crack me with her whip*. A mermaid, a singer, aspiring actress and a skilled horseback rider. No doubt about it, Freyja Beck was one of the most interesting women he'd met in a long time. With Freyja occupying his mind, he ran the whole way back to his beach house unperturbed by the heat or the pain in his side.

* * *

At five minutes to seven he stepped out of the front door of the office. Freyja Beck leaned on the passenger side of the Cougar. *What do you know? I guess she's anxious to get going.* She wore a long, loose-fitting white dress, backless with gold embroidery creating intricate flower patterns around the neckline and waist. The thin fabric rippled against her body in the breeze. Her ashen hair flowed over her shoulders which were wide and tapered to her narrow waist. She gazed westward where the sun dipped near the edge of the North Carolina mainland. The scarred side of her face was turned toward Wolf, but she didn't seem to care.

Wolf said, "There's nothing more beautiful than an Outer Banks sunset."

She pivoted in his direction and eyed him coolly. "We get one sunset a day. I try not to miss it."

"I don't blame you. I like this evening's array." He motioned toward the horizon where the sun's rays lit low-drifting wispy clouds with brilliant reds, oranges and yellows. "Throw in a few clouds, and the view becomes spectacular."

"That's true. Clouds always make things more interesting."

"I hope I didn't keep you waiting."

"No. You're on time. I wandered over a little early to get a closer look at your car."

Wolf ambled down the steps to the driver's side of the vehicle and rapped on the hood. "What do you think? 1969

Mercury Cougar in metallic blue and powered by a 428 Cobra Jet Ram Air V8."

"That matters little to me. I like it because it's old and still in good shape. It's about your age, isn't it?"

Wolf straightened. "Do you always throw daggers on a first date?"

"Do you always brag about what's under your hood?" She yanked the door open. "Let's go. I'm famished." She eased onto the seat and closed the door.

He got in, started the car and gunned the engine. As it idled, the car vibrated. *Is she kidding around with me or what?* He backed out and drove to the end of East Hunter Street. *This might be a long night.*

At the stop sign Freyja said, "I must admit that you do have good taste in cars."

He glanced at her "And women."

She laughed. "Obviously."

That's better. Maybe she just enjoys yanking my chain. "I'm curious. Why the Jolly Rodger?"

"I'm in the mood for . . . karaoke."

Wolf shook his head. "You *are* full of surprises. No better place to have a few beers and belt out a Beatles song."

"I prefer Sinatra."

"You told me you were a singer."

"All mermaids sing. We specialize in siren songs."

"I'll be all ears."

In the middle of Nags Head, Wolf turned west on Gray Eagle Street and north again on Route 158, the main highway. Freyja poked the buttons on his old school radio, jumping from classic rock to country to news. Then she turned the knob on the left, and the sound cut off.

"Can't find a good station?" Wolf asked.

"I just wanted to play with the radio. I've never seen one like that. Very cool."

"It's an original."

"I like originals."

"I'd call you an original."

"Why do you say that?" She shifted in her seat and eyed him.

"You can swim like a dolphin. You ride a horse like Annie Oakley. This morning you told me you were an aspiring actress and a singer. I'd call that an original."

"I didn't say I could sing well."

"If I had to put money on it, I'd bet you do. Where did you learn to ride a horse?"

"I grew up on a farm in Indiana. When I was a kid, I had a palomino like the one I was riding today. I spent my summers on that horse. Rode in every local parade. When I discovered there were stables along the beach south of Nags Head, I had to go ride. Something happens to me when I'm on a horse. It's as if heaven lends me wings."

"I've gone down to those stables a couple times. To me, riding horses is a great escape from the seamy side of the world."

"The world in general, or what you encounter on your job?"

"My job, I guess. I see the dark soul of humanity on a daily basis."

"How did your missing persons investigation go this afternoon?"

Wolf blew out a frustrated breath. "Too well. We solved the case within an hour."

"You sound disappointed. Not enough time on the job to make for a good payday?"

"No." *Another dagger*. Wolf gave her a quick perturbed look. "The girl's body washed to shore near the Whalehead Club in Corolla. Her father was devastated."

"Oh." She slid down slightly in her seat. "Sorry about that."

"The corpse had been in the water a long time. It no longer resembled the girl's photograph, but a scarf washed up nearby, and we got a positive identification on it."

She straightened. "A scarf? What did it look like?"

"It had a colorful flower print on it, very impressionistic. Her co-worker identified it immediately. Why do you ask?"

"Just wondering." Freyja sat quietly for about half a minute. "I see why you need an occasional escape from your work."

Wolf bobbed his head. "Don't get me wrong. I love what I do, but it gets ugly sometimes."

The Jolly Roger Restaurant and Bar was located in Kill Devil Hills about ten miles north of Wolf's bungalow along Route 12, the road that ran along the edge of the ocean. Wolf loved the place. One night about five years ago he had too much fun there. After one too many glasses of wine, he thought he was the best singer in the joint and wouldn't relinquish the karaoke microphone. The crowd complained, and the local sheriff showed up and arrested him on drunk and disorderly charges. Wolf used to work for the lawman as a Dare County deputy. They never did get along.

He turned right on East Second Street and then made a quick left onto Route 12. "Have you ever been here before?"

"No, but I read about it in one of the local tourist brochures. Looks like an entertaining place."

"It is, and good food, too. Very eclectic. I think you'll enjoy it. The place used to be a gas station back in the early 70s. It's been hit hard by hurricanes a few times, but the owner keeps getting back on her feet, rebuilds and reopens."

"Sounds like the kind of woman I'd like to know."

"If she's here tonight, I'll introduce you."

As they approached the restaurant, Freyja's eyes widened. "You're not kidding when you said the place was eclectic. They've got a stoplight hanging next to a black Pegasus, and three statues of goddesses lining the front yard."

"Wait till you see the inside."

Wolf turned left into the parking lot, which was almost full. He found an empty spot in the back, pulled in and cut the engine. They exited the car and walked toward the front of the restaurant.

Brown shake shingles covered the two-story building, and bright red trim set off the doors and windows. A huge glassed-in patio enclosure had been added in front to provide more dining space for customers. A large wooden second-story deck extended above the patio. People gathered on the deck later in the evening to hear local musicians and entertainers when the weather permitted.

Freyja led the way past the bottom of the deck steps to the entrance. A sign between the entrance and deck steps advertised that night's entertainment: Hondo the Magnificent - OBX Renowned Mentalist - Upper Deck at 9:30. They hesitated in front of the sign.

Wolf asked, "Do you want to get your mind read tonight?"

She shook her head. "I wouldn't want to traumatize the poor guy."

Wolf laughed, stepped around her and pulled open the door. "Ahh, a true gentleman," she said.

"And a scholar?"

"I wouldn't go that far."

They entered, and Freyja swiveled her head, checking out the décor. A multitude of Christmas bulbs and trimmings hung from the ceiling with lights dangling and twinkling from the tops of the windows. Although the place wasn't brightly lit, all the decorations and lights made it seem magical. Seascapes and antique framed photographs filled the walls along with old movie posters: Dean Martin, Frank Sinatra, Humphrey Bogart and Lauren Bacall. A wooden pirate stood nearby, with his black captain's hat, scarred cheeks and eyepatch.

"I'll fit right in here," she said.

Waitresses and waiters rushed here and there taking orders and delivering food. Loud laughter erupted now and again above the steady drone of a multitude of conversations, and lively folk music played in the background.

"Nothing like Christmas in September, huh?" Wolf said.

"Why not?" She reached and touched one of the low-hanging bulbs. "Christmas isn't just a day. It's a frame of mind."

Wolf laughed. "Where did you come up with that one? Some quote from an old movie?"

She elbowed his ribs. "Yeah. Miracle on Thirty-Fourth Street."

A plump, redheaded hostess in pirate garb led them to a corner table covered with a red plaid tablecloth. They sat opposite one another on two high-backed wooden benches. The hostess smiled and said, "Captain Jack will be here in a minute to take your orders."

Wolf noticed her name tag. "Arrrrrh, many thanks, and may I say you look splendid tonight, Miss Rita."

She thumbed toward her chest. "I'm the reason Roger is jolly." She winked and headed back to the front of the restaurant.

Wolf peered upwards. Red and silver Christmas bulbs hung from the ceiling above their table. On the wall above Freyja, the fading light of day filtered through a colorful stained-glass window. Below the window hung a painting of a ship flying the skull and crossbones flag on a treacherous sea.

"I think I might have some pirate blood in me," Wolf said.

Freyja lifted her chin. "I have my doubts."

"Arrrrh, me lady. You should never doubt me."

Captain Jack, a tall slim guy with a long black beard, red bandana and eyepatch, strode to the table and placed a couple of colorful menus in front of them. "What can I get you to drink, mateys?"

Wolf held his hands vertically about a foot apart. "A tall glass of red wine for me, Cap'n."

"And for the lady?"

Freyja tilted her head. "Rum."

Captain Jack raised his eyebrows. "Ahhh, a woman after me own heart. Be back in a few to take your orders."

"Red wine," Freyja sneered, "You're no pirate."

Wolf couldn't help smiling as he opened his menu. *She certainly knows how to duel.*

"What's good?" Freyja asked.

"Anything Italian. I'm getting the seafood lasagna."

She ran her finger down the menu. "I'll take the fettuccine alfredo with scallops and a side salad, Italian dressing."

"Good choice."

Captain jack returned with their drinks, and Wolf gave him their orders. He pivoted and headed toward the serving station.

"Where do they do the karaoke?" Freyja asked.

Wolf pointed to the other side of the room. "Back in the lounge. We'll head back there after we eat."

Wolf sat back and gazed at her. The scarred side of her face reflected the colorful lights in an interesting texture. She reached back, twisted her long hair, drew it over her shoulder and down across the scoop neckline of her dress. Her uniqueness gave her an exotic look, one that stirred desire within him.

"What are you thinking?" she asked.

"Probably the wrong thoughts."

She smiled. "Maybe you are a pirate."

"I get into enough trouble."

"I'm sure you see plenty of trouble. I'm curious. What kind of girl was she?"

"The missing girl?"

She nodded.

"The best kind. A hard worker. Talented. Read her Bible every day and loved Jesus. The apple of her father's eye." Wolf shook his head. "Billy Joel had her in mind when he wrote *Only the Good Die Young*."

"That's sad."

"My partner, Angie, took it hard. I'm used to it."

"What kind of talent did she have?"

"Huh?"

"You heard me. Was she an artist?"

Wolf nodded. "A singer. A really good singer. She won some local contests."

Freyja's lowered her chin causing the shadows to deepen on the scarred side of her face. She picked up her butter knife, placed it front of her and spun it slowly. "Was it an accident?"

"I don't know. I don't think so."

She raised her head and met his gaze. "I don't either."

"Any particular reason why?"

She shrugged. "Intuition."

"If her father doesn't get satisfying answers from the sheriff's department, he may call us back. I'd like to find out what happened."

"There's nothing worse than a tragedy with unanswered questions."

"Sounds like you speak from experience."

She lowered her eyes. "I do."

Wolf decided not to pry. He told her about his years serving as a Dare County deputy and decision to resign and start his own detective agency. To his delight, she seemed interested and asked several questions.

Captain Jack approached with a large tray and placed their meals in front of them. "Refills?"

Wolf raised his wine goblet. "Fillerup."

Freyja said, "Why not? More rum!"

With dramatic flair, Captain Jack swooped up their glasses. "I'll be back in the wink of a wench's eye." He twirled and marched away.

Freyja picked up her fork. "This looks really good."

"Dig in."

They ate ravenously for next few minutes until Captain returned with their refills.

Freyja put down her fork and took a big swig of rum.

Wolf pointed to her throat. "Getting your vocal chords ready, aren't you?"

She closed one eye and nodded. "It's been a while since I sang in public."

Wolf wondered if it was because of her disfigurement. "You don't have to answer this if you don't want to, but how did it happen?"

She ran her left hand gently over her damaged cheek and gave him a cold stare.

Chapter 7

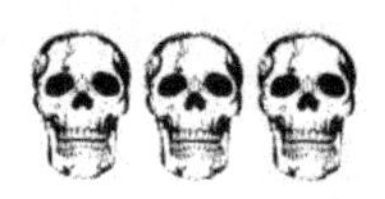

"I was attacked."

"Acid?"

She nodded. "A crazy old man came right up to me out of nowhere and threw a can of hydrochloric acid at me. I turned, and it splattered on the side of my face."

"Did they catch him?"

She swayed her head back and forth. "He vanished like a dust devil. No one else saw him. I gave the cops a detailed description, but they came up empty."

"That's really . . . strange. Do you think it was random?"

"That's what the cops said." Her eyes narrowed. "But I think someone hired him."

"Someone who didn't like you?"

She nodded. "I had rivals. One day I'm going to find out who did it."

"You know, I could help. That's one of *my* talents."

She leaned on her elbows and studied him for several seconds.

He spread his lips tight against his gums and spoke through clamped teeth. "How do I compare to that palomino?"

"I haven't decided yet. I *have* noticed one thing, though."

"What's that?"

She pointed to his incisor. "You've got parsley stuck right there."

Wolf swept his tongue over his tooth. "Thanks. Like I told you this morning, I can turn into a jackass without warning."

"Our meals are getting cold. Do you want to talk or eat?"

"Let's eat."

"Good idea."

* * *

As they were finishing up, a lady approached their table. She was a sharp-looking gal, maybe sixty years old with wavy, golden-wheat colored hair that curled around her shoulders. She wore a red vest, tied in the front with loose strings, over a white t-shirt with a V neckline. She had on a black midi dress with fringe at the hem. A crimson cord around her waist secured a long plastic sword.

"Weston Wolf!" she roared. "How much wine have you guzzled?"

Wolf held up two fingers. "Just two glasses."

"Two too many."

"Don't worry, Kathy Jo. I don't plan on singing tonight."

She raised a hand. "God help us all if you do."

Wolf waved toward Freyja. "I'd like you to meet Freyja Beck."

The woman extended her hand, "Kathy Jo Landon. I own the place."

Freyja shook her hand. "Nice to meet you. I love it here."

She spread her hands. "It's different, isn't it?"

Freyja nodded. "Different is good. I feel comfortable here."

Kathy Jo studied her face. "You're a beautiful girl. You should feel comfortable anywhere."

"Thanks. That's not most peoples' opinion, but I appreciate your kind words."

"You just need to be careful about one thing."

"What's that?"

Kathy Jo pointed to Wolf. "Going out with a guy like this. Did you know he got arrested here a few years ago for being drunk and disorderly?"

"Noooo." A wide grin broke across Freyja's face, and she scrutinized Wolf.

Kathy Jo winked at Freyja and turned to Wolf. "Keeping secrets from your date, huh?"

Wolf picked up his butter knife and pointed it at Kathy Jo. "We've all got skeletons hiding in our closets."

"Yeah, but yours can't sing."

Freyja laughed.

"Geeesh," Wolf said. "Two against one. This ain't a fair fight."

"You're right," Freyja said. "Two women with sharp tongues against a guy with a dull butter knife."

Wolf placed the knife on his plate. "Alright, ladies, you win."

"Are you two sticking around for karaoke?" Kathy Jo asked.

"Wouldn't miss it." Wolf thumbed at Freyja. "She's going to sing some Sinatra for us."

Kathy Jo leaned back and placed her hands on her hips. "Wonderful!"

"Don't expect anything close to Celine Dion," Freyja said.

Kathy Jo smiled. "I'd be disappointed if you sang like Celine Dion."

"Really?"

She nodded. "I want you to sing like Freyja Beck."

"I can handle that."

Kathy Jo leaned and gently touched Freyja's shoulder. "You see, darling, that's the difference between fashion and style. Fashion is trying to be like someone else. Style is being yourself. You've got style."

"Thanks." Freyja peered at the Christmas bulbs above her head. "And so do you."

"Two ladies with lots of style," Wolf patted his chest, "and a guy with a great smile. What more . . . could you ask for?"

Kathy Jo gave him a tolerant grimace, turned to Freyja and said, "There's only a couple slots left. I'm going to put your name down. When you get to the lounge, just let the DJ know the song, and he'll queue it up for you when it's your turn."

"Thanks. Will do," Freyja said.

Kathy Jo headed in the direction of the lounge.

Wolf called out, "I've changed my mind, Kathy Jo! Put my name down too!"

She took a quick peek over her shoulder. "No!"

Captain Jack checked in to see if they wanted more drinks or deserts. Wolf let him know that they were heading to the lounge and asked for the bill.

He raised his finger and said, "Be back in two shakes of strumpet's rump." He pivoted and hurried away.

Wolf grinned. "The Cap'n is definitely an original." He sat back and clasped his hands over his stomach. "Did you enjoy the meal?"

"Delicious."

"I'm curious." He leaned forward. "Why did you decide to vacation on the Outer Banks by yourself?"

"It's more of a business trip."

"I thought you told me you were in between jobs."

"I am."

Wolf waited to see if she wanted to volunteer more information.

"I'm here to finalize my divorce."

Wolf bobbed his head. "I see. Your husband lives down here?"

"Yes, about three months out of the year. He owns four homes—one in California, one in Illinois, one in Texas and one here."

Wolf straightened. "He must be loaded."

"He is. I fell in love with his reputation and mystique." She pointed to her temple. "No brains. I was a foolish wannabe starlet."

"What does he do?"

"He's a movie producer. He's done some work for MGM but mostly independent films. I was scheduled to appear in his next big thriller as a nightclub singer . . ." She brushed the scarred side of her face with her fingertips. ". . . until this happened."

"What's his name?"

"Saul Winterstein."

"I think I've heard of him."

"Most of his movies make good money. Some tank. Once we separated, I went back to my maiden name. I don't like the sound of Freyja Winterstein."

"Sounds cold to me."

Captain Jack returned with the bill. "I'm here to collect the booty."

Wolf gave him a credit card and told him to take a twenty percent tip.

He bowed and said, "May your anchor hold tight, and your cork be loose, sir."

As he walked away, Wolf said, "Your husband ought to give that guy an audition."

Freyja curled her lip. "The Cap'n would have a better chance of impressing Saul if he were young, pretty and female."

Wolf chuckled. "Winterstein's a skirt chaser?"

She nodded.

"May the dissolution of your marriage go smoothly and painlessly."

"It should." She crossed her arms. "We had a prenup."

Captain Jack returned with Wolf's credit card, and they headed for the lounge.

* * *

The people in the lounge buzzed with excitement, their conversations blending with the progressive pop music that jangled over the speakers. The far wall, paneled by large mirrors, set the backdrop for the stage. Colorful lights swirled and flashed, sending specks and dots reflecting off the mirrors, walls and ceiling. The luminous colors glided over faces and bodies, giving the place an otherworldly ambience. The DJ's setup appeared highly professional, his soundboard and laptop computer situated on the left side of the stage. Several large screen TVs hung above the mirrors, and an American flag stood proudly on the right side next to the wall.

Wolf led Freyja through the crowd to a small table in the corner where a young brunette sat by herself. "Do you mind if we take these two empty seats?" Wolf asked the girl.

"No. Please sit down. I'm here alone." Her long auburn hair, parted in the middle, had been plaited into two tails that hung over the front of her shoulders and reached to the top of her blue-checkered sundress. Her big brown eyes gazed up at Wolf from an innocent face with rosy cheeks.

Wolf pulled out a spindled-back wooden chair, and Freyja sat down on it next to the girl. Wolf slid into the seat across from her.

Freyja extended her hand. "My name's Freyja."

The girl shook Freyja's hand, and smiled, her eyes widening slightly. "I'm Judy Gayle. Nice to meet you." She spoke with a Midwest dialect.

Freyja pointed to the left side of her face. "My scars don't scare you, do they?"

She shook her head no. "They make you look . . . unique."

Freyja laughed. "Thanks. That's one way to put it. This is my friend, Weston Wolf."

"Hello," Judy said.

Wolf closed one eye. "What's a young gal like you doing in a karaoke bar all by yourself?"

"I'm nineteen," she chirped and picked up her glass. "This is just a coke. Are you a policeman?"

Wolf smiled. "I use-to-was. Now I'm just a private investigator. Why are you here alone?"

"I'm looking for somebody."

"Your boyfriend?" Freyja asked.

"No, my sister."

"Well, if she shows up, Wes can stand and give her the seat."

Wolf shrugged. "Sure. I'm a gentleman. Maybe not a scholar but a gentleman."

"Do you live around here?" Freyja asked.

"No. I'm from Kansas. I just came to enjoy the beach for a few days."

Wolf grunted. "Clear from Kansas? You and your sister came a long way to see the ocean."

"Kansas is smack in the middle of the United States. There's no shortcut to an ocean from where I live. This is the first time I've ever been to the beach. It's incredibly beautiful here."

Freyja asked, "Did you and your sister drive or fly?"

She shook her head nervously. "I drove by myself. Sammi flew down about a month ago and rented a car. She hoped to find a job down here."

"May I have your attention please," the broad-shouldered DJ announced from the front of the stage. He had short dark hair, just starting to turn gray. The flashing specks of light danced on the lens of his black-framed glasses and square-jawed face. A large silver cross dangled from his neck. "We are ready to get this show started."

The crowd cheered.

The DJ held up one hand to calm them down. "Let's welcome Charlie King, who will be sweeping you ladies off your feet with a great country song, *Ladies Love Country Boys*."

Charlie King stood about five feet five inches tall and weighed close to two hundred pounds. He wore a black cowboy hat and a black, long-sleeved shirt with red roses embroidered on both front pockets. His belly overhung a wide silver belt buckle. He took the microphone from the DJ's assistant and twirled onto the stage, head bobbing to the twangy, upbeat intro. "This is for all you good looking cowgirls out there," he cooed.

Whoops, shouts and whistles burst from the crowd. The flat screen TVs mounted above the mirrors behind him flashed the lyrics. He gazed up at a TV hanging from the ceiling above him. The steel guitars yowled to the steady beat, and he started in, half speaking and half singing the words. His voice was decent but not great. The crowd didn't care. They got swept up in his dramatic poses and gyrations, the more theatrical the better. When he finished, the throng hollered and clapped as he bowed several times.

The next singer looked to be about forty, a thin lady with limp blonde hair and an overbite. She wore a tight blue t-shirt with the Cape Hatteras Lighthouse printed on it, the black and white stripes spiraling up to the light that beamed around her collar. She sang an Adele song, *Rolling in the Deep,* but couldn't carry a tune in a Yeti cooler. The crowd waned in their enthusiasm, but thankfully, no one booed.

After the lighthouse t-shirt lady stumbled to the song's finish line, three sisters took the stage. Their long brown hair framed attractive faces. Wolf wondered if they were triplets because they dressed in the same: loose fitting beige tunic tops and tight blue jeans with matching holes in the knees. They sang a rap song, one Wolf had never heard before. He didn't listen to much rap music. The audience knew it and clapped in time to the lively beat. The girls, repeating something about ba-na-nas, danced and sang with choreographed precision. Wolf figured this wasn't their first karaoke rodeo.

A waitress, a cute blonde wearing a violet mini dress and black boots, came around and took drink orders. Wolf insisted on buying the round. He ordered himself another glass of red wine. Judy wanted a refill on her Coke, and Freyja decided to skip the rum and go with a Coke, too. As they waited for their drinks another country boy took the stage and crooned out an old Alabama song, *Feels So Right*. He was fairly talented, and the ladies in the audience loved him.

The next guy up was an old, bald fart who had been downing one too many Bud Lights. He slurred the words to Elvis's *I Can't Help Falling in Love with You*, not coming close to hitting the right notes. Wolf couldn't watch. It was too painful. He turned to the young brunette and said, "Doesn't look like your sister is going to show."

She shook her head slowly, eyes downcast. "I haven't been able to reach her on my phone. I've messaged her ten times."

"Where is she staying?" Freyja asked.

"I don't know for sure. Some guy's big beach house. She met him here at the Jolly Rodger. I was hoping she would show up tonight."

Something didn't sound right to Wolf. He could tell by the tone of her voice and uncertainty of her sister's whereabouts that she felt uneasy. "So you haven't seen her since you arrived?"

She wagged her head and took a deep, calming breath.

The old, bald guy finished up and staggered by their table as the DJ announced, "Ladies and Gentlemen, our next singer has come a long way to delight us with a beloved classic. Clear from Emporia, Kansas, let's welcome Judy Gayle."

The young girl stiffened, eyes wider than twin full moons. "That's me!" She scooted the chair back and stood. "I signed up to sing. I hope I don't mess up."

"You'll do fine." Freyja reached and patted her back. "Go get 'em."

Judy about-faced and marched to the stage. The DJ's assistant handed her the microphone, and she panned the crowd and swallowed. "I've a feeling . . . " The rustling and voices of the throng quieted. "I've a feeling we're not in Kansas anymore."

Mumbling and soft laughter ensued for a few seconds, but then the place became silent.

Judy closed her eyes and slowly tilted her head upwards. As the familiar strains of *Somewhere Over the Rainbow* began, she lowered her head and gazed at the audience. Her voice was angelic. Wolf felt chills rush down his back. The scene transported him thirty years into the past to the first time he sat in front of his grandfather's television with his family and watched *The Wizard of Oz*. The young girl hit every note with perfection. Wolf glanced at Freyja and noticed the girl's voice had captivated her. Every stanza about hopes, dreams, wishes, lemon drops and chimney tops was charged with emotion. An older lady sitting nearby began to sniffle, and Wolf noticed several people wiping their eyes. The song ended with the question: *Why can't I*? and the room exploded with cheering and applause. The clapping went on for almost a minute. Judy smiled and nodded as they lauded her. Finally, she handed the microphone back to the assistant and pranced to their table.

Freyja stood, reached and gripped her shoulders. "You were fantastic!"

"Do you really think so?"

"Are you kidding?" Wolf said. "They had to send a waiter to get a crate of Kleenex before the place flooded."

She sat down and tried to slow her breathing.

"Where did you get that kind of talent?" Wolf asked.

"I come from a musical family. My sister is a good singer, too."

"I look forward to meeting your sister," Freyja said.

"I'll check my phone to see if she answered my text."

The DJ introduced another singer, a muscle-bound guy wearing a pink tank top emblazoned with the image of a surfer in the curl of a huge wave. He had on pink sweatpants that resembled tights. Wolf laughed to himself, thinking the guy is right where he feels comfortable: in front of a giant mirror. The drumbeat started, and he danced around the stage like a rusty robot. His voice sounded robotic, too: "I'm too sexy for my shirt, too sexy for my shirt, too sexy."

Freyja tilted her head toward the stage. "What do you think of that specimen?"

"I think he looks like a pink nightmare," Wolf sneered.

The singer lifted the bottom of his tank top to reveal a solid eight-pack. "I'm too sexy for my shirt, to sexy for my shirt, too sexy."

A half-drunk woman yelled, "Then take the damn thing off!"

Unfortunately, he obliged.

"I can't watch this," Wolf grumbled. He shifted in his seat, faced the women and noticed Freyja shaking her head and shifting her focus away from the stage, too.

Judy gazed at her phone. "Sammi finally answered me. She says she's busy for the next few days but hopes to meet up with me later in the week." Her shoulders slumped and the corners of her mouth drooped.

"Maybe she got that job she was looking for," Freyja said.

"Maybe."

"So you're staying all by your lonesome in some hotel room?" Wolf asked.

Judy nodded. "Don't worry about me. I'll find something to do for the next few days."

"Do you like to ride horses?" Freyja asked.

"Sure. I'm from cowboy country."

"Come over to my place tomorrow morning, and we'll head to the Outer Banks Stables south of Nags Head."

"That would be great. Give me your address." Judy dug for a pen in her small handbag and handed it to Freyja. She jotted a few words on a napkin and handed the pen and napkin back to Judy.

The Pink Nightmare finished his I'm-Too-Sexy song and dance. He strutted back into the crowd, and the drunk lady, who told him to take off his shirt, goosed him as he walked by. He rocketed three feet into the air. Fortunately, the short cowboy caught him as he tumbled forward. "Steady there now, partner," the cowboy chortled.

The DJ ambled to the center of the stage. "Ladies and gentlemen, before I introduce our last singer, I'd like to remind you that Hondo the Magnificent will be appearing on the upper deck at 9:30. You don't want to miss Hondo, he's a mind reader of extraordinary powers. Now . . . with no further adieu, let's welcome to the Jolly Roger karaoke stage Miss Freyja Beck!"

"My turn." Freyja scooted her chair out, stood and strode to the left side of the stage. She leaned over the soundboard and said something to the DJ. He scrolled down the screen of his laptop and nodded to her. The assistant handed her the microphone, and she took her place in the middle of the stage.

When she turned and faced the audience, a few people gasped. The red and yellow lights flashed across her face, creating a dichotomy of beauty and terror. She appraised the onlookers as if she dared them to look away. The song commenced with the spattering of piano keys and the deep moan of stringed instruments. With a husky but exquisite voice, she sang the first line to *My Way*. The tone of her words sent a eerie shiver through Wolf: "So now, the end is near and I will face the final curtain." He glanced at Judy. She sat utterly still, transfixed on Freyja's face as if she were seeing a phantom.

Chapter 8

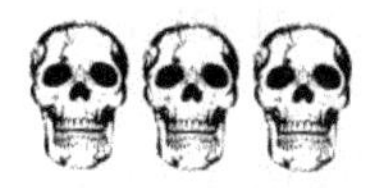

The song became her tragic story. With each line of facing the hard knocks of life, taking the blows but refusing to cave, doggedly placing one foot in front of the other, she began to win the audience over. With every movement of her body and facial expression, the lyrics flowed with dramatic artistry. The words to the final stanza became an anthem uniting the listeners with her: their hard-fought battles, their bitter disappointments, their heartfelt losses, but yet the determination to press on and live life with hope and ferocity. Wolf sensed a communal jubilance as Freyja belted out the final: "I did it my way!"

The crowd stood to their feet, applauded and cheered as if a great victory had been won. Freyja scanned their faces and nodded, binding the union between them. The woman on the stage was no longer an oddity but one of them: a sufferer, a loser, a winner, a fighter, a survivor, a human being. As the cheering diminished, Freyja smiled, a smile that said I know the battles you are facing, and I stand with you. At that moment Wolf was overcome by her beauty. It beamed from the inside and transformed her disfigurement into something ethereal.

She glided back to their table, and Judy embraced her, planting her head against her chest. They stood there holding each other for almost a minute. Finally, the young girl stepped back and said, "I feel like I've met you before, like I've known you my whole life."

"I think we're going to be very good friends," Freyja said. "Sometimes you just know in your heart when you make a connection with someone."

They sat down, and Wolf couldn't keep from staring at Freyja.

"What's wrong with you?" she asked.

He shook himself out of the trance. "I'm sorry. Your performance . . . stunned me."

Freyja laughed. "Good. Consider it a gift."

"What do you mean?"

She spread her hands. "Surprise! What's a better gift in life than being surprised?"

Wolf chuckled to himself. Her words rang with truth, and he recalled seeing her on the surface of the ocean and then disappearing beneath the waves for minutes like a mermaid. *You are my wonderful surprise.*

The crowd filtered out of the lounge, many of them praising Freyja and Judy as they passed. Wolf felt like he was sitting with two celebrities. A strange emotional high charged through him, and he wondered if their performances had triggered some chemical reaction in his body.

Judy reached across the table and grasped Freyja's hand. "Where did you learn to sing like that?"

"Your voice is better than mine."

She shook her head. "You made people feel something deep inside. I can imitate other singers, but I can't do what you did."

"Yes, you can." Freyja placed her palm on her heart. "You moved me."

Wolf raised his hand. "I can second that."

"Really?"

Kathy Jo Landon approached their table. She carried a small gift box in one hand and a pen and a piece of paper in the other. She leaned over slightly, holding the objects in front of her. "Can I get your autographs?"

"Sure," Wolf said. "Give me the pen. I'll sign my John Hancock for you."

She frowned. "Bob Dylan sings better than you. I'm talking about these two Divas. Those were the most memorable songs ever sung in this place." She handed Judy the pen and a piece of stationary with the restaurant's letterhead.

Judy's mouth dropped open. "Are you serious?"

"Yes!"

"What should I write?"

Wolf pointed to Kathy Jo's plastic sword. "How about: To Kathy Jo, may your blade always be sharp and your powder dry."

Kathy Jo laughed. "That's actually pretty good, but no. Write: *To Kathy Jo at the Jolly Rodger – a night to remember*. Then you both can sign your name."

Judy wrote out the words and passed the pen and stationery to Freyja. She signed her name and added a few more words.

Kathy Jo picked up the paper and read it. "That's good!" She lowered it so that Wolf could see it."

In his best pirate inflection, he read: "BE WHO YOU ARRRRRRGH!"

Kathy Jo set the small gift box on the table, stepped back, slipped her phone out of her vest pocket and took their photograph. "I'll print out the picture and attach it to the stationery. Then I'll put it in a nice frame and hang it right over there." She pointed to the wall next to the American flag. Several framed pictures hung there.

Wolf picked up the gift box. "Is this for me?"

Kathy Jo pointed to Judy. "Give that to the young lady, you scallywag,"

Wolf handed her the box.

"Why me?"

"Some woman asked me to give it to you. She loved your song. It brought back some wonderful memories. She said she placed a personal note inside the box."

"What did she look like?" Freyja asked.

"I'd say she was about forty, short black hair, a good-looking lady. She left right after she handed me the box."

"I wish I could have thanked her." Judy examined the container. It was about six inches long and giftwrapped in a ruby shade of foil. "Maybe she wrote her address on the note. If so, I can send her a thank you card tomorrow."

"I've got to get going," Kathy Jo said. "Hondo the Magnificent is about ready to get started on the upper deck. I don't want to miss it. Thanks for the autographs. You'll both be famous one day." She winked, turned and headed to the front of the restaurant.

Judy placed the box in her small handbag. "I don't want to go back to that lonely hotel room yet."

"Why don't you hang out with us?" Freyja asked.

Judy shifted her focus to Wolf, her eyes pleading.

"I don't mind." He spread his hands palms up. "I feel lucky to be in the company of two beautiful and talented women."

"You must be Irish," Freyja said.

Wolf raised his empty glass. "I should be drinking whiskey."

Judy planted her hands on the table. "I know what we can do. Let's check out Hondo the Magnificent."

Wolf gave a thumbs up. "That might be fun. Just so he doesn't charge too much to read our minds."

Freyja chuckled. "He'll probably give you a big discount."

"You misjudge me, madam." Wolf tapped his forehead. "A person could get lost wandering the galaxy of these neural pathways."

Freyja reached and gently tapped his cheek. "C'mon, Galileo, let's get up there before the show starts."

They stood, and Freyja led the way out of the lounge.

"I hope Hondo the Magnificent is truly magnificent!" Judy trilled.

Wolf followed the women, reaching and brushing his cheek where she had touched him. *Freyja is truly magnificent.* With every minute spent with this eccentric lady, he felt his insides altering, something forming in a place once empty. Was it the excitement of a new relationship? Or the discovery of her unusual personality? Maybe it was the stirrings of romance or the rising flames of desire. He couldn't quite put his finger on it. *Man, oh man, this woman has got me feeling a little bit lost.*

They exited the restaurant and climbed the long wooden stairway to the upper deck. Wolf judged the space to be about fifteen feet by thirty feet. Perhaps fifty people had gathered, half sitting at tables and the other half standing. A fresh breeze blew in from the ocean, and the rumble of surf could be heard in the distance. A spotlight beamed down on Hondo the Magnificent and his assistant at the far end of the deck. Smaller lights and Christmas lights were strung on poles around the railing, adding a colorful glow to the onlookers. Hondo, an older man with grayish-bronze hair, thick eyebrows and a bulbous nose, was dressed in a black suit with a green vest and bowtie. He looked like he just stepped out of a 1910 barbershop. His assistant, a nice-looking young blonde, wore a black top hat and cape over a flimsy red mini dress.

All the seats had been taken, so the three of them stood against the back railing. Wolf slipped his hand around Freyja's back. She glanced at him, smiled and leaned against his shoulder. Her skin was warm, and she smelled of vanilla muskiness. The sensations made him a little dizzy and excited. He took in a deep breath and savored the scent. *Yeah, I think I'm getting lost.*

"Tonight, ladies and gentlemen," Hondo began, "you will see an amazing demonstration of extrasensory powers. I was born with this gift. When the moment is right, I can hear your thoughts and see your visions."

His assistant weaved through the crowd and stopped in the middle of the deck.

He continued, "Is there a lady here by the name of Leah . . . or Linda . . . or Lisa."

"My name's Lisa!" a woman gasped.

"Please stand up."

She wore a yellow top with puffy shoulders. Her wide face, red from sunburn, and plump body reminded Wolf of his third-grade teacher, Mrs. Roberts. *Damn, that lady smacked me with her ruler one too many times.* He shook the memory away. Lisa took a big breath and faced Hondo.

He slipped a green, glittering blindfold over his eyes. "Madam, I cannot see you with this blindfold on. I don't want people to think I am reading your expressions. First I thank you for the opportunity to connect with you mentally."

"You're welcome." She had a southern accent.

"You are vacationing on the Outer Banks with your family, correct?"

"That's right."

"You're from the south, not too far away."

"I'm from southern Virginia, Suffolk County."

"Yes, just north of here. Let's see . . . you spent the day at the beach."

She nodded. "All day."

Hondo rubbed his chin. "You've vacationed here in the past."

"That's correct. Almost every September for the last ten years."

A spattering of applause tinkled around the deck.

"You are a mother with several children."

"That's right!"

"And you have a dog."

"Noooo."

"I mean a cat."

"Yes! Two cats."

Wolf leaned and whispered in Freyja's ear. "Two cats equal a dog."

She shook her head and giggled.

"Lisa," Hondo intoned deeply, "I would like you to take an object, any object out of your purse and hand it to my assistant, Emily."

"Okay." Her purse sat on the table beside her. She opened it, withdrew a set of keys and handed them to the top-hatted blonde.

"Hondo, this *kind* lady has handed me the object." The assistant raised the keys and made a complete turn for the crowd to see.

Hondo touched his temple. "This object is very important to you. With it, doors will open for you, and without it, you'll be left out in the cold. The object is a set of keys."

Lisa gasped, and the audience clapped loudly.

"How did he know that?" Judy exclaimed.

Freyja's applause was less enthusiastic. She eyed Wolf and smiled skeptically.

"I know what *you're* thinking," Wolf said in a low tone. "This guy's the next Kreskin."

"Not even close," Freyja said coolly.

Hondo removed his blindfold. "Is there an older gentleman in the audience tonight from Ohio?"

Three old guys raised their hands. Hondo pointed to the one standing near Wolf. "You sir, what part of Ohio are you from?"

"Youngstown!" he shouted. A few people applauded. Wolf judged him to be about seventy years old. He was bald on top with close-cropped gray hair on the sides. He wore a black and yellow football jersey with the number twelve on it.

"What is your name, sir?"

"John Harris."

Hondo slipped his green-glittering mask over his eyes again. "Mr. Harris, I sense that you've labored hard all of your life with your hands."

"That's true."

"I see a large building . . . a factory. I hear lots of noise."

"That's the steel mill where I worked for thirty-five years."

Murmurs resonated throughout the crowd.

"You are a big football fan."

"That's right."

"But you're not a Cleveland Browns fan."

"Damn straight! Go Steelers!"

Applause erupted.

Wolf said, "Lots of Steeler fans here tonight."

Hondo raised his hands to quiet the audience. "Mr. Harris, I would like you to take out your wallet and remove any object from it—your license, your insurance card, whatever. Then hand the object to my assistant, Emily."

The blonde made her way through the crowd to where Mr. Harris stood. He slipped a one hundred dollar bill out of his wallet and handed it to the girl.

Emily raised the bill and waved it in the air. "Mr. *Harris* has given me the object."

Hondo raised and lowered his head several times slowly. "It's a one hundred dollar bill."

"That's amazing!" Harris cried, and the upper deck reverberated with cheers.

Hondo the Magnificent took off his blindfold. When the crowd quieted, he said, "Are you amazed enough to contribute the one hundred dollars to my rainy-day fund?"

"What's that?" The old man reached for the bill, but Emily backed away.

"I'm only kidding," Hondo said. "Emily, please give Mr. Harris back his money."

With a wry smile, the assistant handed over the bill. The crowd laughed and a gray-haired woman slapped him on the back and said, "Johnny, you told me you were down to your last dime."

Hondo cleared his throat, and the laughter and talking diminished. "There is a young woman here tonight who is a talented artist."

Wolf leaned back and thumbed toward Judy.

Hondo caught sight of his gesture and pointed at her. "You, young lady."

Judy placed her hand on her chest. "Me?"

"Yes."

The assistant stepped beside her.

Hondo closed his eyes. "You are a very talented . . . singer! Correct?" His eyes popped open.

Heads bobbed around the audience, and several people clapped.

"I don't know. I guess so," Judy said.

"You're also very modest." He slipped the blindfold over his eyes. "You are from a western state. You've come a long way from home."

Judy nodded. "That's right."

"You are from Kansas."

Judy straightened and sucked in a quick breath. "Yes."

"You are on a journey in life, looking for something."

Her face muscles tightened, and her eyes focused intensely. "Yes, I am."

"Young lady . . ." He templed his hands in front of his chest. ". . . you will find what you are looking for if you believe with all your heart."

Judy's eyes widened. "I'll do my very best."

"I want you to take an object out of your purse, any object, and hand it to my assistant."

Judy reached into her handbag, pulled out the gift box and handed it to Emily.

The assistant held it up for all to see. "Hondo, the young lady has *bestowed* upon me the object."

"Very good." He touched his forehead. "This is some kind of container. There is an object within an object."

A few people clapped, and Emily smiled broadly and waved the box again.

"It is a box."

"Yes," the assistant said, "but can you tell us what's in the box."

"It's something very beautiful, perhaps a gift."

"That's right," Judy said. "Someone gave it to me tonight."

"What's inside could be the key to your future."

"Really?" Judy clasped her hands in front of her.

Hondo bobbed his head. "It may lead you to what you are searching for."

Judy turned, gripped Freyja's arm just below her shoulder and asked, "How does he know that I'm looking for my sister?"

Freyja dipped her head closer and said, "He doesn't. He's just guessing."

Judy faced Hondo again.

Emily held up the box. "Could you open it and see what's inside?"

"I . . . I guess so."

The assistant handed the box back to Judy, and she carefully peeled away the crimson foil. After giving the foil to Freyja, she lifted the lid. With her thumb and forefinger, she pinched the corner of the object and pulled it from the box. The wind fluttered a beautiful scarf patterned with impressionistic flowers.

Wolf stared at the flowing silk cloth, his heart thumping.

"There's something else in the box," Emily said.

Judy handed Freyja the scarf, lifted a piece of paper from the bottom of the box, unfolded it, and read it. Her face brightened. She raised her head and focused on Hondo the Magnificent. "It's an invitation! An invitation to an audition!"

Chapter 9

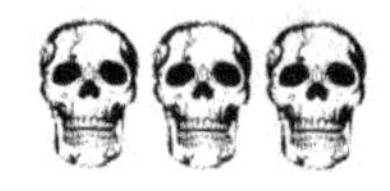

Wolf and Freyja walked Judy to her car, an older Chevy Malibu in need of a new coat of paint. Wolf sensed that Judy might be in danger but didn't feel he had enough evidence to prove his notion. He wanted to know more about the scarf and invitation. Somehow he had to warn her about the threatening possibilities without scaring her. He knew he didn't have all the facts. The body and scarf that washed up at the Whalehead Club may have nothing to do with any of this. Yet, something deep inside told him it did.

At her car door, Judy turned and said, "This was such a wonderful evening. I wish my sister would have been here to share it with us. Oh well, I'll see her later this week."

"I'm looking forward to meeting her," Freyja said.

"You'll love her. She's a great girl and talented, too. She's got an incredible voice."

"How about you?" Wolf pointed to the gift box. "An invitation to a big audition. Do you know where and when it will be?"

"It's tomorrow night. All the information is on the invitation. I'm so excited."

"And that scarf," Wolf said, "it's beautiful. Do you mind if I take a closer look at it?"

"Not at all." She pulled the scarf out of her handbag and handed it to Wolf.

The parking lot light above them offered Wolf sufficient visibility to inspect the cloth. It matched exactly, same patterns, same colors, same flowers, same staff and notes, same silky feel. He handed the scarf back to Judy.

"I don't want to lose this." She tucked it back into her purse. "According to the invitation, I need to show the scarf to the doorman to get into the audition."

"Just curious," Wolf said. "Where is the audition to be held?"

Judy shrugged. "It's a Corolla address. I guess I'll find out when I get there."

"You'll knock 'em dead," Freyja said.

"I'll do my best."

"Where are you staying?" Wolf asked.

"At the Best Western in Kitty Hawk."

Wolf patted her shoulder. "You know that a young girl staying by herself needs to be very careful. Make sure you keep your eye out for anyone who looks suspicious. We live in a dangerous world."

Judy's smile broadened her innocent face. "Don't worry about me." She patted her handbag. "I keep pepper spray with me all the time. Whenever I walk alone, I carry it in my hand."

"That's a good idea," Freyja said. "Always be prepared. I'll see you tomorrow morning about ten."

"I can't wait to ride horses with you." She hugged Freyja.

"Don't I get a hug?" Wolf asked."

"How could I forget you?"

As she hugged Wolf, a helpless feeling seeped through him like copper into a fresh stream. He wasn't her guardian or longtime friend. He had just met her. Yet he felt a responsibility to protect her. When she released him, he didn't want to let go. But he did. She opened the door, entered her car, backed out and drove away.

Freyja reached for his hand as they walked to the back of the parking lot. "Are you okay?" she asked.

He intertwined his fingers with hers. "I just have this strange feeling."

They separated at the back of the car, got in and sat in the darkness. Freyja grasped his hand again.

"You're worried about her," she said.

"Yeah."

"You think she might be in danger."

"Yeah."

"You're wondering what that audition is all about."

"Now you're starting to sound like Hondo the Magnificent. Are you going to put on a blindfold?"

"Not yet." She gave him a sensuous smile.

"He was a half decent mentalist."

"He knew the code."

"How did he know about Kansas?"

Freyja tilted her head and narrowed her eyes. "Obviously, he was there when they introduced Judy to the karaoke crowd. It's called pre-show research. Everything else was guesswork."

"Makes sense. I guess the thing that bothered me most was the scarf."

"Was it the same kind of scarf that washed up near the dead girl?"

"Perfect match."

"Was the missing girl a singer?"

Wolf nodded. "She won a major local contest."

"Hmmmm." She pulled her hand away from his and touched the scarred side of her face. "I wonder if she received an audition invitation, too."

"It's possible. Her co-worker mentioned she seemed hopeful that something good was about to happen."

Freyja sat quietly, staring out the windshield. Wolf started the car, backed out, headed for the exit and turned south on Route 12.

"What are *you* thinking?" Wolf asked.

"If the audition is tomorrow evening, then I would assume she should be safe tonight."

"I agree. I wouldn't want to jump to conclusions, though, and suspect that the people putting on the audition are killers. Maybe they are legit."

"Maybe. But circumstantial evidence has raised some questions."

Geeesh. She's talking like a detective. Wolf slowed for the first red light on the outskirts of Nags Head and came to a stop. "We don't know if the singer in the sound was murdered. She may have drowned accidentally. We're waiting for autopsy results."

"Until we know, we can't take any chances."

"That's true." The light turned green, and he eased his foot onto the accelerator. "So what do we do?"

"I'm not sure, but there's something else to consider."

"What's that?"

She shifted in her seat and faced Wolf. "This whole *Wizard of Oz* show tonight wasn't random."

"What do you mean?"

"Think about it, the way she fixed her hair, the blue-checkered dress, the song. That was all planned."

"Okay. What was her motive?"

"She has a strategy and knows more than she's letting on."

Wolf made a left onto Old Oregon Inlet Road. "You think Judy may have been disingenuous with us?"

"I wouldn't call it disingenuous."

Wolf chuckled. "She acted as innocent as Dorothy in Munchkin Land."

"I think she's a good kid. She's just not showing us all her cards."

"Maybe you can look over her shoulder and get a peek at them tomorrow."

"I'll see what I can do."

Wolf turned onto East Hunter Street, drove down the lane and pulled into his driveway.

He cut the engine. "Would you like to come in for a glass of wine?"

"No. I've had enough to drink tonight. It's been a long day."

Wolf's shoulders slumped along with his hopes.

"You could walk me to my door, though."

He straightened. "I think I can handle a thirty-foot walk."

They got out of the car, crossed the yard to her cottage, passed the old Jeep Renegade and climbed the steps to the front porch. Standing in the shadows, they faced each other. The few lights from the other houses on the street did little to alter the violet hues of the evening.

"Did you have a good time tonight?" Wolf asked.

"Yes. Did you?"

"Yeah. I had fun."

"It was interesting."

Wolf nodded. "The two words I would use to describe the evening are surprising and unexpected." Wolf drew closer and put his arms around her waist.

"Hmmmm. Are you about to surprise me?"

He kissed her, a quick kiss, and leaned back. "Surprised?"

"No." She gripped the back of his head, pulled him close and kissed him, a warm, wet kiss that lasted for several seconds. She broke it off. "Surprised?"

Wolf took a deep breath. "Yeah." He drew her tight against him and kissed her harder this time. After about a half minute, he opened his mouth slightly, hoping she would respond.

She pushed him away. "Whoa!"

He stepped back. "What's the matter?"

"You told me this morning not to ride you hard and put you away wet."

"C'mon now, you haven't even put the saddle on me yet."

She laughed. "If we ever get to that point, I'll ride you bareback. Good night, Detective Wolf." She turned, unlocked the door and entered the cottage.

As the door closed, Wolf wobbled his head like a stunned bobblehead doll. "Surprise, surprise."

Wolf crawled into bed around midnight but couldn't sleep. He kept thinking about Freyja, Judy and Jennifer Cobb. He turned on the TV to the classic movie channel and conked off watching an old crime flick. The sun beaming through the window and the sound of the surf finally stirred him awake. He checked the digital alarm on the nightstand: 8:55. By the time he showered, ate breakfast and dressed, it was almost ten. He entered the office and saw Angie at the front desk computer. She wore her usual gray Polo shirt and jeans.

"What are you doing, Angel? Watching those goofy cat videos on YouTube again?"

She gave him a perturbed glare over her shoulder. "I've been doing background checks and investigative work for the last two hours. Where've you been?"

"In the back doing some important investigative work of my own."

"Trailing femme fatales in your dreams doesn't count."

"What can I say? My mother always told me to follow my dreams."

"So that's why you sleep so much."

"Enough of the jabber. What's new, anything?"

She rolled back from the desk on the wheeled chair and spun toward him. "I called the Currituck County Sheriff's Office to check on the autopsy results."

"And . . . ?"

"Not in yet. Maybe this afternoon or early tomorrow."

"Figured it might be a little soon."

"Something else came up, though. Deputy Jenson told me a yellow kayak washed into shore a few days ago. Someone reported it, but they didn't think much about it until the body washed up yesterday."

"Now they figure it was an accidental drowning."

"Right. They believe she went kayaking after work that day, paddled too far out into the sound, got tipped by a wave and drowned."

"Did they check to see if it was a rental?"

"Yeah. No identifying markings. The local beach equipment and rental stores couldn't confirm anything."

Wolf raised his chin. "What do you think?"

"No way."

"I agree. If she were a kayaker, we would have heard about it."

"Her father agrees too. He called about twenty minutes ago. He reminded me about her car being left in the Food Lion parking lot. Why would she park it there and walk two miles back to the Whalehead Club to go kayaking?"

"Good point. Does he want us to keep working the case?"

"Yep."

"We can start checking with that list of friends he gave us."

"I've already called two of them."

"You are Sally on the spot."

"Golly gee, thanks, Mr. Wolf," she said in a mocking little-girl voice. "I couldn't get hold of one of them, but I'm meeting Willa Freedman at three. She works for the Outer Banks Conservationists at the Currituck Beach Lighthouse."

"What does she do?"

"Takes tickets. Keeps a head count of the people climbing to the top. That sort of thing."

Wolf bobbed his head slowly. "I'll check out the local restaurants and bars that offer karaoke. Maybe I can dig something up that can give us a lead."

"Sounds good." Angie scooted back toward the computer desk but stopped halfway. "How'd your date go last night?"

"We had a great time. Went to the Jolly Rodger. Had a good meal. Some karaoke."

Angie sneered, "How'd it go once you got back here?"

"Why do you ask?"

"Because Freyja seems like a cautious lady, and you think you're Casanova. I bet you didn't even get to first base."

Wolf expanded his chest. "I got to first base. We kissed."

"Really. I'm surprised."

"I tried to steal second base."

Angie chuckled. "What happened?"

"I held her close and said that I considered her body a temple."

"What'd she say?"

"'Sorry, no services tonight.'"

Angie shook her head and scooted back to the computer. "Denied! And your jokes suck."

"Something else happened last night that you'll want to hear about."

Angie angled away from the computer. "What?"

"We met a girl named Judy Gayle at the Jolly Rodger. She sang one of the best renditions of *Somewhere Over the Rainbow* that I've ever heard."

"That's nice."

"That's not all. When the karaoke was over, Kathy Jo Landon delivered a gift to our table for Judy. She said it was from an admirer."

Angie stiffened. "A scarf?"

Wolf nodded.

* * *

Wolf sat on the back deck at noon in the warm sunshine, eating a ham sandwich and drinking a cold Michelob, when he caught sight of two horseback riders trotting along the beach. He stood and shaded his eyes. *Freyja and Judy. Surprise, surprise.* Freyja rode the same palomino she had ridden yesterday. Judy's horse, jet black and slightly smaller, trailed a few yards behind. They loped up to the back of Wolf's deck.

"Howdy ho, ladies," Wolf called. "Back in the saddle again, huh?"

Judy waved. "Hi, Mr. Wolf." Her long auburn hair flowed down her back, unfettered by any ties or clasps. Her blue tank top fit her sleek torso snuggly, and her white shorts and pale legs beamed against the background of the saddle and black horse.

Freyja wore an outfit similar to the one she had on yesterday, a blue plaid shirt with cutoff sleeves, faded jeans and white-framed sunglasses. "Hi, Wes. We stopped to talk to you."

"Great. Park your ponies at the railing. I'll get us some Michelobs." Wolf turned but hesitated and spun back to the women. "Sorry, I forgot." He pointed to Judy. "You're only nineteen. I'll get you a Coke."

"Screw that. The act is over," she said. "I'm twenty-three years old. Get me a cold one."

Freyja raised her eyebrows and tilted her head.

Wolf noticed her accent had changed completely. East coast? "Okay. Three brews coming up."

Wolf headed to the kitchen. *Freyja nailed it. This gal put on a helluva show last night. Fooled me. What is she up to?* He opened the fridge and pulled out three brown bottles of beer. *She intended to get an invitation to that audition. Why? Is her sister in trouble?* He headed back down the short hallway, through his bedroom and out the sliding glass door. The girls sat at the round wooden table in the middle of the deck. Wolf lowered the beers, and they each grabbed one.

Wolf screwed off the cap and took a swig. "I guess were not in Kansas anymore."

Judy twisted off the cap with ease. "I'm from Jersey."

Wolf grinned. "I can tell by your accent. And you can ride a horse?"

She scowled at him. "Jersey girls ride horses."

"What's your real name?"

"Melissa Bianco, but you can call me Mel."

Freyja smiled and took a drink. She sat her bottle down with a clunk. "We had a long ride and a long talk."

"Soooo . . . " he eyed Mel, "You got what you wanted—an invitation to an audition. You're off to see the Wizard."

She shook her head. "More like the witch's castle."

Freyja leaned on her elbows. "Mel believes her sister is being held against her will."

"That's serious."

"It's my younger sister, Sammi. She sang at the Jolly Rodger and got the same scarf." Judy reached behind her and pulled a cell phone from her back pocket. "The last six texts I got from her were sent by an imposter."

"How do you know?"

She placed her thumb on the ID button to access her phone. "It's not her style. Someone must have seen her enter her code or else threatened her to give it up." She brought up her sister's message account and handed the phone to Wolf.

He scrolled down through the messages. They were filled with emojis and slang. In one she described a boy as juiced with a muscleman emoji. She called an ex-boyfriend a backpack and added a ball and chain emoji. There were lots of hearts, broken hearts, poop piles and smiley faces. One of the later posts said she stepped on a landmine.

"What does that mean: stepped on a landmine?"

"She teased the wrong kinda Romeo."

"Oh." Wolf felt like a grandpa talking to a teenager. "In other words, she was nice to some guy, and he came on too strong."

"Right. He went head over heels."

Wolf scrolled down through the remaining texts. "The landmine text is where the emojis stopped."

Mel gulped down about a third of a bottle and wiped her mouth. "Yeah. Those last six are blow-off texts. *I'm busy right now. I'll message you later. Can't talk now.* And last night's *I'll see you later in the week.* After the landmine text she wouldn't answer her phone, and I kept getting these kinds of I-don't-have-time-for-you messages."

"So what's your plan?" Wolf asked.

"I'm going there tonight to find my sister."

"I told her it could be very dangerous," Freyja said.

Mel finished off her beer and spun the bottle on the table. "I don't give a monkey's ass if it's dangerous! If one of those bastards did something to my sister, I'll cut off his kiwis!"

Wolf grimaced. "You're from Jersey alright."

Freyja patted the top of the table gently with her palms. "You need to calm down and think straight."

"Did Freyja tell you about the other girl?"

"The singer that drowned in the sound?"

Wolf nodded. "Same scarf."

"She told me. If they snuffed her and dumped her in the deep, they wouldn't hesitate to do it to Sammi. I'm going in there tonight."

Wolf leaned toward Mel. "They wouldn't hesitate to do it to you too either. That's why we need to *think* about this."

"There's something else that came up," Freyja said.

"What's that?"

"The address on the invitation . . ."

"What about it?"

"It's my husband's beach house."

Both women eyed Wolf as he processed the revelation.

"Shiiiiiit! Does your husband hold auditions there for his films?"

She nodded. "I told you I was in line for a part as a nightclub singer in his next big thriller."

"Yeah, I remember."

"He's still trying to raise the funds to produce that movie. It's his pet project."

Wolf stood, circled the deck and came back to the table. "A yellow kayak washed into shore by the Whalehead Club a few days ago. The other girl's death might have been an accident. We have no proof that she went to an audition. I wish we could be absolutely sure about this before we made any drastic moves."

The girls shifted their focus to the doorway. Wolf turned to see Angie standing there.

She stepped onto the deck and clasped a book with a solid brown cover to her side. "Hi, Freyja."

Freyja smiled and waved. "Hello, Angie."

Wolf motioned to Angie. "Mel Bianco, I'd like you to meet Angie Stallone, my partner."

"Nice to meet you," Mel said.

Angie stepped closer. "Are you the girl that received the scarf and invitation last night?"

"Yeah."

Angie's lips tightened. She held the book in front of her and glanced from it to Mel.

"What do you got there, Angel?" Wolf asked.

She placed the book on the table. "Jennifer Cobb's Bible."

Chapter 10

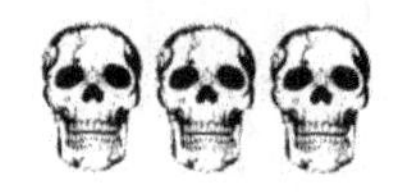

Angie opened the thick book towards the back to where she had bookmarked it with a Post-it Note. "For the last two hours I've been reading the passages and notes in the margins."

Wolf scooted his chair closer to the Bible. "Did you find something?"

"I think so. I've read so many scriptures I could pass the Pope's ordination exam. Look at this one from First Peter chapter five: *God opposes the proud but shows favor to the humble. Humble yourselves, therefore, under God's mighty hand that he may lift you up in due time."*

Wolf leaned closer and read the note in the margin next to the verse. "The Lord has opened a door for me. My time has come. I am claiming this verse for tonight's audition and screentest."

"Look at the date." Angie pointed below the note. "August 28, that was eleven days ago."

Wolf rubbed his chin. "The dots are starting to connect, but we don't have a complete picture." He focused on Freyja. "You were married to the guy. How coldblooded is he?"

She bit her lip for a few seconds. "I don't think Saul would commit murder. I don't know about his inner circle. He hired a new girl to recruit talent a couple months before I left. Her name is Elaine Maxell. We never got along. His security guy, Jake Cleaver, has a shady background. There's a housekeeper and a cook. They seem harmless. His mother lives in an upstairs apartment. She's in her late seventies and has health problems."

"How about people on the fringe?" Angie asked. "Does he keep a tight rein on who comes in and out?"

"He's careful, but his business requires networking. He can't make a film without the financial backing. He'll invite movie stars and millionaires to his parties in hopes of raising interest and possible commitments. If he can get a major star to sign on, the fundraising gets easier."

"Sammi wanted to be a star," Mel said. "The last time I talked to her on the phone, she said she had found her ticket to Hollywood."

Freyja leaned back and eyed Mel. "I thought Saul Winterstein was my ticket. I was wrong."

Angie sat down next to Freyja. "Were you invited to an audition?"

"Yes, in Chicago. I had a part in *South Pacific* at the Cadillac Palace Theater. Saul came back to my dressing room after the play. He invited me to an audition at his house, a big mansion on Hutchinson Street. He wanted to do a remake of *Somewhere in the Night.* He thought I would be perfect for the part of Christy, the lounge singer. I was in awe of his influence and power, and he became obsessed with me. Within a month, he proposed. We were married a few weeks later."

"Did he run around on you?" Wolf asked.

"No." She pointed at the scarred side of her face. "Not until this happened. He was a lovesick schoolboy. We were very happy for about a year. Things were falling into place. I cared for him. He adored me. Hank Cruse agreed to co-star. That was a big break. Money from backers started rolling in, and then I was attacked."

"And things fell apart," Wolf said.

She nodded. "His search for a leading lady started over. I was pushed to the side. He hired Elaine Maxell to recruit talent. She was a studio musician in New York and sat in on recording sessions for some well-known singers. He thought she'd be perfect to set up the auditions. He wanted to find a new face, someone he could turn into a star. Finding a beauty who can sing and act is not an easy task."

Angie twirled her hand. "So, Maxell started to bring in potential replacements."

"Yes. Most of them were good but not great. Saul knew it. His ability to judge talent was the key to his success." She lowered her head. "I knew what was happening. He offered the possibility of stardom to these girls, and they jumped into bed with him. Then he tossed them out. It's as if he and Maxell had this perverse agreement. Until the right girl came along, she would provide a regular supply of wide-eyed women. That's when I left."

Mel narrowed her eyes. "Sammi is incredibly talented. She can act and sing with the best of them. Maybe he fell for her. She's been there nearly a month."

"That's possible," Freyja said.

"How old is the guy?" Mel asked.

"Forty-one. He's about ten years older than me."

Mel shook her head. "That's a big age difference between him and Sammi, twenty-two years."

"Not in the movie business," Wolf said. "Humphrey Bogart was twenty-five years older than Lauren Becall. And then there's Ashton Kutcher and Demi Moore."

"Wait a minute," Angie said. "If Winterstein has fallen for Mel's sister, then why would he continue to audition singers?"

"Good question," Freyja said. "There may be other roles in the movie."

Angie frowned. "Or Winterstein may have become addicted to the sexual pattern that Maxell established for him."

"That's probably it." Mel said. "Sammi wouldn't do the pants-off dance unless she loved him."

Wolf sat back and stared at the empty bottle that Mel had spun on the table. *Jennifer Cobb wouldn't do the pants-off dance either. What do you do with the ones who say no? Thump 'em and dump 'em?* "I think Angie and I should stop by and talk to Mr. Winterstein and his crew this afternoon."

Freya straightened and eyed Wolf. "Good luck with that proposition."

"Why?"

"Saul is very particular about who enters his camp."

Wolf grinned. "I can be very persuasive."

* * *

About four that afternoon Wolf planned to meet Angie at the Currituck Beach Lighthouse. They wanted to compare notes before heading to Saul Winterstein's beachfront mansion. He parked the Cougar in one of the spaces along Corolla Village Road and hurried along the path toward the circular clearing where people gathered to climb the spiral staircase to the top of the lighthouse. A brick walkway circled the clearing. Tall loblolly pines and live oaks on the outskirts of the clearing offered generous shade to the tourists. The looming redbrick tower, nearly 200 feet tall, dwarfed the trees.

Angie sat on the steps of the Lightkeeper's House, directly across the circle from the lighthouse. The three-story abode had been fully restored: new wood siding, white paint, black shutters, new shingles and scrolled wood decorations on each of the gables. Angie studied her cell phone as Wolf approached.

Wolf plopped down next to her. "How'd your talk with the Freedman girl go?"

Angie slipped her phone back into her shoulder bag. "Good. Learned a few things. How about you?"

"Not much luck. Jennifer was definitely a popular fixture at the karaoke bars, but no one knew much more than that. Kathy Jo Landon at the Jolly Rodger recognized her photo, but that was about it. She couldn't recall if someone gave her a gift."

"Willa Freedman told me she was with Jennifer at the Jolly Rodger when a lady came to their table and handed her a small giftbox. She didn't know anything about the contents of the box or the audition. Jennifer must have kept it to herself."

"Did you get a description of the woman?"

"Yeah. Thin but well built. Early middle-age, maybe forty or so. Black hair cut in a bob style. Very friendly and lavish with her praise toward Jennifer's talent."

"Wow. That's the exact description we were looking for."

"Elaine Maxell, Winterstein's love connection."

Wolf rubbed his hands together. "That tidbit may be the key that gets us into Winterstein's palace."

"Any instructions you want to give me before we go knocking on that pig's door?"

"Follow my lead. Be observant. Don't expect me to huff and puff and blow the house down."

Angie stood. "You must have caught up on your summer reading list. What's next, Hansel and Gretel?"

Wolf got to his feet. "No. A book by a guy named L. Frank Baum." He took a few spry steps along the brick walkway.

Angie caught up with him. "Of course. We're off to see the Slimeball."

As they approached the Cougar, Wolf said, "I've got the address in the car."

"I know exactly where it is. I looked it up on Google Maps while I was waiting for you."

"You are Sally on the spot. How far from here?"

"Not far. The last house on the right where the road ends and the Wild Horse sanctuary begins."

They settled into the Cougar, and Wolf backed out and headed to the main highway. He turned left on Route 12 and passed the Currituck County Sheriff's Office. "I've got an idea," Wolf said. "I want to approach this from two different angles."

"Okay. What angles are you talking about?"

"Good cop—bad cop, just like you see on the television crime shows."

"So one of us will get on their good side and make them feel all warm and fuzzy, and one of us will rattle their cages and yank their chains."

"That's the idea. We'll observe their reactions and see what we can stir up."

Angie pointed to her chest. "Who am I?"

"You're the bad cop."

Angie chuckled. "I like that."

"I thought maybe you would."

They passed Lost Lake Lane on the left, and Wolf tilted his head in that direction. "This one's for Jennifer Cobb."

"Amen to that." Angie pointed out the windshield. "There's an access lane a couple hundred yards before the road ends. It's up here on the right."

"I see it." Wolf turned onto the short lane which led to a cul-de-sac.

"That's the palace," Angie said. "The big green one."

There were two gates separated by a copse of pine trees. Wolf parked in front of the gate on the right and cut the engine. "Man, that is a huge beach house."

The building was three stories high and sided with green shake shingles. Wolf had never seen a similar design on the Outer Banks. The main part of the house curled at the end like the letter J. Two sections connected to the J, the left one on the curve and the other against the flatter side to the right. The section on the right looked to be the entrance. Both sections were wide at the bottom and narrowed as they rose, giving them the appearance of castle towers. Hipped roofs covered both sections and connected them to the main roof. Long narrow windows with white trim were spaced evenly along the second floor. The top floor was patterned with a series of smaller square windows. There were no windows on the bottom floor, except for the small windows on the top sections of three garage doors. The two driveways, composed of green paving stones, united on the other side of the patch of pine trees and widened into a spacious area stretching across the length of the house.

"What do you think?" Wolf said.

"I wouldn't want to pay Mr. Winterstein's utility bills."

They exited the car and walked to the gate. An intercom box mounted on a steel pole stood on the right side of the gate.

Wolf took a quick breath and blew it out. "Here goes nothing."

"Let's hope for a little more than nothing."

Wolf pressed the call button on the intercom box.

"Who is it?" a deep voice replied.

"My name is Weston Wolf. I'm a private detective. My partner, Angie Stallone, and I would like to speak with Mr. Winterstein."

"What's this about?"

"Lester Cobb hired us to look for his missing daughter, Jennifer Cobb. We believe Mr. Winterstein may have some information that could shed some light on the case."

"One moment please."

They stood there for about a minute, checking out the lavish property. A volleyball court and putting green took up a large space on the left side of the building. Tall, thick shrubbery lined the perimeter of the estate, insuring privacy from the few other beach houses in the area.

"Sorry, Mr. Winterstein is busy and doesn't have anything to say about the girl."

"It will only take a few minutes."

"You need to leave. Goodbye."

"Hello." He pressed the button again. "We talked to a witness who identified Elaine Maxell as the woman who gave Jennifer Cobb the invitation to an audition here. We don't want to cause trouble or involve the local authorities. We just want to clear things up."

"Hold on." A long silence followed. "Mr. Winterstein has agreed to talk to you. I'll be down in a minute to open the gate."

They stepped away from the intercom. Wolf winked at Angie. "Your investigative work paid off."

Angie held out her hand, and it trembled. "I'm a little nervous."

Wolf doubled his fists. "Courage."

A tall man, maybe six feet six with wide shoulders, emerged from the doorway on the left side of the right tower. His dark brown hair, parted on the side, and tight black t-shirt gave Wolf the impression that the guy just stepped out of a Bond movie. It wasn't a good feeling. He strode toward them across the green paving stones, his quad muscles rippling with every step under thin gray pants. He had neatly trimmed sideburns and small ears compared to the size of his head. His heavy brow gave him a simian look.

"Here comes Magilla Gorilla," Wolf uttered.

He stopped at the left side of the gate and put his hands on his hips. "After I open the gate, park your vehicle in front of the house." He had a bass voice that rumbled like a rockslide.

"Whatever you say." Wolf smiled ingratiatingly.

As Gorilla Man punched a code into the gate access box, Wolf and Angie got back into the car, and Wolf started the engine.

"This guy makes Lurch look like Big Bird," Angie said.

"Ahhh c'mon, he's not that scary." The gate swung open. Wolf shifted into drive and pulled the Cougar up near the right entrance. He cut off the engine, and they got out.

"Follow me," Gorilla Man growled. He led them into a wide doorway at the base of the right tower. Several flowering plants sprung from large pots around the room, giving the air the thick smell of tropical orchids. Reddish flagstones covered the floor and gleamed with a clear-coat polish. On the left, a modern stairway, with taut wires threaded through holes in the posts, ascended to the next two floors. Wolf gazed up to the third floor, guessing the ceiling must be forty or fifty feet above him. A mobile sculpture made of gleaming metal hung from the ceiling. It must have been twenty feet long and looked like a DNA helix.

Gorilla Man gestured to the back wall. "We'll take the elevator up to the third floor." He crossed the flagstones and hit the button. Angie and Wolf trailed him. The gleaming steel doors separated, and they entered the roomy elevator. Mirrors paneled the inside.

When the doors closed, Wolf said, "Nice place."

The man grunted.

The G-force kicked in as the elevator shot up to the top floor. The doors opened, and Gorilla Man led the way into a spacious great room. The wall facing the ocean consisted mainly of windows and a couple French doors that opened onto a wide deck. Brown leather chairs with beige cushions sat around an oversized mahogany coffee table. A glass-topped table that looked like a big kettle drum was positioned between two cushiony beige couches laden with pillows. Other cushioned chairs were spaced around the room. A grand piano stood in the corner surrounded by potted tropical plants. A golden oak cathedral ceiling gave the place an imperial atmosphere.

To the right next to the same modern railing that Wolf noticed downstairs, a man and a woman sat in cushioned armchairs at a round, wooden table. Just beyond them, the steps descended to the lower floors. Wolf figured the stairway led right back down to where they entered. As he and Angie walked in their direction, they stood.

The man looked like an ex-athlete whose fitness level had slipped over the last several years. He was about Wolf's height, six feet two inches, but probably weighed at least thirty pounds more. He had short receding bleach-blonde hair, thick lips and dark eyebrows. He wore a shiny black and crimson Adidas sweatsuit with white stripes down the sleeves and pantlegs.

The woman appeared exactly as Wolf had imagined: about five feet six inches tall, well built, and despite the arrival of middle age, still very attractive with her short black hair and fair complexion. She wore an emerald green jumpsuit with matching heels. Her vee collar dipped to the middle of her chest.

"Thanks for giving us some of your time, Mr. Winterstein," Wolf said. "I'm a big fan of all your movies."

He forced a smile. "And you are?"

"Oh, I'm sorry. My name is Weston Wolf." He patted Angie on the back. "This is my partner, Angie Stallone."

Winterstein waved his hand toward the woman. "This is Elaine Maxell, my assistant. You've met Jake Cleaver, my security man."

Standing behind them by the stairs, Gorilla Man grunted again.

"Now what's this all about?" Winterstein asked.

Wolf tightened his lips and bobbed his head a couple times. "Well, you see, Mr. Winterstein, a young woman has been reported missing for eleven days. The local sheriff's department investigated but couldn't figure out what happened to her. Her father, Lester Cobb, hired us to see if we could find her."

Maxell and Winterstein briefly eyed each other, their faces somber, but quickly refocused on Wolf.

"You believe she's here?" Winterstein said.

"No," Angie said, her voice flat and hard as a slate floor. "We believe she's dead."

Elaine Maxell stiffened, her lower lip trembling.

"We *think* she might be dead," Wolf said more gently. "A body washed up near the Whalehead Club yesterday, and we're waiting for identification confirmation."

A door opened on the far wall, and an older woman entered the room. Her light-blue dress, patterned with pink flowers, drooped down to her knees. A string of pearls circled her sagging neck, and her silvery hair was stacked atop her head in an oversized bun. She had piercing blue eyes and wide nostrils.

"Saul," the old woman piped, "you didn't tell me you were having guests over this afternoon." She waddled in their direction.

"We weren't expecting guests, Mother." Winterstein smiled patiently, waiting for her to draw near. "This is Detective Wolf and Detective Stallone."

"Detectives?" Her eyes widened. "Did something happen?"

"They are looking for a missing girl."

"Gracious me." She raised her hand to her mouth. "Do we know the girl?"

Wolf bowed slightly. "We think she spent some time here. We don't want to upset you, Mrs. Winterstein, but we need to clear some things up."

"Yes, of course. Please, don't let me interrupt."

Wolf cleared his throat. "Detective Stallone interviewed a friend of the missing girl today. She said that Miss Maxell gave Jennifer a giftbox containing a scarf and an invitation to an audition for a part in a movie. The screentest was to take place here, according to the address on the invitation."

Elaine Maxell swallowed and nodded. "Y-y-yes, that is true. Miss Cobb came and sang for us about . . . t-t-ten days ago." She took a deep calming breath. "We were undecided whether or not to give her a screentest. Her voice wasn't quite right for the part."

"That's correct," Winterstein said. "She had a great voice, but I was looking for something more raw, a nightclub singer's voice."

"So she left after her audition?" Angie asked.

"No." Maxell kneaded her hands. "W-w-we were still undecided, so we invited her to stay the night and prepare for a screentest the next morning. We gave her the script, and s-s-she went to her room to study it." She separated her hands, and they trembled like two abandoned kittens.

"The next morning we sat down with her," Winterstein said. "Together we came to the conclusion that she wasn't quite right for the part. She seemed to take it well. Shortly after that, she got her things together and left."

"Do you remember the color and make of her car?" Angie asked.

Winterstein shrugged. "I don't know the make. It was a red compact."

"Jennifer lives a couple hundred yards down the road from here," Angie said. "Her red Ford Focus was left abandoned in the Food Lion parking lot five miles from here. Her body washed up at the Whalehead Club ten days later. How do you explain that, Mr. Winterstein?"

The old woman's mouth dropped open. "What are you suggesting?"

Winterstein raised his hand. "Stay out of this, Mother." He faced Angie. "I don't have to explain anything. I just told you what I know."

"What you don't know, Mr. Winterstein," Angie seethed, "is that another girl has been reported missing. She received the same giftbox, same scarf, and same invitation."

Winterstein expanded his chest. "We give out invitations for auditions to hundreds of singers and actors all over the country. We make movies. Big movies. I have no control over what these people do after they leave here."

Angie pointed her finger at him. "But you do have control over them while they are here. That's some coincidence that two of your guests have disappeared within a ten-day period."

"How dare you level such a vile accusation against my son!" Mrs. Winterstein fumed. "He's a world-famous movie producer. Anybody that's somebody knows he would never do such a thing."

Wolf stepped in between them. "Hold on now, Mrs. Winterstein. No one's accusing anyone of anything." Wolf took a deep breath and let it out slowly. "We are simply trying to gather all the facts and make rational deductions." He strolled in the direction of the windows. "Let me ask you this." He stopped near one of the couches and faced them. "Do you use this room for your auditions?"

Winterstein motioned toward the grand piano in the corner. "We'll listen to a singer up here occasionally. Screentests take place downstairs in a room specifically designed for that purpose."

"I see. Did Jennifer Cobb sing up here?" Wolf drifted over to the windows.

Elaine Maxell said, "Y-y-yes, I believe she did."

Wolf peered out the window toward the ocean. Below at ground level, a wooden deck surrounded a long swimming pool divided into three lanes by blue lane-line floaters. Teal cushioned chairs and lounge chairs were scattered around the pool, and long wooden benches and booths edged the fencing on each side. An outdoor bar and huge gas grill were stationed to the right of the pool. Pines and shrubbery grew tall on each side of the fences. Beyond the pool a long wooden walkway led to a gazebo. From there the walkway extended to the beach. *Excellent. Another entry into this place that would avoid the front gates. That's good to know.*

Winterstein cleared his throat. "We're very busy, Detective Wolf. Do you have any other questions?"

Wolf turned to his left and gazed out the windows that faced the north. A steel spiral staircase wound its way up to nowhere like a corkscrew, reaching to the building's roof level. A walkway from the deck led to it. "Yeah. What in the world is that thing?"

"That's an outside observation tower." Winterstein said. "It has high-powered binoculars mounted at the top to see miles out into the ocean. But, again, you're wasting my time here."

"I'm so sorry, Mr. Winterstein." Wolf ambled back to where the group stood by the railing. "I know you are a very busy man with lots of connections to important people. Like I mentioned before, I truly admire your work. Your movies are great."

Winterstein raised his hand like a traffic cop. "Enough of your compliments. Get to your questions."

Wolf smiled politely. "Let's get back to the second missing girl. Her name is Samantha Bianco. Does that ring a bell?"

"Y-y-yes," Maxell said. "She left here about a week ago." Her whole head quivered.

"From what we have uncovered," Angie said, "she arrived here back in early August. Correct?"

Maxell glanced at Winterstein. "That sounds about right."

"She was very talented," Winterstein said. "We really liked her audition and put her through several screentests. It takes time to memorize scripts for different scenes. She felt comfortable here and couldn't afford to stay in one of the local hotels. We almost offered her a contract."

"But you didn't," Angie said.

"No. Bottom line: She didn't check all the boxes."

"Bottom line," Angie sneered, "Samantha Bianco is the second girl to go missing after spending time here."

Mrs. Winterstein's face turned red, her lips disappearing as her face muscles tensed.

Winterstein furrowed his brow. "We've told you everything we know about those girls."

Angie raised her chin. "We know more than you think we know, Mr. Winterstein. You've been stacking lies like a drunk stacks beer cans."

The old woman stepped forward, her eyes flaming. "Did you just call my son a liar?"

Angie glared at her. "That's right, Mrs. Winterstein. I believe he's a liar and a coldblooded killer."

She gasped. "You insolent bitch!" She took another step forward and slapped at Angie, catching her slightly across the face.

Angie leaned back and raised a fist. "You touch me again, old hag, and I'll knock those false teeth down your throat."

Winterstein stepped in between them. "Get out of my house!"

Gorilla Man clamped his hands on Angie's shoulders and pulled her backwards.

"Whoa! Whoa! Whoa!" Wolf raised his hands like a bank teller during a holdup. "No need to get physical. Let my partner go! We'll leave peacefully."

Winterstein nodded, and the security guy released his hands.

Angie took a quick breath and eyed Gorilla Man. "Letting me go was the smartest move you made all day."

He snarled like an agitated silverback.

Wolf pulled Angie toward him. "Everybody take it easy. Like I said, we're just trying to clear some things up here."

"Your partner made some serious allegations against me," Winterstein said. "If you've got proof to back it up, then go to the police. I'll gladly allow them to do a full search of my premises. But you are no longer welcome here." He pointed to the elevator. "Get out of here and don't come back!"

Wolf raised a finger. "If you don't mind, we'll take the steps."

"I don't give a damn how you leave! Just leave."

"Okay. No problem." Wolf led Angie down the first couple steps but hesitated and turned. "Just one more thing, Mr. Winterstein."

"What!"

"Could I get an autograph?"

Winterstein glared at Gorilla Man. "Get them the hell out of here!"

"Okay, okay, we're leaving," Wolf called over his shoulder as he and Angie hurried down the steps.

Chapter 11

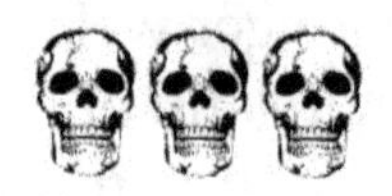

Gorilla Man followed them all the way down the steps and out to the car. Then he marched across the green paving stones and punched the numbers into the gate access box. The gate swung open. He stood there like Frankenstein and glared at Wolf as he drove by. Wolf slowed the Cougar and waved, wiggling his fingers and grinning.

Wolf glanced at Angie. Her hands shook visibly. Even her knees wobbled. "Relax, Angel, it's over."

"I know. The whole scene shook me up. I've never felt so scared in my life." She breathed haltingly, and tears streamed down her face.

"Listen, kid, you handled it like a pro. I couldn't have done it better."

"Thanks, but I barely kept it together." Her breathing steadied.

"What are you talking about? You rocked. Not only did you rattle their cages, you turned them upside down."

She wiped the tear streaks away with her hands, and a smile tugged at the corners of her mouth. "Do you think all that drama did any good?"

Wolf made a left onto Route 12 and accelerated. "Sure. Couldn't you tell? They were scrambling like skunks on a slippery slope."

"That's true. I thought Winterstein's pants might catch fire. Lying bastard."

"And Maxell, she practically stuck out her hands and said, 'Put on the cuffs.'"

"I wouldn't go that far, but she is their weak link. What a nervous bird."

"How about Winterstein's mother?"

Angie laughed. "I'd say she's a cross between Aunt Bee and Joan Crawford."

"What a witch."

"Can you believe she slapped me?"

"She's the epitome of the mom that thinks her boy never does anything wrong."

"What's our next step?"

"Good question. We know they're lying, but we don't have much evidence against them."

"Should we stop by the sheriff's office and let them know what's going on?"

Wolf rubbed his chin. "We could, but I don't think they'll do much. They certainly don't have enough evidence to obtain a search warrant. I guarantee you that Winterstein was bluffing when he said the cops could search his whole estate. He won't let them do anything without a warrant."

"Still, we should probably stop by and let them know. I'll see if the autopsy report on Jennifer Cobb is in yet."

"Alright." Wolf pointed to his left. "There's the sheriff's office right on cue." He turned left, rumbled into the parking lot and found an empty space near the office entrance.

Angie shifted in her seat toward Wolf. "Is my face okay?"

Wolf reached and wiped a couple wet spots on her cheek with his index finger. "Now you're good."

"Thanks. Be back in a few." Angie stepped out of the car and entered the office.

Wolf tried to run through all the possible options in his mind. *How could they get back in there and check every nook and cranny? That might be a waste of time. They may have taken Mel's sister somewhere else, or worse, snuffed out her life and dumped her in the sound. A search and rescue may turn into a double murder case. If Mel decides to walk into the lion's den tonight, who knows what could happen? Triple homicide?*

Wolf raked his fingers through his unruly hair, and squeezed his eyes shut. *No doubt, Winterstein has the best security system available. We could try to break in tonight, but that would be risky. Without solid evidence, the law would be on Winterstein's side.* Wolf opened his eyes. There wasn't many more options. Mel's best chance to find her sister was Mel herself. And that option stunk like a dead marlin at midnight.

Angie exited the sheriff's office and trotted to the car. She yanked the door open, slid in and slammed it shut.

"What did you tell them?" Wolf asked.

She took a few seconds to catch her breath. "That we had proof that both missing girls spent time at Winterstein's place."

"What did they say?"

"That they had no information about a second missing girl."

Wolf shrugged. "That's true. We're the only ones who know. Mel hasn't filed a missing-persons report yet."

"Something else came up." Angie frowned. "Still no positive ID, but the toxicology report came back on the victim."

"And?"

"Jennifer Cobb didn't drown. There was very little water in her lungs. She died from a combination of alcohol and sedatives."

Wolf spread his hands. "What more proof do they want. Someone drugged her and dumped her in the sound."

"That's not how they see it. They think it was an accidental overdose. She had a few drinks at a local bar, took some nerve medicine to calm herself and paddled out into the Currituck Sound on a kayak."

"You've got to be kidding me?"

"The deputy said he'd pass on the information I gave them to Sheriff Rawlings. He may go up and talk to Winterstein."

"That's not going to help us."

Angie nodded. "If Sammi Bianco is still alive, every second counts. We need to make a thorough search of the place."

"Right, but I don't see how. The place is a fortress, and there's only one person with a ticket in—Mel Bianco."

* * *

When they got back to the office, Angie checked her watch. "I still got time to get to my self-defense class. I need to work off some of this tension. We're learning Judo kicks tonight."

"You are a paragon of self-improvement. Did I ever tell you that I had a black belt?"

"In karate?"

"No. It's just a black leather belt hanging in my closet."

She slugged his arm. "Every once in a while you get one in on me."

Wolf snapped into a Bruce Lee pose. "Jack be nimble, Jack be quick, Jack better duck my roundhouse kick."

Angie held up her hand in front of his face. "I'm leaving before I hear another lame poem."

"Hey, before you leave, I need to let you know something."

"What?"

"I'm going to give Mel Bianco an alert button and program my cell phone number into it. She hasn't hired us. This is a favor for a friend. If she goes to that audition tonight and gets into trouble, she can press the button, and I'll be notified."

Angie nodded. "If they take her phone away from her, she'll still have the button."

"Right. It's small and thin. She can hide it easily in her shoe or wherever."

Angie took a deep breath. "Program my cell phone number into it, too."

"Are you sure? Remember, we're working for Mr. Cobb, not Mel Bianco."

"I'm sure. I'm volunteering in memory of Jennifer Cobb."

"That's how I feel, too, Angel." Wolf placed his hands on her shoulders. "If we have to storm the castle, we'll do it together."

"Should I stay at the office with you tonight in case she presses the button?"

He released her shoulders. "No. Go to your class and then head on home for your date with Deputy Joel. Business as usual. Tomorrow's Saturday. Don't worry about coming into the office. Just keep your cell phone charged and on hand."

"If I get the alert, what's the plan?"

"There's a back entrance to Winterstein's place. When we were there today, I walked over to the window and checked it out. A wooden walkway leads out to the beach. There's a gate along the walkway, but it shouldn't be hard to maneuver around it."

Angie tilted her head and raised her eyebrows. "A back door into the castle."

"Exactly. Wait for me on the beach by the walkway. We'll go in together."

"What about the security cameras?"

Wolf shrugged. "Hopefully, Jake Cleaver won't be paying attention."

"Hopefully, Mel's sister shows up, and we won't have to worry about it."

"There's always hope."

* * *

After programming the alert button, Wolf headed over to Freyja's cottage. He skirted around Mel's old Malibu and Freyja's dusty Jeep Renegade, noticing new tires on the Jeep with deep treads. *Bet that beast could climb a sand dune.* He took his finger and wiped a light coating of dust away. A metallic olive-green sparkled underneath. Wolf chuckled to himself. *What's on the surface doesn't always tell the story*. He trotted up the steps and rapped on the door. While he waited, he checked his watch: 6:15. *Mel will be leaving in a few minutes*.

The door swung open, and Freyja appeared wearing a white terrycloth robe.

"Shower time?" Wolf asked. "I'd be happy to join you."

"Don't get your hopes up. I'm going for a swim after Mel leaves."

"I'll settle for a swim."

"I can agree to that. The ocean is big enough for both of us."

She stepped to the side, and Wolf entered. The front room served as the living room, the walls and ceiling painted a bright white. A row of colorful pillows was spread across a white couch stationed below a wide window. Wolf could see his bungalow through the window. In the corner next to the couch, a large fern almost reached the ceiling. A glass coffee table stood in front of the couch on a pink oval rug that covered most of the hickory floor. A gray upholstered armchair and a gray recliner filled the opposite corners.

Wolf wheeled toward Freyja. "I didn't realize how nice this place was on the inside."

"I like it. Plenty of room for me, and the sea is a few steps away out the back door."

"Very convenient for a mermaid. Sink any ships or drown anybody lately?"

"Not lately, but the day's not over."

"Where's Mel? I need to talk to her."

"Getting ready for her audition. Would you like a cup of coffee while you wait?"

"Sure, with a couple shots of cream."

"Have a seat." She motioned to the gray recliner.

"Do you have anything good to eat?" Wolf plopped down and kicked the recliner back. "I'm starved."

The corner of her mouth turned up. "Ham sandwich?"

"Perfect. Got any cookies?"

She rolled her eyes. "I'll dig something up." Freyja headed to the back of the cottage.

Wolf clasped his hands behind his head. He felt somewhat helpless where Mel Bianco was concerned. He couldn't blame her for wanting to go to the audition in hopes of finding her sister. Was it possible that he had misinterpreted all the evidence they had uncovered: the scarves, Jennifer Cobb's note in the margin of her Bible, her cause of death attributed to alcohol and barbiturates, the texts from Mel's sister, the coincidence of two young women disappearing after venturing into Winterstein's lair? Their interrogation at Winterstein's place convinced him otherwise. Something was amiss in the merry old land of Silver Screen Dreams.

Freyja returned with a large cup of coffee in one hand and a plate bearing a ham sandwich and three chocolate chip cookies. Wolf sat up, collapsing the recliner. She handed him the plate and placed the coffee on a glass-topped stand next to the chair.

Wolf drew in a deep whiff. "Those smell fresh."

"Just made them."

"You can bake, too? What can't you do?"

"I can't tolerate fools for more than a few minutes."

Wolf pointed to his chest. "Are you timing me?"

She laughed. "Like sand through the hourglass."

"When it runs out, just flip it over."

"I already have . . . several times."

Wolf took a big bite of the sandwich and nodded to Freyja as he chewed. "Goood," he garbled. It didn't take long for him to scarf down the food.

"You are a human garbage disposal," she said.

He wiped his mouth with his hand. "Thanks. I'm not used to getting compliments from you."

Mel entered the room wearing a black satin mini dress with a lowcut vee neckline. The multi-colored scarf adorned her neck, tied into an attractive bow. She carried a small black purse with a long thin strap.

"Whoa, Nelly!" Wolf said.

She spun around, the bottom of the dress swishing. "How do I look?"

"Very sexy," Freyja said.

Wolf screwed up his face. "What happened to Dorothy and *Somewhere Over the Rainbow?*"

"She went back to Kansas." Mel spread her arms on a diagonal slant. "The Jersey girl is ready to flip the script on these dirtballs!"

"They may not be expecting the Jersey girl," Wolf said.

"Freyja told us they're auditioning for a nightclub singer. If that's the case, then I'll sing like Rita Hayworth."

Wolf motioned to the other gray chair. "Have a seat, Jersey girl. We need to talk."

Mel sat down and leaned on her knees. "What's up?"

"You are stepping into a danger zone, and we can't go in with you."

"I understand that, but my sister's in there."

Wolf reached into his pocket and pulled out the alert button. Composed of plastic, it was about an inch square and a quarter inch thick. "Listen. If you get into trouble tonight, press this."

Mel smirked. "Do you mean if I fall, and I can't get up?"

"I'm serious. If you press this button, both Angie and I

will be alerted on our cell phones." Wolf lifted his gray Polo shirt and revealed his Sig Sauer handgun strapped to his side.

Mel's eyes widened. "You *are* serious."

"We'll storm the castle, so make sure you don't press it accidentally."

"What degree of danger should prompt me to hit the panic button?"

"You'll know when you're in trouble. They might take your cell phone away so you can't communicate with us. They may toss you in a room and lock the door. You'll know." Wolf reached and handed her the button.

"Where do I put it?"

"Somewhere they won't look," Wolf said.

Pinching the corner of the plastic square between her thumb and finger, Mel stared at the button. "I know." She lifted the vee of her dress's neckline and slid the button under her bra, inching it to the bottom of her left breast. "There. I'll slap the guy who dares to ignore my no trespassing sign."

"Good," Wolf said. "Now the next item. We'd like an update sometime tonight."

"Okay." She patted the black purse on her lap. "I've got my cell phone handy. Who do I call? I've got Freyja's number on my contact list."

"That's fine," Wolf said. "We can hang out together until you report in. Let me give you my number, too."

Mel took out her phone and entered Wolf's number. "Anything else?"

Freyja knelt next to her. "If you leave after the audition, pull off to the side of the road and call as soon as you can. If they offer to give you a screentest tomorrow and want you to stay the night, don't call from your room."

"Why not?"

"The room may be bugged," Wolf said. "Those bedrooms probably all have deck access. Step outside. Check for cameras. Get away from windows. Once you feel isolated enough, then make the call."

"How do you plan on finding your sister?" Freyja asked.

Mel shrugged. "I'll play it by ear. I'm sure there'll be opportunities to break away and look through the house."

Wolf lowered his eyebrows. "It's a big house, ten or twelve bedrooms."

"Then I hope they ask me to stay the night. I'll get up at three in the morning and go exploring."

Freyja stood. "Be careful. Jake Cleaver takes his security responsibilities seriously. If he thinks you're an intruder, he'll come at you in attack mode."

"Don't worry." She patted her purse again. "I'll carry my pepper spray with me."

"If you find your sister, and she's in danger," Wolf said, "hit that alert button immediately."

"Got it." Mel glanced at her watch. "I'm late." She stood and hugged Freyja.

"One for me, too?" Wolf asked.

"I couldn't forget you." She gave Wolf a quick hug and stepped back. "Don't worry. I can handle myself. I'll call tonight and let you know what's happening." She turned and hurried out the door.

Freyja sat on the gray armchair. "I don't know what to think."

"She's determined to go. We stopped at the sheriff's office today. They may question your husband, but they don't have enough evidence to obtain a search warrant. It's up to Mel to find her sister with whatever help we can give her."

"He's only my husband for one more day."

"Tomorrow is the day of dissolution?"

"Tomorrow morning at ten at his lawyer's office in Kitty Hawk."

"Are you glad?"

"Of course, but I don't know what to think about Saul. He wasn't a monster when we were together. He may have been shallow, but he wasn't a murderer."

"Maybe somebody turned him into a monster."

"That's possible. Elaine Maxell is a good candidate. She's a manipulator and knows his weaknesses. She got him hooked on sex with wannabe starlets to gain control over him."

"When we were there today, Maxell could hardly say a word without stumbling over her tongue."

"She feels safe in the shadows. You turned on a light."

"If Sheriff Rawlings would put her in an interrogation room and turn the screws, I bet she'd crack."

Freyja chuckled. "Like mud in the sun."

"Too late for that now."

"Mel's on her way, and there's no stopping her."

Wolf grunted and nodded. "I met your mother-in-law today."

Freyja sat back and grinned. "What did you think of her?"

Wolf raised his eyebrows and blew out a low whistle. "She's a work of art, something Picasso would paint."

"We didn't get along. She was overprotective and jealous."

"I bet she still changes his diaper. Don't tell her that her boy is a monster."

"She would lose it."

"She slapped Angie."

Freyja shook her head. "That's typical Margaret. She was an actress for years in the 60s and 70s. B movies. Once her looks faded, she worked in the makeup department for MGM. Saul grew up in the business. From an early age he made connections with important people at the studio. I guess he was destined to make movies."

"And she nourished the dream."

"More likely, she force-fed him."

"Well, you'll be free of that family tomorrow."

Freyja stood. "Freedom! I love it." She offered her hand to Wolf. "Let's go for a swim."

He took her hand and got to his feet. "I'm ready."

"Do you need to go home and get your swimsuit."

Wolf shook his head. "I've got boxers on under these baggy jeans."

Freyja grasped his belt buckle and tugged him toward her. "Good enough for me. Let's go."

Chapter 12

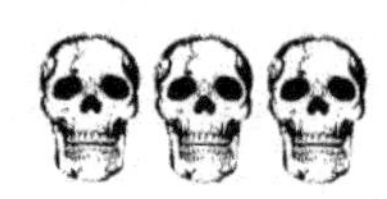

On the back deck, Wolf quickly kicked off his shoes and stripped off his clothes. He removed his holster, placed it on one of the deck chairs and covered it with his shirt.

Freyja tossed her white robe over the back of the chair. She eyed his boxers. "Tartan?"

"Maybe I'm Scottish." Wolf ogled her black bikini, the same one she wore yesterday.

"What are you looking at?"

"Just admiring the view." *Geeesh. With a body like that, no wonder she was on her way to La La Land.*

Freyja turned, scampered down the steps and ran toward the water. "Catch me if you can!"

Wolf double-timed it but still trailed her into the surf. She dove beneath the curl of a wave and disappeared. The wave smacked Wolf, almost knocking him over. He recovered his balance and scanned the surface of the water. No Freyja. Her head popped up about twenty yards in front of him.

"Can't keep up?" she called.

He thrust forward, slicing into the surface, and swam as hard as he could. With every few strokes, he glanced up to see her backstroking farther out to sea. *I'm not going catch her if she keeps this up.* Finally, she treaded water beyond the breakers, and he closed in on her. When he reached her, he checked to see if he could touch bottom. *Ah, barely. Good, I can still stand.* As he caught his breath, the water rose and fell from his chin to his chest with the rhythm of the incoming waves.

"The water's warm tonight," Freyja said.

"We're the beneficiaries of a southern current."

"Feels good."

Wolf shifted toward the shore. "The sun will set in about half an hour."

She smiled approvingly. "I don't want to miss it. Hopefully, there'll be some clouds to make it even better."

He focused on her face. The sun's reflection off the water colored her scars. "My view couldn't get more beautiful than it is right now."

"Are you trying to seduce me with lies?"

"Never."

She eyed him, as if she could see to the deepest layers of his hidden thoughts. "Do you really think I'm beautiful?"

"Yes."

"Why?"

Wolf wasn't expecting a pop quiz. "Uhhhh . . . you just are."

"I hope you can do better than that."

"Well . . . I've known women who were beautiful on the outside but ugly on the inside. I've dated a few."

"And it didn't work out?"

"No. The more time we spent together, the more their outer beauty faded. I'd look at their faces and feel repulsed. I guess what was inside transformed their appearance in my mind. But it's different with you."

"How so?"

"The more time I spend with you, the more beautiful you become on the outside. Who you are on the inside has altered my vision." He reached and caressed the scarred side of her face. "You truly are beautiful."

"Good answer." She drew closer and clasped her hands behind his neck. "I'm getting tired of treading water."

Wolf wrapped his arms around her and lifted her, their noses brushing. He turned his head slightly and kissed her. She responded intensely. As the seconds slipped away their mouths opened, and they kissed more deeply. An unexpected wave flowed over them, lifting them off the seafloor. They sank into the water, rolling with the flow, still kissing intimately.

Wolf felt lost in a wonderful dream. The sensation of the warm water and her heavenly body enclosed him in an enraptured cocoon. Under the surface, the sound of the surf against the shore seemed far away. They sank, whirled and rose with the surge and backflow of the ocean. They held on to one another, lips sealed together, untied against the forces of nature. The seconds slipped by without cognition or memory, only incredible bliss. In the throes of ecstasy, he felt a great need: the need to breathe.

He tried to pull away, but she held him steadfastly. Fighting off the urge for air, he twisted and pressed his hands against her shoulders to break her embrace. He shook himself free and shot upwards. When he penetrated the surface, he gasped, heaving in oxygen.

A few seconds later she surfaced. "Are you okay?"

"You almost drowned me!" he snarled.

"I'm so sorry. I forgot you can't stay under like me. I – I - I didn't want to let you go." Anguish clouded her features like a young girl about to cry.

"It's okay. I survived."

She sank into the water and shot up toward shore, swimming at a rapid pace.

"Don't go!" Wolf shouted. "I'm sorry I yelled!"

He thrust upwards, catching the momentum of a wave and swam after her. When she reached the shallows, she stood and marched toward her cottage. Another wave walloped him into the shore, but he staggered to his feet and sprinted after her. He caught her about halfway across the stretch of sand.

"Slow down! I'm not mad."

She halted, head down, her hair matted against her face. "It's okay. You don't have to pretend."

He gripped her shoulder and turned her toward him. "Who's pretending?"

"I know you don't want me."

"Are you kidding?"

She gazed up at him.

Wolf cleared her hair from her face and clasped her cheeks with both hands. "Listen. I'm telling you the absolute truth. That was the greatest kiss of my life."

"But you pushed so hard away from me."

Wolf drew his hands away. "That's known as the survival instinct."

She lowered her head. "I feel so embarrassed."

Wolf lifted her chin with a curled finger. "If you feel so bad, then you owe me another kiss." He lowered his face, and their lips met tenderly. She clasped the back of his head, entwining his hair in her fingers. He ran his hand down her wet back and drew her closer. The breeze from ocean threatened to chill them, but their body heat staved off the shivers. The minutes passed, and Wolf slipped back into the euphoria of their intimacy, his mind and body adrift in a cloud of delight.

They slowly separated, and Wolf drew in a deep breath. "That's more like it."

Freyja smiled. "You survived the kiss of a mermaid."

"And lived to tell about it."

"I hope you're not one to kiss and tell."

"Don't worry. I plan on keeping these moments all to myself."

She clasped his hand. "Let's get dressed and drive over to the Bodie Island Lighthouse and watch the sunset. We still have time."

"Sing me a siren's song, and I'll follow you anywhere."

She began to hum a familiar tune. Was it Danny Boy? She sang the words with her rich alto voice: "O Weston boy, the pipes, the pipes are calling, from shore to shore, to see the setting sun."

Wolf followed her to the back of the cottage and up the steps, feeling like a lovestruck teenager.

* * *

After getting dressed, they headed out the front door, crossed the porch and rambled down the steps.

They turned toward Wolf's Cougar, but Freyja held out her hand and stopped him. "Let's take my Jeep."

"Sure. I'd love to see how it runs."

"Oh, it runs good."

Freyja had removed the doors and vinyl top, leaving a rollbar just above the headrests and its supports that slanted to the tail where the large spare was mounted on the back. Wolf angled to the passenger side, stepped up into the vehicle and settled into the bucket seat.

Freyja fished her keys out of her cut-off jeans pocket and stepped up into the car. Her orange t-shirt with a dolphin skimming over waves reminded Wolf of his first glimpse of her in the ocean. She started the vehicle, and the engine rumbled and purred.

"Wow," Wolf gushed. "That engine hums like a Navy Hellcat."

"I keep it in good shape. 1982 Renegade."

"1982? That's the year I was born."

Freyja shifted into reverse and backed out. "I knew there was something about you I liked."

"Right. I'm old, and I still run good."

She drove to the end of East Hunter Street and turned left onto Old Oregon Inlet Road. The lighthouse was only about three miles away. After a couple miles, she made a left onto Route 12, drove another mile and turned right onto the lighthouse access road. Tall loblolly pines and woods lined the lane all the way to the lighthouse. The spire, about 160 feet tall and painted with wide black and white stripes, stood halfway between the ocean and Roanoke Sound. Freyja drove past the parking lot, rounded a curve and parked off the side of the road.

They got out of the Jeep, met in front of the vehicle, clasped hands and walked toward the sound. Stepping over a few small bushes and patches of weeds, they found a clearing about ten yards from the edge of the water. The sun had just kissed the skyline, slowly dipping below it. Bright yellows bled into oranges on both sides of the blazing ball just above the horizon. The dying light set aflame a swath of clouds above it with reds and crimsons that faded into violet-blue higher in the sky. Below, sea grasses waved in the breeze along the shore, brushing the reflection of the fiery colors in the rippling water.

They stood in silence, watching the sun slowly slip below the edge of the world.

"You're right about the clouds. Wolf slipped his arm around her shoulders and pulled her close. "They add beauty to a sunset. Maybe we should take a photo with our phones."

"No."

Wolf stole a quick peek at her and then refocused on the sky. "Why not?"

"Photographs are illusions. Clouds are free. Like love, they can't be captured."

Her words bewildered him. "If we can't capture love, what hope do we have?"

She linked her arm around his waist and met his gaze. "The next sunset."

Wolf kept silent, thinking about her words but not quite understanding. The sun disappeared, and the colors faded, draining away into twilight. He wanted to freeze those exhilarating moments in time, but they slipped away. He took a deep breath and let it out. Finally, he said, "I feel like a tall glass of wine."

She glanced at him and winked. "You look like a tall glass of wine."

"Let's say we go back to my place and pop a cork on a bottle of Napa Valley Cabernet?"

"Bring it over to my place. We can watch an old movie and relax for a couple hours."

"Perfect."

Wolf felt contented on the drive back to her cottage. It was a good feeling. He wouldn't be spending the night alone. There was something about sharing the evening with Freyja that lifted him. She filled an empty space with life. Was it the beginning of something that would last? He didn't want to go there. She had come to the Outer Banks for a purpose—to be set free from her husband. In a few days she would go on her way and leave him behind. Yet he remembered how she held on to him under the sea. *The same feelings must be stirring inside of her. Is she afraid of falling in love?* Her words echoed in his mind: *Clouds are free. Like love, they can't be captured.* He wondered about his past relationships with women. Most of them were shallow. Was she taking him into the deep?

He parked the Jeep Renegade in her driveway. "Be back in a few."

"I'll be here."

He got out of the car and hustled over to his bungalow. As he hurried through the front office toward the hallway, he stripped off his shirt and unhitched his shoulder holster. He entered his bedroom, tossed the shirt on the bed and slung the holster around the bedpost. *Won't need that tonight*. He made a quick trip to the bathroom to add a layer of Old Spice under his arms. *What's the old slogan? Brisk and bracing as a sea breeze, or is it: Smell like grandpa*? He chuckled to himself After gargling with Listerine, he went back to the bedroom and pulled a fresh t-shirt out of the top drawer of the dresser, a black one with the Wolf and Stallone logo stamped in white on the chest. He funneled into it and flattened the wrinkles.

Before heading to the kitchen, he decided to check his collection of movie DVDs on top of the dresser. He shuffled through and picked out *The Shawshank Redemption, North by Northwest* and *Casablanca*. He held them up and smiled. *Can't beat the classics*. He rushed into the kitchen, snatched a bottle of wine from the cupboard next to the fridge and headed back over to Freyja's.

He wondered if he should open the door and go right in but decided to knock. He checked his phone while he waited. Nothing from Mel. Freyja opened the door, wearing the same dolphin t-shirt and cutoff shorts.

She closed one eye. "What took you so long?"

"The anticipation of my arrival must be difficult to suffer."

"I'm suffering alright."

Wolf entered and noticed a big bowl of popcorn between two wine glasses on the coffee table in front of the white couch. "Brought a few good movies." He handed her the DVDs.

"Nice selection." She pointed to the couch. "Have a seat."

He toted the wine bottle to the couch and noticed a corkscrew next to the bowl of popcorn. *Hmmmm. Always thinking ahead.* He tore the foil from the top of the bottle, reached for the corkscrew, twisted it in and popped the cork. "Voila! Did you know that men are like fine wine?"

"Yeah, they take years to mature."

Wolf filled the glasses, replaced the cork and set the bottle on the table. Freyja sat next to him and placed the DVDs on the coffee table along with her phone.

Wolf raised his glass. "To immaturity."

She took her glass and clinked his. "You're only young once, but you can be immature until you're drowning in dirt."

"Cheers."

They both took a long drink.

"That's really good," Freyja said.

"Have you heard anything from Mel?"

"No, have you?"

"Huh-uh. I wonder what's going on over there?"

"Sometimes Saul's auditions are more like parties."

"How's that?"

"Plenty to eat and drink. Invited guests. Lots of laughing and talking. The audition ends up being the entertainment."

"Hmmph." Wolf scratched his chin. "Who comes to these parties?"

"His friends. Potential backers. Sometimes movie stars."

"I see. It's an opportunity to raise funds and sign actors."

Freyja took another sip of wine. "Exactly. Depending on who's there, Mel may be overawed."

"Let's hope she keeps her head."

She nodded. "In more ways than one."

Her words sent a cold blade through him. The image of Jennifer Cobb floating in the Currituck Sound flashed across his mind, but he shook it away. To shift his thoughts, he focused on the DVDs. "What about the movies? Any preferences?"

She lifted one off the table. "I've never seen Casablanca."

"Is that possible? It's one of my favorites."

Freyja got up and crossed the room. A medium-sized flatscreen TV sat on a stand against the opposite wall. She picked up the remote, clicked on the television, opened the case and slid the disc into the DVD player. She returned, picked up the bowl of popcorn and snuggled next to him.

As the opening credits rolled, Wolf savored the vanilla musk and the warmth of her body. He grabbed a handful of popcorn and tossed it into his mouth, a couple at a time. The familiar scenes of the movie drifted him into a cloud of comfort and security. Although he had seen the flick many times, watching it with Freyja made everything seem new: the play-it-again-Sam scene, Rick and Ilsa falling-in-love in Paris, the inspiring singing of La Marseillaise back at Rick's bar, the gin-joint scene where Rick gets drunk and complains to Sam, and the final scene, the departure, when Ilsa leaves with her husband Victor Laszlo, and Rick walks off into the darkness with Captain Renault.

As the final credits scrolled down the screen, they turned toward each other.

"I'm no good at being noble," Wolf said, "but the problems of three people don't amount to a hill of beans in this crazy world."

She patted his cheek. "I assume you're talking about me, you and Mel."

He nodded. "We'll always have Nags Head."

"Now you're being silly."

He winked. "Here's looking at you, kid."

She pulled him close, and they kissed. She slid back onto the couch, and he managed to lay beside her without falling off. They nuzzled, caressed and kissed each other playfully and then sensually, unaware of the passing of time. Their breathing and moaning accelerated, and she reached for the bottom of his t-shirt and tugged it up his torso. He sat up to pull it off, and she ran her hands over his abs and up his hairy chest. Pounding of piano keys, the notes from Beethoven's Fifth Symphony, blasted from her cell phone on the coffee table.

Her eyes grew wide. "That must be Mel!" She pushed him away, sat up and dove for her phone.

Wolf fell off the couch, his rear thudding on the floor. "Ouch!"

Chapter 13

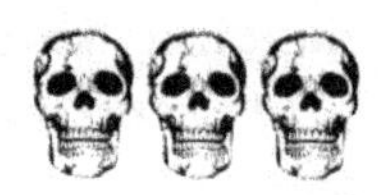

She picked up the phone. "It is Mel." She tapped the answer button. "Hello . . . yes, it's me. I'm going to put you on speakerphone so that Wes can hear, too." She held the phone in front of her and activated the speakerphone.

Mel's voice was just above a whisper. "I'm on top of the tower. It's beautiful up here."

Freyja glanced at Wolf. "Saul has an observation tower next to the house."

"I know, I saw it when I was there today. It looks like a giant corkscrew."

"Why did you go to the top of the tower?" Freyja asked.

"I'm in a bedroom on the second floor. There's a sliding-glass door that leads to the deck. I wanted to get away from the house to call you. I went out to the deck and saw this walkway that led to the tower. I figured no one could hear me if I climbed to the top."

"How'd the audition go?" Freyja asked.

Silence.

"Mel . . . . ? Mel . . . . ?"

"I'm sorry. I was looking through the binoculars that are mounted up here. There's a cruise ship out on the ocean, and the stars are incredible."

"How did the audition go?"

"It was fantastic. I got here about ten after seven. Some big guy let me in the front gate. There were a bunch of cars parked in front of the house. We rode the elevator to the top floor. You're not going to believe this . . ."

"What?"

"Hank Cruse is here. Hank Cruse!"

"Shhhhhhhh." Freyja's eyes widened as she met Wolf's gaze.

"Sorry . . . sorry . . . I'm just so pumped. I've seen all his movies, the impossible spy mission ones, the jet fighter one, the war movies and the one where he's stranded on an island for a year."

"We know he's a big star," Freyja said, "but keep your voice down."

"I will. I need to be careful. Anyway, there were about twenty people in this huge room with lots of windows and a grand piano. They had different types of hors d'oeuvres—shrimp cups, water chestnuts, stuffed mini-peppers, stuffed mushrooms. And then they brought more food—the chicken with the cheese inside, calamari, lobster tails. I nearly made a pig of myself."

"Did you sing for them?" Freyja asked.

"Yeah, but not until later. Everybody seemed to know each other. Mr. Winterstein introduced himself. He led me around and introduced me to everyone else. I can't remember their names, but they seemed like very important people in the movie business. I did recognize one actress—Ella Stonewall. She's incredibly beautiful."

"What happened after you ate?"

"There was plenty of drinking, whatever kind of drink you wanted. Some people smoked weed. I had a couple Margaritas just to fit in."

"You need to be careful." Freyja shook her head with an annoyed look in her eyes. "Remember, you're on a mission to find your sister."

"I know. I didn't want them to think I'm some innocent schoolgirl. The more comfortable they feel around me the better."

Wolf leaned closer to the phone. "Did any of the men try to make a move on you?"

"A couple of the old coots became friendlier after a few drinks, but they didn't cross any lines. Then Mr. Winterstein's assistant, Elaine Maxell, started to play the piano. She's really good. Everybody gathered around, and Mr. Winterstein asked Ella to sing first."

Freyja asked, "Is she auditioning for the part, too?"

"I think so. She gave it her all. She sang *At Last* and *You'll Never Know*. She's got a good voice and really connects with the audience. Everybody loved her."

"That's nice," Freyja said, "but you shouldn't get caught up in all this Hollywood glitz. You need to keep your head about you."

"Right." She took a deep breath. "I'm trying to stay focused, but it's hard not to get juiced up."

"What happened next?" Wolf asked.

"Miss Maxell started playing *Somewhere Over the Rainbow*, and Mr. Winterstein ushered me to the piano and introduced me as Judy Gayle from Kansas. I told him I'd rather sing something jazzy. He seemed impressed that I showed some chutzpa. I asked Miss Maxell if she knew *Back to Black*. I can do a great Amy Winehouse. She started prancing on those piano keys, and I wailed out the song, slurring my words just like Amy."

"How'd they react?" Freyja asked.

"They went crazy. You'd have thought that Amy had been resurrected from the dead. Then Winterstein asked me to sing something more traditional. I guess he wanted to test my range. Miss Maxell suggested *La vie En Rose*. That's one of my favorites. I tried to channel Lady Gaga's version from *A Star Is Born*."

"How'd that go?" Wolf asked.

"I played it to the max and paraded around the room like some jazz-singing floozy. A couple of the old guys about went toes up when I nuzzled against their cheeks. Then I wrapped my arm around Hank Cruse's neck and took his martini away from him. Everybody laughed. I stopped singing and eyed him like I was going to haul him off to my bedroom. Finally, I let them have it with that last line and held it forever: La vie en rooooooooose. They went nuts again and kept making requests. I must have sang seven songs. Winterstein's mother even came up to me, kissed me on the cheek and said she loved every one of them."

"Mel . . ." Freya's voice was fraught with trepidation. ". . . it sounds like you're having too much fun. I'm not kidding. This whole scheme is incredibly risky."

"I know what I'm doing. It's working. Winterstein took me aside later in the evening and gave me a script. He wants me to do a screentest tomorrow at noon. That gives me plenty of time to go over it. Tonight, I'll search all the empty bedrooms on the second floor. There must be at least five with no lights on. The second-floor deck goes all the way around the house. It's easy to see which rooms are unoccupied. They might have her locked in a bathroom or closet. Who knows? I'll set my phone alarm for three a.m."

Wolf said, "Mel, you need to watch every step you take. Remember what happened to Jennifer Cobb."

"Don't worry. I'll carry my pepper spray with me. Shhhhhh. I hear somebody coming. I'm going to slip my phone into my pocket."

Wolf shifted his eyes from Freyja to the phone and back to Freyja. She raised her forefinger to her lips, and he nodded.

A distant voice called, "Is that you up there, Judy?"

"Hi, Mr. Winterstein. Yes, it's me. I just had to climb up here and look at the stars."

"I'm coming up."

Freyja's face muscles tensed, the lines of her scars darkening.

Winterstein's voice grew louder. "I knocked on your bedroom door, but no one answered. I wanted to make sure you had everything you need."

"Miss Maxell lent me these pajamas and a robe. I'm good to go."

"Wonderful. When you didn't answer the door, I wondered what happened to you."

"I saw this tower out my window, and I couldn't resist."

"Yes, it's one of my favorite features at this house."

"I looked through the binoculars and saw a cruise ship on the ocean. The stars are incredible."

Winterstein laughed. "I often come up here by myself at night and look at the stars. It's a good place to get some inspiration and vision."

"In your business, you need a good source of inspiration."

"That's right, Judy. I create new worlds and give people a break from the drudgery of their lives. I take my work very seriously."

"I appreciate you giving me a chance to audition."

His voice became louder. "You amazed us tonight."

"Really?"

"I was expecting a farm girl act, but you dazzled us with your sensuality. We're looking for someone who can play a talented nightclub singer."

"I thought Ella Stonewall's songs were incredible."

"She's great, but your audition topped hers. Hank Cruse came up to me and said that you're the one."

"Wow! That's huge coming from him."

"He knows talent when he sees it."

"I hope I don't disappoint him."

"Just study that script I gave you. Tomorrow at noon, dazzle us like you did tonight. If you do, the part will be yours."

"I'll do my best. I always give everything I got."

Winterstein's voice grew even louder. "That's my girl. Let me give you a good luck hug."

Silenced ensued for almost half a minute, except for some soft rustling. Freyja narrowed her eyes and stared at Wolf.

Finally, Mel said, "Thanks for the pep talk."

"I'll be rooting for you."

"You're sweet."

"You're a very beautiful young woman."

"You've got warm hands."

"Once you really get to know me, you'll discover I have a warm heart, too."

"I hope I get that chance."

"Do your homework. Tomorrow could change your life forever."

"I'll learn those lines better than a Hell's Angel knows his Harley."

"I know you will. I'm heading back down. You better get to bed soon. I want you to be at your best."

"Don't worry, Mr. Winterstein. I'm going to spend a few more minutes stargazing, then I plan on getting a good night's sleep."

"Young lady, I have a feeling that stargazing falls short of your future. I believe you are going to be a star. Goodnight."

"Goodnight, Mr. Winterstein."

"Oh, one more thing. My friends call me Saul."

"Goodnight, Saul."

Things grew quiet for more than a minute. "Okay, he's gone," Mel whispered.

"Good," Freyja said. "Did he make you feel uncomfortable?"

"A little. He gave me one of those too-long hugs. Then he put his hands on my cheeks. He didn't try to feel me up or anything. I was worried he might."

"He didn't want to scare you off," Freyja said. "He's trying to establish trust."

"I bet that's what he did to my sister. What a lech."

Wolf asked, "Do you have the alert button with you."

"Yeah. It's in my robe pocket."

"Don't forget to take it wherever you go."

"Don't worry. It's my lifeline. Make sure you keep your phone charged."

"Will do."

"Listen," Freya said. "When you go exploring tonight, call me once you step out of the room. We don't need a play-by-play account. Just leave your phone on so we can hear in case anything happens."

"If you insist."

"I insist."

Mel yawned. "I better get some sleep."

"Good idea," Freyja said.

"I'm heading back down now. Talk to you later."

"Bye." Freyja met Wolf's gaze with worried eyes.

He tapped the phone to end the call. "You look like a mom who just saw her daughter ride off on the back of a motorcycle."

"With a Hell's Angel."

"Mel's in over her head."

Freyja sat back on the couch and let out a strained breath. "I need another glass of wine."

"That'll make four for you."

She pointed to the glass. "Filler up."

Wolf emptied the bottle into her glass. "We can't allow ourselves to fret over what we can't control." He handed her the glass of wine.

"I know. I'm trying to think if there's something else we can do."

Wolf leaned back next to her and grasped her hand. "I'm glad you told her to call later tonight when she goes investigating. That didn't occur to me. You'd make a great detective."

"You better stay here tonight. I want you with me when she calls."

Wolf grinned. "I'm all for that."

"I'm sure you are."

"Can you lend me some pajamas and a robe?"

"Your tartan boxers will do."

Wolf patted the couch cushion. "Do I have to sleep here?"

Freyja grasped his chin and turned his face toward her. "Not if you behave yourself."

Wolf leaned and kissed her softly. "I'll be on my best behavior."

Chapter 14

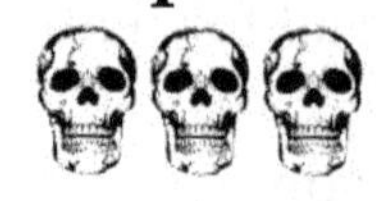

Wolf stepped out of the sunshine into the third-floor great room of Winterstein′′s palace. As his eyes adjusted to the darkness of the interior, he panned the room. He noticed Elaine Maxell sitting at the grand piano in the corner. She pounded the keys four times and then four more times. Wolf recognized the tune--Beethoven's Fifth. To the right, Winterstein and his mother stood in front of the railing near the steps.

"Where are they?" Wolf demanded.

Maxell pounded the keys again.

Wolf stepped closer. "Where are the Bianco sisters!"

They stared at him with blank faces.

Maxell played the next stanza, striking the keys higher and higher, faster and faster.

Muscled arms clamped around Wolf's chest, and a large man lifted him off the ground. Wolf couldn't see his face but knew it was Jake Cleaver. The piano notes intensified and accelerated.

Cleaver carried him over to the railing. Winterstein and his mother separated as Cleaver lifted him. Wolf couldn't break free. The giant hoisted him above the railing and heaved him over. Wolf whirled and managed to clasp the top of the rail with one hand and a baluster with the other. Cleaver pried his hand off the top rail. Wolf swung to the left, clenching the baluster. He glanced over his shoulder and down to the red flagstone floor three stories below. He reached and tried to grasp another post but kept missing. The piano notes echoed through the tall entryway. Cleaver pried his other hand loose and held him dangling, away from the rail.

"No! No! Don't drop me!" Wolf cried.

Cleaver grinned like a heel wrestler about to terminate a WWF hero. He let go. Wolf fell, his stomach leaping into his throat. Just before he hit the stone floor, he opened his eyes and sat up. Someone stirred beside him, and Beethoven's Fifth played on. The cell phone on the nightstand lit up, vibrating with the music. Wolf stretched over the sleek body beside him and reached for the phone.

"What are you doing?" Freyja grumbled.

"It's Mel." He tapped the answer button and fell back onto the bed beside her. He touched the speakerphone button. "Hello . . . Mel?"

"I'm in the hallway," Mel whispered. "I'm putting the phone in my pocket while I check the bedrooms."

"Okay," Wolf said. "We'll listen."

Freyja propped herself up against the headboard. "My head hurts."

Wolf held his finger to his lips. "Shhhhhh." He checked the digital alarm on the nightstand: 3:10.

Freyja's eyes widened. She mouthed the words: *Mel's on the phone?*

Wolf nodded.

Freyja rubbed her eyes and massaged her temples.

The subtle sounds of doors opening and closing emitted from the phone. They sat on the bed against the headboard, shoulder to shoulder. Wolf held the phone in front of them. Fifteen minutes passed.

Finally, Mel whispered, "I've checked four bedrooms. No sign of my sister. One more to go."

Freyja's eyes, tense and unblinking, stared at the phone.

Wolf heard the sound of a door being gently opened.

A muffled voice said, "Don't move." The voice was low and rough.

Freyja stiffened.

"Stay right where you are," the man growled.

"Oh, I'm sorry," Mel said. "I thought this was my bedroom."

"What are you doing, walking these hallways in the middle of the night?"

Wolf recognized the voice—Jake Cleaver.

"I'm too excited to sleep. I needed to walk off some energy. I guess I lost my sense of direction. I thought this was my room."

"Your bedroom is in the middle of the hall, not at the end."

"That's right. Now I remember."

"You're not that dumb. What do you got there?"

"Ow! Lemme go!"

"What are you holding? Give it to me." Seconds slipped slowly by. "Pepper spray? What the hell are you doing with pepper spray?"

"I carry it with me to protect myself. Two of the old guys at the party tonight hit on me. I'm not taking any chances."

"Bullshit. You're taking a big chance walking these halls at three o'clock in the morning. I could have pounded you first and asked questions later."

"I'm sorry. I'll go back to my room. I didn't know I was a prisoner here."

"I didn't say you were a prisoner. I don't know what you are, but I guarantee you this: Nothing gets past me."

"I was invited here. You're the one who let me in the gate. I had an audition tonight, and I've got a screentest tomorrow. My mind's in a whirl. That's all. If there's a problem, then let's go talk to Mr. Winterstein."

"We're not going to wake up Mr. Winterstein."

"Then if you don't mind, I want to go back to bed."

"You may be a guest here, but you don't have permission to wander the halls and open doors."

"Can I have my pepper spray back?"

"No. Go back to your room and don't come out until breakfast is served."

"Okay. I'm going."

A few seconds later Wolf heard the sound of a door opening and slamming. "Mel, are you there? Mel, are you there?"

Another minute passed. "I'm under the covers," Mel whispered. "If this room is bugged, I don't want them to hear me."

"Good thinking," Freyja said. "Don't leave that room again tonight."

"I'm not stupid. That big-ass gorilla out there suspects I'm up to something. I'm going to lay low until the coast is clear."

"Did he hurt you?" Freyja asked.

"No, but he took my pepper spray. I should have kicked him right in the gonads."

"Yeah, that would have helped your cause," Wolf said. "Did you see anything in those empty bedrooms?"

"Nothing. I checked the walk-in closets and the bathrooms. I never got to check out the bedroom at the end of the hallway. Maybe I'll take a quick peek in there when I go to breakfast tomorrow morning."

"It's too risky," Freyja said. "You need to leave that place as soon as you can."

"No way. Not until I look in that other bedroom and see what's on the bottom floor. The top floor is just a giant great room and Mrs. Winterstein's apartment. I doubt if they stuck Sammi in there, but you never know."

"Did you remember to take the alert button with you tonight?" Wolf asked.

"Would a skydiver forget his parachute?"

"Keep it on you in case they come to question you tonight."

"It's in my pajama pocket."

"Please, Mel," Freyja begged, "leave that place as soon as possible."

"I'm not going to stay much longer. My sister's mistake was living here. She couldn't afford the hotel costs. As soon as I get through my screentest tomorrow and check the bottom floor, I'm outta here."

"Good," Freyja said.

"I need to get some sleep. I still haven't memorized the script. Big day tomorrow. I'll check back in with you after the screentest."

"Okay," Wolf said. "Stay safe."

"Bye."

"Goodbye," Freyja sighed.

Freyja slid down the headboard and settled onto her pillow. "Could you get me a glass a water and some ibuprofen?"

"Not a problem. Too much wine?"

"Yes. I usually limit myself to two drinks. Four did me in."

"Where's the meds?"

"There's a bottle in the bathroom."

Wolf made his way into the bathroom, flipped on the light and found the headache pills. He saw a dixie cup on the sink counter and filled it with water. He stared at himself in the mirror. Bags had formed under his eyes, but other than that, he didn't look too bad. *I wonder what she thinks. I'm seven years older than her. That's not too big a gap. Am I in love? I've only known her two days. It feels like love, but what do I know. I'm the strikeout king.* He shook his head and headed back to the bedroom.

Freyja sat up, downed the ibuprofen and slumped back into her pillow.

Wolf crawled into bed and lay on his side facing her. "How bad does it hurt?"

"Don't get any ideas."

"You think that's what's on my mind?"

"Is it?"

"I don't think of women as sex objects. I would ask, but they would object. I've learned my lesson."

Freyja laughed. "Ohhhhh. It hurts when I laugh."

"Seriously, though, I know you're worried about Mel."

"I think the risk isn't worth the possible payoff."

"Chances are, she's not going to find her sister."

"Right. There's a better chance of her ending up in trouble."

"She's a risk taker."

Freyja massaged her temples again. "Obviously."

"Do you want me to give you a nice massage?"

"You stay right where you are."

Wolf turned in the opposite direction and clicked off the light on the nightstand. "Go to sleep. You'll feel better in the morning."

"Wes?"

"Yes."

"My mind's a little foggy. Did I do anything last night that I'll regret in the morning?"

"No. You did everything just right."

She snorted, "Ohhhhh, my head."

Chapter 15

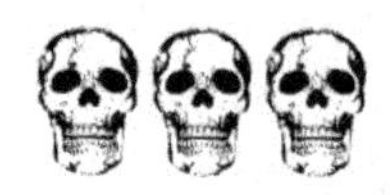

About ten o'clock the next morning, Wolf decided to take a long beach walk. He missed Freyja already. They had eaten breakfast together at her place and said their goodbyes. She had gone off to Kitty Hawk for her appointment with her husband and his lawyer. He had wanted to tell her he loved her before she left, but he knew that would sound crazy and immature. He had drifted back over to his bungalow, showered and shaved. It was the first time he had shaved in three days. Feeling refreshed, he had decided to go for some ocean therapy.

He walked barefoot along the wet sand, the wash of the up-rushing waves splashing his feet. About a mile south of his bungalow, he caught sight of a sea turtle. It had crawled about thirty yards onto the shore and rested in the dry sand. He stepped up to it, bent over and took a closer look. The creature breathed with great difficulty, opening and closing its eyes. Wolf figured it was about ready to die. By the scarring on its shell and weathered texture of its scales, he could tell it was ancient. Had it lived a long and satisfying life? Probably. Regrets? Probably not. Hell, it was a sea turtle.

Wolf angled back toward the shore. *That's a good way to die – after a long, satisfying life with no regrets.* He drifted lower on the bank, and the water poured over his ankles. It felt good. Did he have any regrets? He was almost forty, and he still hadn't married or conceived children. Time was slipping away. Clearly, that was his biggest regret: not finding love, entering into a long-term relationship and having a family. *Is it too late for me? Maybe that's not in my cards.* Images of his night with Freyja played over in his mind. Was she the one in a hundred million who could fill that empty space in his life? When they were together, it sure felt like it. Then again, he always believed that if you can't be happy by yourself, don't count on someone else making you happy.

He took a deep breath and pulled his cell phone out of his cargo shorts pocket. *I need to talk to Angie.* He tapped the contacts icon, scrolled to her number and initiated the call.

She answered, "Good morning, Wes."

"Hey, Angel. I didn't wake you, did I?"

"You're the one who sleeps 'til noon and avoids work like the plague. I was up at seven. What're you doing right now?"

"Avoiding work."

"See what I mean. What's going on with Mel?"

"She almost blew it last night. Gorilla Cleaver caught her wandering the halls at three o'clock in the morning."

"What'd he do?"

"Gave her a lecture and sent her to her room."

"She got off easy. Do you think he suspects anything?"

"Probably, but she refuses to leave until she checks out the rest of the house."

"That's not good."

"No. She's got a screentest at noon. Hopefully, she'll get a chance to look around afterwards and get outta there. Keep your phone near you just in case she hits the alert button."

"It's right here in my pocket. I'll be home all day stripping wallpaper."

Wolf grinned. "I missed that. Did you say, 'stripping'?"

"Yeah, I've got a pole set up in my living room. Joel's coming over with all his buddies from the Dare County Sheriff's Department. Do you got wax in your ears? I said, 'stripping wallpaper'!"

"Oh, okay. I thought maybe you picked up a side job."

"Remind me to smack you the next time I see you."

"I'm sure you'll remember without me reminding you."

"What's up with you and Freyja?"

"I think I'm in love."

"Did you spend the night with her?"

"Yeah."

"Wasn't that a little rushed? You've only known her two days."

"Special circumstances."

"What circumstances? You're old, and time is at a premium?"

"No, but that's true." Wolf knelt and cupped a hand full of sand. "My life is slipping away like sand through my fingers. I'm nearly forty years old. Never been married. No kids."

"You're pathetic. You've known her two days, and you think you're in love."

"How long did it take you to fall in love with Joel?"

"Two minutes. I'm more pathetic than you."

"That's why I hired you. I need someone to look up to me."

"Let me give you some advice."

"I'm listening."

"Treasure the moments you've shared. Focus on the now. Keep low expectations for the future."

Wolf rubbed his chin. "Very wise advice, Angel. Low expectations and insensitivity are the keys to happiness."

"Don't be a bonehead! If you expect fireworks, and they go off, you got what you expected. If you expect fireworks, and they don't go off, you're disappointed. If you don't expect fireworks, and they go off, you're delighted."

Wolf stood and stared at the few remaining grains of sand in his hand before flicking them away. *That's actually sound reasoning.* "You want to know something, Angel, I think I'm going to take your advice."

"It's about time."

"Listen, I've got some more work to avoid. If that alert goes off on your phone, meet me on the beach by Winterstein's walkway. If I don't show up, stay there and wait. I don't want you storming the castle alone."

"You want me to wait all day? Maybe I should bring a beach towel and some suntan lotion."

"That's not a bad idea, if you still want to be a stripper."

"I'm going to smack you silly next time I see you."

"Adios."

"Goodbye, Bonehead."

Wolf slipped his phone back into his pocket, turned around and walked back to his bungalow. Talking to Angie always made him feel better.

* * *

When he got back to his beach house, he checked his watch: 10:55. He decided to catch up on some background checks for a client, tedious work that he had been neglecting. He sat at the computer in his office, trying to concentrate, but thoughts of Freyja kept infiltrating and disrupting his progress. He did discover that two of the men he was checking on had criminal records. One had been arrested for shoplifting and the other for beating up his girlfriend. His client, a local businessman who owned a slew of souvenir shops along the Outer Banks, wanted to know potential employees' missteps before putting them on the payroll.

Wolf checked his phone to make sure he didn't miss Mel's alert call. Nothing. He walked to the kitchen and made a pot of coffee. While it was brewing, he grabbed a piece of leftover pizza out of the fridge, slapped it on a plate and popped it into the microwave for forty-five seconds. *This has been my life for fifteen years. In and out of shaky relationships or hanging out by myself eating leftover pizza. It's time for me to grow up*. The microwave dinged. The coffee maker sputtered. He slid the pizza onto a plate, poured a cup of coffee and dumped a couple teaspoons of powered creamer into it.

He decided to take his lunch onto the back deck. The sun beamed down from a bright blue sky, as if welcoming him like an old friend. The sea always offered consoling company. He needed the companionship of the sun and the sea. He didn't quite know why he was feeling low. Then again, maybe he did. He had fallen hard for Freyja Beck but doubted that she was equally enamored with him. *I might be wrong. She'd make a good poker player. Is it possible that she loves me but doesn't need me? Maybe that's the best kind of love. No matter what happens, life won't fall apart. You can stand with the person you love or stand alone, if necessary.* Wolf figured that kind of independent spirit was good, but it didn't diminish the gnawing possibility of living the rest of his life as a lonely bachelor.

He checked his watch again—11:55. Almost time for Mel's screentest. He imagined her standing in front of the camera, going through her lines with dramatic flair. *If she acts as well as she did at the Jolly Rodger, she'll impress the hell out of those Hollywood hustlers. What would she do if Winterstein offered her a big contract? Good question. Do you look for your missing sister or deposit a million dollars into your bank account? I guess she could do both. Chances are, though, Winterstein just wants to use her. Get her into bed until he gets bored with her. What a slimeball.*

Wolf finished off his pizza and downed the last few gulps of coffee. He closed his eyes and enjoyed the feel of the breeze off the ocean. Seagulls screeched in the distance, and the rhythm of the waves lulled him into a half sleep. The sounds and sensations relaxed him. He felt small in this dreamy state, as if he were a feather floating on the breeze above the ocean. The sea had a way of making him feel small—a good small. It reminded him of his place in the world—not all-important yet not insignificant. He was a part of the fabric, responsible for doing his part to hold things together.

"Hey, stranger," a woman's voice called.

Wolf bolted upwards, bracing himself on the arms of the chair.

Freyja laughed. "Sleeping on the job again?" She wore a white frock dress patterned with seashells that reached to her knees.

He took a calming breath and faced her. "I was meditating."

"I see. Hanging out in the space between your thoughts."

"Yeah. There's lots of space between my thoughts. How'd the divorce proceedings go?"

She raised her arms like a runner crossing the finish line. "I'm a single woman. Are you ready to get married?"

"Whenever you are." *If only she were serious.*

"Let's take a walk along the beach and celebrate. Maybe we'll run into a preacher."

Wolf stood. "Or we can build a sandman and pretend he's Parson Brown." He slipped his phone out of his pocket and checked for alerts. Nothing. He noticed the time on the face of the phone—12:31. "Mel's screen test is probably over by now." He descended the steps to the sand and joined Freyja in front of her deck.

"That sounds about right. Thirty to forty-five minutes depending on how many takes they do." She held out her hand. "What direction do you want to go?"

Wolf pointed southward and grasped her hand. "That way. I want to check on a sea turtle that crawled onto shore earlier this morning."

They walked to the wet sand near the edge of the ocean, trying to skirt the up rush of water from the incoming tide but not always succeeding.

"Did you talk to your husband much?

"Not much. I asked him how the star search was going. He said they may have finally found someone to take my place."

"Mel?"

"I would assume."

"How were his mannerisms?"

"Twitchy and nervous."

"Is he usually that anxious?"

"No. I could tell something was bothering him."

"Maybe finalizing the divorce got to him."

"Maybe."

"Or murder."

"Possibly."

"I'd say probably."

"He told me to stop by for old times' sake."

"Hmmmm." Wolf froze in his tracks and faced her. "That might be helpful."

She smiled. "A way in, if we need one."

Wolf tugged on her arm and began walking again. "Hopefully, we won't, but it's a good option to have."

"Options are good, but I like choices better."

"What do you mean?"

She raised his hand. "I choose you. Do you choose me?" She lowered it.

He raised her hand, and said, "Yes, I choose you," and lowered it.

"We're chosen. That's better than being options."

Wolf wanted to tell her that he loved her right then and there but kept silent. *Keep the expectations low, you bonehead.* Was her talk of choices and marriage for the fun of it? Just kidding around? As long as he wasn't sure, he'd play along. Up ahead he saw a white circular object in the sand. As they neared, he could see it was a large sand dollar. He let go of her hand, crouched to his knees and picked it up. Kneeling, he faced her. The wind rippled her ash blonde hair and white dress. With the sun illuminating her face, her scars appeared more like the markings of a Viking goddess.

He held the sand dollar up to her. "In lieu of a ring, this is my engagement gift to you."

She took it. "I accept. This is much better than a ring. Like me, it comes from the sea. Shall we seal this covenant with a kiss?"

Wolf stood, and they kissed for several minutes, lovingly and unmindful of the few onlookers scattered across the beach. The incoming tide washed over their sandals and splashed up to their calves. They broke apart, gazed into each other's eyes and smiled.

"Did you know the eyes are the mirrors of the soul?" Freyja asked.

"I've heard it said. I wish I were better at soul gazing. I'm not certain of what I see in there."

She tapped his cheek gently with her palm. "Look deeper and you'll see everything you need."

Wolf's eyes narrowed. "What does that mean?"

"That's the definition of love." She grasped his hand and headed down the beach. "Let's go find that turtle."

Wolf shook his head. *Did she just say she loved me? Or did she give me a definition, and I'm supposed to figure it out?* The turtle appeared at the peak of the upsloping shore about a hundred yards away. With the tide was coming in, the water had risen much closer to the turtle than earlier in the day. They broke away from the firmer sand and walked up the slope toward the turtle.

"I can't believe it," Wolf said.

"What?"

"This morning he was pointed in the opposite direction, headed into shore. I thought he crawled up here to die. Now he's managed to turn back around toward the sea."

"He's old, but he's not ready to die. He just needed a rest."

The turtle moved its legs and inched forward. The effort seemed to strain the creature.

"Let's help him out," Freyja said. "You lift on that side."

Wolf figured it weighed about 150 pounds. He bent over, grasped the shell with both hands and lifted. Freyja heaved her side, and they carefully slid the turtle down the slope. The water rushed up the incline and helped raise the creature. In less than two minutes it was swishing through the waves and heading out to sea. Freyja raised her hand, and Wolf slapped it.

"We accomplished our good deed for the day," she said. As if on cue, Beethoven's Fifth played from her dress pocket. She fished out her phone and read the screen. "It's Mel."

Chapter 16

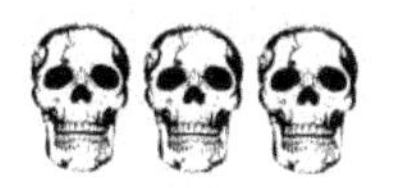

"Hello." Freyja switched to speakerphone.

"It's me," Mel whispered.

"Where are you?" Freyja asked.

"On the bottom floor. It's dark down here, but I don't want to turn on a light."

"There's not much down there," Freyja said, "some storage rooms, utility rooms, a garage and the cook's and housekeeper's quarters."

"I've looked through a couple of the storage rooms. Lots a tools and crap like that. There's a Mercedes, a red Humvee and an ATV in the garage, but that's about it. I went through a door into the next room, but it leads to a small open space and a wall with no door. It can't be the end of the house."

"A wall?" Wolf asked. "What kind of wall?"

"It feels solid and cold. It might be made of steel."

"I don't remember a steel wall," Freyja said.

"I checked out the other bedroom on my way to breakfast this morning. No luck."

Wolf said, "I'd say you're lucky to still be free and unharmed."

"That's true, especially after that screentest."

"Why? What happened?" Freyja asked.

"I had to do a steamy love scene with guess who?"

"Hank Cruse," Freyja said.

"I wish. He left last night along with most of the other guests. Winterstein stepped in for him. The scene required passionate kissing and some groping. I almost threw up. Winterstein must have enjoyed it. He wanted four retakes. He couldn't get enough of me. Fortunately, afterwards he went to a local restaurant to meet with potential backers. I thought he was going to invite me up to his room for more practice."

"It's time to get out of there," Freyja said.

"You're right. I've reached a dead end. As soon as I find my way out of this dungeon, I'm heading to my car and . . . Oh . . . Oh . . ."

"Mel?" Wolf said.

"There you are," a low voice growled.

Wolf met Freyja's stare and mouthed, *Jake Cleaver.*

"I was t-t-trying to find the way outta h-h-here and must have made a wrong turn."

"Sure you were, just like last night. Wandering where you shouldn't be wandering."

"Could you please take that light out of my eyes."

"Who are you talking to on your phone?"

"My mother. I was telling her about my screentest. H-h-here. Do you want to talk to her?"

"Gimme that phone."

"Oh no, Mom must have hung up."

The screen went black.

Freyja gripped Wolf around the bicep. "What're we going to do?"

"Relax. He might just give her the right-foot-of-fellowship out the door and send her on her way."

Her face drained of color. "What if he checks the recent calls on the phone. He'll see my name."

"That won't make sense to him, but he'll know she's lying. He'll want some questions answered."

"He'll take her up to Maxell, and they'll grill her."

"Let's head back. We'll drive up to Corolla and watch for the alert signal on my phone. If she can come up with a good story, maybe they'll let her go. If not, we'll at least get a head start. Can you jog a mile back to the cottages?"

Freyja took off running and yelled over her shoulder, "Try to keep up!"

* * *

By the time he reached his bungalow, Wolf had fallen about 200 yards behind. Freyja stood on her back deck, completely recovered.

"Let's take your Jeep," he heaved. "We can park on the beach just beyond the house. My Cougar will get stuck in the sand."

"Okay. I'll meet you out front."

"I'm going to grab a big hat and sunglasses. You can introduce me as your boyfriend. Hopefully, Cleaver won't recognize me."

"Hurry up!" Freyja rushed into her cottage.

Wolf trotted up the steps and into his bedroom. He stripped off his black Polo shirt and strapped on his holster. He whirled and yanked the closet door open. Seeing a Hawaiian shirt, he whipped it off a hanger, slipped into it and fastened a couple buttons. On the top shelf he spied a wide-brimmed, straw beach hat and crammed it on his head. He stepped out of his sandals, wriggled his feet into his loafers and swiped his black-framed Oakleys off his dresser. As he rushed through the front office and out the door, he caught sight of the Jeep Renegade in the street, engine rumbling and Freyja at the wheel.

She reached and pounded the dashboard. "C'mon, get the lead out of your ass."

He rushed around the front bumper and sprung into the car. Freyja peeled out, slowed for the stop sign at the end of the street, checked for traffic and gunned it, squealing around the turn onto Old Oregon Inlet Road.

Her eyes focused intensely, and she gripped the wheel with both hands. "What do you think they'll do with her?"

"If they check her recent calls and see your name, they won't stop there. They'll look through her purse and check her ID."

"Then they'll find out she's Sammi's sister."

"Yeah. That's a no-brainer. Even a guy like Gorilla Cleaver can figure that one out."

"What's their next step?"

Wolf brushed his knuckles against his clean-shaven jaw "Maybe they'll lock her away with her sister."

"Right. Let's hope so. That'll give them time to figure out what to do."

"Mel said that Winterstein was meeting with potential backers. Maxell and Cleaver will want to talk to him before making any moves."

"That gives us a window to make our move."

Wolf drew his phone out of his cargo shorts and checked it. No alerts. "Let's not get too worked up. Mel hasn't hit the alarm button yet. Maybe they let her go."

"If she's got it tucked in her bra, she's not going to press it until she's alone."

Wolf nodded. "That's true."

"What if we do get into the house? They may play dumb or tell us she left. How do we find out where they're hiding her?"

"That's where my friend Siggy comes in."

"Siggy?"

Wolf patted his shirt where his gun was strapped beneath the fabric. "Sig Sauer, my semi-automatic pistol."

"Nice to meet you, Siggy." Freyja glanced at him. "Where'd you get that shirt? A hand-me-down from your great uncle?"

"Yeah, Uncle Leo. He gives me all his old shirts and tartan boxers."

After turning onto Route 12 and plodding through the busy town of Duck, Freyja picked up the pace."

"Better watch your speed," Wolf said. "There's a few traps along this road."

Freyja sighed and slowed the Jeep. "How's fifty in a forty-five?"

"That's pushing it."

"It's worth the risk."

When they entered the town of Corolla, she brought the car down from fifty to forty mph.

They passed the Food Lion, and Wolf thumbed out the window to his right. "That's where they found Jennifer Cobb's car."

Freyja took a shaky breath. "I hope Sammi and Mel don't end up like her."

"Not if we can help it."

Wolf's cell phoned dinged, and he checked it. "Mel hit the button."

"Shiiiiiiiit. This is really happening."

"It's about to hit the fan. Let's keep our heads. We're only about four miles from the house."

They flew past a cop car, and Freyja checked her speed. "Five miles over the limit."

Wolf twisted in his seat and peered back at the cruiser. "No sirens, no lights. Must be the middle of the month."

They passed the sheriff's office, and Freyja tilted her head to the right. "Should we give them a call? Maybe they could help."

"Sooner or later, but not now. Let's see what happens."

"Okay. I hope you know what you're doing."

"I might not know much, but I know it fluently." As they approached the end of the road, Wolf extended his hand straight ahead like a traffic cop. "Go on past the house and into the Wild Horse Sanctuary."

Freyja glanced to her right. "There's Mel's old Malibu parked in the front."

"We know she's still here."

Freyja slowed the Jeep for the upcoming turn. Fifty yards past Winterstein's palace, a wooden fence, about five feet high, fronted each side of the road. A wide steel grate, one horses could not cross because of the gaps between the bars, traversed the road where the fences met the asphalt edges. The Jeep rumbled over the grate. The road turned toward the sea and ended after another 150 yards.

"Go straight and park near the sea fence," Wolf said.

The Jeep thudded over the edge of the asphalt and into the sand, its large tires sinking in but managing to burrow steadily across the soft surface. Freyja peeled off to the right where a tall fence composed of poles and thick wires extended into the ocean. The fence kept the wild horses from entering the vacationers' beach area and neighborhoods.

She stopped the Jeep about fifty yards from the shore. "We can leave the car here."

"Right. People park along the beach to fish and look for shells. Your ex-husband's walkway is right on the other side of this fence."

"I know. I used to cut through and jog down the beach. There's a place in the fence where pedestrians can weave in and out, but horses can't."

"When I looked out the window yesterday, I noticed a tall gate along the walkway to the house. We'll have to climb over it or work around the side to get by it."

"Maybe not," Freyja said. "It has a combo lock on it. I'll punch in the old combination and see if it works—1980."

"The year of his birth?"

"Yes. Easy to remember." Freyja reached and grabbed Wolf's wrist. "Look!"

A well-built woman with short black hair threaded through the fencing. She wore a one-piece emerald swimsuit and green-framed sunglasses. The sun flashed off an object she carried in her hand. As she passed in front of them, Wolf noticed her face was lined with stress. A scarf adorned her neck, a white scarf with a multi-color flower print.

Wolf leaned forward, his mouth dropping open. "Elaine Maxell."

"That's her."

"Give me three minutes with her, and I'll find out where they're keeping Mel and her sister." Wolf stepped out of the Jeep.

"Do you want me to come with you?"

"No. Stay here."

Wolf dropped in behind her along the sloping wet sand. She walked briskly. He scanned the beach. The closest people to them splashed in the shallows a few hundred yards ahead. *Perfect.* He picked up his pace to a jog, running as softly as possible.

She raised the object to her ear, her cell phone. "Saul . . . you need to get back here as soon as you can. We've run into a big problem."

When he got to within a few feet, she whipped around and faced him.

"Hi Elaine," he beamed and stopped directly in front of her.

She lowered the phone. "Who are you?"

"You don't recognize me?"

Her mouth dropped open. "You're that private detective."

"That's right." Wolf reached, clamped onto the scarf and twisted it.

She dropped the phone and reached for her throat. "Stop it! You're hurting me."

He gave the scarf another twist. "That's my plan unless you come up with some answers."

She gagged and rasped, "What are you talking about?"

"Two missing girls and Melissa Bianco."

She tried to slap him, but he grabbed her hand. "No, no, no. None of that."

"I don't know anything about them."

Wolf bent her hand back, and she shrieked.

"Do you want to play the piano again?"

She bobbed her head rapidly, face muscles tensing.

"I'll turn your hand into a useless claw. Do you understand me?"

"Yes, yes, yesssss. Please, let go."

"That's up to you."

"It was an accident. She had too much to drink, and then Margaret gave her some sleeping pills."

"And she overdosed?"

"Yes. Saul didn't want to face a scandal."

"So you dumped her body into the Currituck Sound and dropped a kayak into the water to make it look like an accident."

"I didn't. Jake Cleaver took care of the body."

Wolf tightened the scarf, and she struggled to breathe. "Who gave him the order? You?"

She gagged, her face reddening, and Wolf let up on the tension.

She caught her breath. "We discussed all the options, but Saul made the final decision."

"Then you shouldn't be in too much trouble. Just tell me where they are, and I'll let you go."

Her lips tightened, and she glared at him.

He bent her hand back again.

She gasped, "They're in the secret room."

"Where is it?"

"Saul had it constructed on the bottom floor."

"How do I get into it?"

It's a solid steel wall. It can only be opened electronically with the right combination. Then you'll need the key for the door."

"Who has the combination and key?"

"Jake Cleaver."

Wolf let up on the pressure against her hand. "Last question. What did Winterstein plan on doing with his prisoners?"

"I don't know for sure. He doesn't know about Melissa yet. Jake told Saul he knew people who could take care of things."

"What kind of people?"

"They . . . they run an industry."

"The sex-trafficking trade?"

She nodded.

"When are they coming to pick them up?"

"I don't know. Maybe this afternoon, maybe tomorrow. They told Jake to be patient and keep her healthy."

Wolf pointed northward down the beach. "You walk in that direction and keep walking. Someone from the sheriff's department will pick you up. If you don't cause me any more trouble, I'll let them know you cooperated."

She glanced down at her phone.

Wolf grinned. "I'll take that with me." He spun her around. "Get going."

As she walked away, she wept, inhaling quick breaths followed by uncontrolled sobs.

Wolf picked up her phone and put it to his ear.

"Elaine! . . . Elaine! . . .We've got a bad connection. What problem are you talking about? . . .Elaine!"

Wolf made an odd noise similar to static mixed with garbled speech.

"I can't hear what you're saying," Winterstein complained. "I'm heading home now. I'll be there in twenty minutes."

Chapter 17

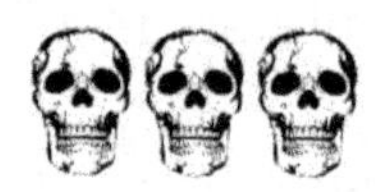

Freyja leaned against the front of the Jeep as Wolf approached. He jammed Maxell's phone into one of the deep pockets of his cargo shorts. Freyja pushed off the car and strode toward him. The sea breeze winnowed her long ashen hair and whipped the thin cloth of the white frock dress, offering a chimeric outline of her lovely body.

"What did she tell you?"

Wolf motioned toward the passageway in the tall fence and headed in that direction. "Let's go."

Freyja caught up and strode beside him as he marched toward the opening. "Well?"

"They locked Mel and Sammi in a hidden room on the bottom floor."

"I knew it. When Mel described that steel wall, it didn't match my memory of that part of the house. They added that room after I left."

"She said we'd need the combination to get through the wall and a key to open a door."

"How do we get the combination and key?"

"Jake Cleaver."

They reached the fence opening and zigzagged through the passage to the other side. The surf thundered on the shore to the left, and a few beachgoers stretched out on towels or sat in beach chairs under large sun umbrellas. Some kids splashed in the waves. Wolf peered to the right across the stretch of sand and spied the steps that ascended to the walkway. They hustled toward the steps and stopped at the bottom.

"Dammit," Wolf said. "I told Angie to meet me here. We left before the alert went off. She's probably twenty minutes behind us."

"We can't wait that long."

"No. Winterstein will be back before then. I overheard him on Maxell's phone."

"What should we do?"

"We don't have time to waste. Let's storm the castle."

They charged up the steps and hurried down the wooden walkway to the tall gate. Massive thickets and tall thorny bushes grew on each side of the walkway beyond the gate, creating a natural security wall. A combination lock with numbered buttons controlled access to the latch.

"I hope 1980 was a good year," Wolf said.

Freyja punched the numbers into the lock. A green light flicked on above the buttons. "Open sesame." She pushed the gate, and it swung open.

They walked through, and Wolf closed the gate. "I told Angie not to approach the house without me. I have a feeling she'll wait a few minutes and come anyway." He examined the tall, thorny bushes on each side of the walkway. "If she tries to work around the gate by climbing over the railing and skirting the edge, those thorns will be painful."

"What if she shows up at the wrong time?"

"That wouldn't be good. Then again, she might show up at the right time. It's a coin flip. It'll be up to her."

They strode down the walkway to a gazebo that covered a large octagonal hot tub. A wooden privacy fence surrounded the tub with openings on opposite sides to the walkway and the house.

Wolf caught Freyja's arm and stopped her. "Let's check it out from here and go over the plan."

"There's a plan?"

"If we can come up with one."

They edged to the opening that led to the house and stood behind the tall fence.

Wolf took off his straw hat and peeked around the side of the opening. Jake Cleaver stood on the third-floor deck and leaned on the railing, smoking a cigarette. His blue denim shirt and jeans made him look like an over-grown Marlboro Man.

"There's Cleaver," Wolf said.

"Let me see." Pulling Wolf back, she leaned and looked. She withdrew her head and pressed her back against the fence. "What if I lead the way. He knows me. I'll wave and pretend like I'm glad to see him. Then I'll introduce you."

"What if he's made the connection between you and Mel?"

"He only has bits and pieces of information. He won't know what to think. Inviting us into the house will give him an opportunity to sort things out."

Wolf chuckled, placed the wide-brimmed hat back on his head and tilted it downward. "Okay. I hope you know what you're doing."

"I don't know much, but I know it fluently."

Wolf pointed to the opening. "Lead the way."

Freyja strutted into the sunlight, gazing at Cleaver and waving. Wolf followed closely behind. She edged around the long, three-lane pool, still waving. "Jake Cleaver! Long time no see!"

Cleaver straightened and blew out a stream of smoke. "Hold it right there!"

"It's me! Freyja!" She kept walking along the wooden deck next to the pool.

He dropped his cigarette and stamped it out. "What are you doing here?"

She stopped near the steps that led up to the decks and stared up at him. "I met with Saul this morning. We finalized our divorce on friendly terms. He invited me over for old time's sake."

Cleaver nodded slowly. "Who do you have with you?"

Wolf stepped up beside her, and she said, "This is my boyfriend, Jerry . . . Attricks."

Cleaver tilted his head, and an odd smile formed on his face. "Come on up and have a drink. Saul's not here, but he should be getting back soon."

"Great! C'mon, Jerry." Freyja led the way up the steps.

Wolf caught up with her and whispered, "Where did you come up with that name—Jerry Attricks? I'm not that much older than you."

"I said the first thing that came into my mind."

"Thanks. Sounds like a Freudian slip."

"Just keep Sigmund handy when we get up there."

"Huh?"

"Siggy, your gun."

"Oh, yeah."

They hurried up the last section of stairs and stepped onto the third-floor deck. Cleaver held open a French door and motioned them through. As they entered, Wolf noted that the gorilla was as least four inches taller than he and twice as wide. Cleaver followed behind and closed the door.

"Have a seat." He motioned across the room to the beige couch next to the glass-topped kettle-shaped table. "What can I get you to drink?"

Wolf raised a finger, and with a high, nasally voice said, "I'll take a cold beer."

"I'll second that," Freyja said.

They crossed the room, and Wolf pushed aside several pillows so they could sit down. The open floor plan gave them a clear view of Cleaver as he entered the kitchen area and opened a large stainless-steel refrigerator.

"How's a couple Coronas sound?" Cleaver called.

"That'll do," Freyja said.

He came back with three bottles of beer and placed two on the table in front of them. After twisting off the cap on his, he flipped it into the air.

"Heads," Wolf called.

The cap landed bottoms-up on the table. "You lose," Cleaver sneered. He took a long swig and sat down on the matching couch across from them. "So how ya been, Freya?" He eyed her, one eyebrow raised.

"Pretty good. Can't complain."

"You look good." He raised his chin. "Except for the scars."

Her eyes narrowed, and she took in a slow breath.

Wolf straightened and said, "Nice place you got here. Your boss must have a lot of dough." His voice sounded slightly tweaked by helium.

Cleaver raised his bottle and tilted it in Wolf's direction. "Don't I know you?"

"I don't think so."

"You look awful familiar."

"Yeah. People mistake me for that one movie star. What's his name?"

Freyja said, "Steve Buscemi?"

Wolf shook his head. "No, I was thinking more like Matthew McConaughey."

"I don't see the resemblance," Cleaver said.

"So how's the movie business going?" Freyja asked.

"It's going."

"Did they ever find my replacement for that film noir Saul wanted to remake?"

"I think they did. I overheard Mr. Winterstein mention a gal by the name of Judy Gayle. Both he and Elaine were quite impressed with her."

"I know her," Freyja said. "I met her at the Jolly Rodger the other night. We went horseback riding yesterday."

His face muscles froze as if he just stepped into a meat locker. "Is that right?"

"Yes, but her name's not Judy Gayle. It's Melissa Bianco."

He lowered his thick brows, and his eyes darkened. "Judy Gayle must be her stage name."

"That's right." She patted Wolf's forearm. "We heard her sing. She has a beautiful voice. Is she still here?"

Cleaver plunked his beer bottle on the table. "Nope." He leaned back against the pillows and stretched his back. "She finished up her screentest and left about forty-five minutes ago."

Wolf slipped his hand under his shirt. In his normal voice he said, "Then why is her car still parked in front of this house."

Cleaver shrugged. "Maybe she went for a walk. I don't know."

Wolf pulled out his handgun and pointed it at Cleaver. "Enough of this bullshit. We know she's here."

"How could you know that?"

"Stand up and move over to that open space." Wolf waved his gun toward the middle of the room."

Cleaver held up his hands. "Take it easy. You're making a big mistake."

"Move!"

Across the room to the left a door opened. Margaret Winterstein peeked out. "What's going on?" In her baggy black dress with a white collar, she looked like a fashion reject from a nunnery.

"Get back in your room and lock your door," Cleaver commanded.

"He's got a gun!" she shrieked.

"I said get back in your room!"

Wolf stood and shouted, "I said move!"

Cleaver sidestepped between the table and couch and edged slowly backwards.

"Far enough." Wolf took deliberate steps between the furniture and moved to within a few feet of him.

Freyja followed and stood slightly behind Wolf.

Wolf flipped the straw hat off the back of his head. "Now do you recognize me?"

"Yeah. As soon you stepped in the door, I recognized you. You're that private dick that was here yesterday. And I do mean dick."

"Listen, you pile of ape shit, I want the key and combination to the hidden room."

"What the hell are you talking about?"

"You know what I'm talking about."

"Damned if I do."

"Melissa Bianco had an alert button that sent an SOS to my phone. I know she's in the secret room downstairs. Maxell told me. I'm going to say this one time. I'm counting to three. If you don't produce the key and combination, I'm putting a bullet through your leg. One . . .Two . . ." Wolf aimed the gun at his quad.

"Okay, okay! I'll give it to you." He reached into his pocket and pulled out a key with a black triangular keychain. "The code's written on the keychain." He tossed it over Wolf's head. It sailed passed Freya and clanked against the glass of the French door.

"Freyja, get the key," Wolf ordered. "Now that wasn't nice."

"Sorry, I'm a little nervous with that howitzer pointed at me."

"I don't blame you. It would nearly blow your leg clean off."

An odd buzzing surged through Wolf's quad. He jerked and glanced down. Maxell's phone! Cleaver whirled and kicked the gun. It flew across the room, ricocheted off a table and tumbled down the entry steps. Wolf glanced up to see a huge fist collide with his sunglasses. They shattered as the fist crunched against his eye. He slumped onto the floor, head smacking the ground. His vision twirled. A work boot slammed into his stomach, expelling the air from his lungs. He struggled to breathe.

"I've got the key!" Freyja yelled. "Come and get it, King Kong!"

"You scar-faced bitch!"

In the background fog of his mind, Wolf heard a door open, and two sets of footsteps thudding away.

Chapter 18

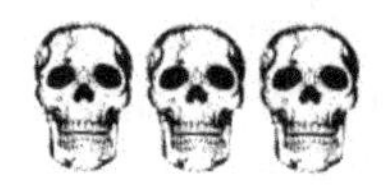

Wolf tried to focus, but the room swirled. His left eye swelled and throbbed. Little by little his lungs opened as he huffed in air. He placed his palms on the oak floor, pushed upwards and drew his knees forward. The room spun more slowly. He crawled to the kettle table and planted his hand on it. Pushing down on the tabletop, he managed to stand. The swelling had narrowed the vision of his left eye to a little more than a slit. The French door hung open. *Freyja didn't get much of a head start.* He swiveled to the left and saw another French door on the south side of the great room. The corkscrew observation tower rose above the deck beyond that door.

He plodded toward the door, focusing on the corkscrew tower. His head ached, and blood had dripped onto his Hawaiian shirt, adding dark red to the tropical colors. He swiped his hand across his cheek and felt the warm wetness. At the door, he stopped and took a deep breath. His brain slowly cleared, the fog lifting. He opened the door, feeling steadier, and walked onto the deck. A metal bridge spanned the gap between the deck and the tower. He walked across the span and anchored his hand on the tower railing. The staircase spiraled up to just above roof level. He climbed the steps, holding tightly to the rail. At the top, vertigo kicked in again, and he closed his eyes to stop the spinning.

"Gimme that key," Cleaver's harsh voice commanded.

"Come and get it, Ape-face," Freyja taunted.

Wolf opened his eyes and tried to focus. Freyja stood on one side of the narrow lap pool, and Cleaver on the other. They faced each other across the three lanes. He moved cautiously back toward the house keeping his eyes on her.

Wolf figured at any second he would charge around the end and try to chase her down. She edged along the pool in the direction of the ocean. He took off, circling the end of the pool, and she sprinted toward the walkway. She had a thirty-yard lead as she disappeared under the gazebo and shot out the other side onto the walkway.

Cleaver dashed after her with surprising agility. She reached the gate and fumbled at the latch. He closed in. She flung the gate open and charged through, but he caught the gate before it shut. He had cut the distance between them to five yards. She sprinted down the remaining length of the walkway. Her white dress flowed behind her, giving her a wraithlike appearance. Wolf blinked several times to clear his vision.

She bounded down the steps but stumbled when she hit the sand. *Get up, Freyja. Don't let that gorilla catch you.* He swiped at her as she recovered her footing, catching the end of her dress. She whirled, bent over, allowing the dress to rip from her body. Making a full pirouette, she kept her balance and bolted toward the ocean. Cleaver tossed the dress to the side and rushed after her.

Clad only in a white bra and panties, she high stepped into the sea. Cleaver dove for her and clasped her ankles, toppling her into the water. She kicked and jerked free, struggled to her feet and dove under a wave. He splashed through the curling breaker, unphased by its power. She surfaced a few feet ahead of him and swam with graceful, quick strokes. He took a few more steps and dove again, just missing her. With long, loping arms and strong kicks, he swam after her.

Wolf noticed the binoculars mounted on a post in front of him. Although he could barely see out of his left eye, he tried looking through the oculars. The ocean appeared to be a gray-green chaotic jumble. He turned the focus wheel, and the choppy water crystalized. He glanced up to get a fix on the chase. They had swum beyond the breakers to the deeper water. Now he could barely see Freyja a few yards ahead of Cleaver.

He angled the binoculars as best he could in that direction and peered into the eyepieces again. Shifting the barrels slightly back and forth, he caught sight of them. Freyja had opened a three- or four-yard lead, but Cleaver pressed on like a shark after a swift seal. *Go Freyja! Don't stop. He'll give up.* Freyja disappeared under the surface. *What're you doing?* Cleaver swam a few more strokes, stopped and treaded water. He turned his head, searching for her. Wolf tilted the barrels up slightly to find Freyja. Nothing but empty ocean. He lowered them again, but Cleaver had disappeared. *What's going on?*

Someone surfaced—Cleaver. He thrashed at the water as if he had difficulty staying afloat. He sank again, but his hands splashed the surface as if trying to get a grip. Slowly, his fingers disappeared below the surface. One hand shot up again but quickly submerged. Something was pulling him down. An undertow? Where's Freyja? Did it get her? He shifted the binoculars around. A minute and a half ticked by. Wolf felt helpless. A head popped up where Cleaver went down. He adjusted the focus wheel. Freyja treaded water. No sign of Cleaver. *What happened?* Freyja swam toward shore. Wolf straightened. Although the swelling around his eye hurt like hell, a wide smile broke across his face. *I just witnessed a genuine, true-and tried, bona fide mermaid homicide.*

Wolf descended the spiral metal steps, taking his time. The blood had dried on his face, and the pain around his eye eased, but his head still hurt. *My gun. Where's my gun?* He remembered Cleaver kicking it out of his hand and seeing it careening toward the stairway. Did it tumble off the steps and onto the flagstone floor in the entryway? He couldn't remember hearing it clatter down there. Cleaver's solid punch to his eye didn't help his memory. His ribs still ached from the kick to his gut. He chuckled to himself. *No more kicks for that gorilla, thanks to Freyja. I need ice for my eye. Better get my gun first, though.*

He crossed the metal bridge onto the deck and entered the French door. Steadying himself, he gazed across the room at the stairs that descended to the entryway. He remembered the buzz of Maxell's phone sending a shock through his quad. *She had it on vibrate. Figures. She'd be the vibrator type.* He reached into the deep pocket, extracted the phone and glanced at the screen. A notice appeared: Missed call from Saul Winterstein. *That call about ended my life.* He slid the phone back into his pocket.

He trudged across the room and inspected the first set of stairs. No gun. *Crap! It must have fallen all the way down.* He descended a few steps but stopped when he heard footfalls echoing in the entryway. They ceased, and someone said, "What's this doing here?" It sounded like Winterstein.

Now what? Wolf tried to think, but his head still throbbed. The footsteps began again. *Did Winterstein pick up my gun*? He wondered if he should hide behind the couch or just face the man. He wasn't in the mood to hide. He stood, leaning on the railing, and waited at the top of the steps.

A half minute passed, and Winterstein made the turn around the post. His gray suit, white shirt and black tie seemed incredibly formal for the circumstances. He stopped on the landing and looked up at Wolf. "What're you doing in my house?"

"Waiting for you."

Winterstein raised Wolf's gun. "What happened to your face?"

"I punched your security man in the fist with it."

"Where is my security man?"

"He went for a swim."

"Put your hands up and back up."

Wolf took his time backpedaling up the few steps. He kept walking backwards toward the middle of the room.

"That's far enough." Winterstein climbed the last few steps and waved the gun to his right. "Stand against that railing and face the entryway. Empty your pockets."

"You've got my gun. Why are you worried?"

"You heard me," Winterstein growled. "I could shoot you right now and claim that I was defending myself from an intruder."

"Okay. I won't argue with you." Wolf walked to the railing, and Winterstein circled behind him. He leaned on the railing and gazed up at the DNA metal sculpture suspended from the cathedral ceiling. It dangled about twenty-five feet into the entry hall, slowly spinning. The red flagstone floor was another twenty feet below the sculpture. He remembered his dream. "That would be a helluva fall."

"I told you to empty your pockets."

Wolf took his keys out first and then his wallet and phone. He leaned and dropped them on the floor.

"Turn around and lift up your shirt."

Wolf pivoted, grasped the bottom of his Hawaiian shirt and pulled it above his holster. "See, no gun. Oh . . . I forgot something that belongs to your buddy." He reached into the deep pocket of his cargo shorts and pulled out the other phone.

"Who's phone is that?"

"Maxell's."

"How did you get it?"

"We took a walk on the beach. She left it behind with me."

"Where is she?"

"Still walking. That leaves you all alone to handle this mess."

The door to Wolf's right opened and Margaret Winterstein stuck her head out.

Wolf grinned. "I guess you're not alone."

"Saul, is that you?"

"Yes, Mother."

"Who's out there?"

"Detective Wolf."

"He had a gun. I saw it. He pointed it at Jake Cleaver."

"I have the gun now, Mother."

"Oh . . . good." She stepped out of the room and waddled toward them. "Should we call the police?"

"Not yet. I'm trying to figure out what's going on."

Wolf laughed. "You know what's going on, and so does she."

"Suppose you tell me what I know."

"Suppose we take a walk to the bottom floor and open up the secret room."

The color drained from Winterstein's face. He glanced at his mother, and her eyes widened.

Wolf looked beyond Winterstein and caught sight of Freyja and Angie standing in the doorway.

Angie raised her Smith and Wesson revolver. "Put down the gun, Winterstein."

He lowered the gun but didn't turn around.

"I've got a .44 Magnum aimed at the middle of your back. It will blow your heart clean through your chest. Drop it onto the floor."

He shook his head no.

"I said drop it!"

"It's you!" Margaret Winterstein shrieked. "You're the insolent smartass that I bitch-slapped yesterday."

Angie sneered, "You're the old crone that gave birth to that sack of shit in front of me."

She gasped. "I'm calling the police."

"Good," Wolf said. "The sooner they get here the better."

She pivoted, waddled back into her room and slammed the door."

Winterstein turned slowly and faced Angie.

She kept her handgun trained on his chest. "Are you going to drop that gun, or am I going to drop you?"

Freyja stepped out from behind Angie. "Put the gun down, Saul."

His pale face twisted into a knot. "Freyja, what are you doing here?"

"You told me to stop by for old time's sake."

"Do you know these people?"

"I'm afraid I do. And I know Melissa Bianco, too."

"Who?"

"Judy Gayle."

"What about Judy? We may offer her a contract for a part in *Somewhere in the Night*."

"You really don't know what happened to her, do you?" Freyja said.

"Did you say her name is Bianco?"

"That's right," Wolf said as he circled around Winterstein. "Cleaver locked her in your hidden room when he found out she was Samantha's sister."

Winterstein closed his eyes and hung his head. "It's all crashing down around me. I should have never listened to them."

"It's over," Angie said. "There's no way out. Put down the gun."

He raised his chin. "There is a way out."

The door to his mother's bedroom flew open, and she stomped out carrying a metal bucket. Her eyes, like burning coals, focused on Angie. Her mouth turned into a pit bull's snarl. As she neared, she tilted the bucket.

Freyja's eyes widened. "She's got acid!"

Angie whirled and kicked the bottom of the bucket.

The liquid doused Margaret Winterstein's face and head. She shrieked. Her skin sizzled and melted. "I can't see!" Smoke rose from the crackling burns. Raw flesh appeared as skin dripped off her face. "Water! I need water!" She stumbled around randomly and then ran toward the railing. Winterstein went after her. She crashed into the railing at full speed and flipped upwards. Winterstein collided with her legs and knocked her over the wooden rail. Her scream resounded in the tall entryway and ended with a loud thud and a faint echo.

Winterstein leaned over the rail. "Mother! Mother!" His chest quivered as he took in breaths. He turned and faced them.

"Put down the gun, Winterstein," Angie said. "Your mother couldn't save you. You're out of options."

His mouth tightened into a vicious frown. "You're wrong," he seethed, "there is another way out." He raised his head and stuck the gun under his chin. The blast blew off the top of his skull, splattering his brain on the cathedral ceiling. His body slumped onto the floor in front of the railing.

Angie gasped and stepped back. Her eyes widened as she stared at the gory mess that was once Winterstein's head. She turned away and faced the windows that looked out on the sea. "Jeeesh. I think I'm going to be sick."

Wolf approached her and put his hands on her shoulders. "Steady yourself, Angie."

Her hands and head trembled. She laid the gun down on a nearby lampstand. "I don't know if I'll ever get used to this, Wes." She shook her head. "Why did he do it? I don't understand. Suicide is the coward's way out of your problems."

Wolf glanced at Winterstein's empty skull. "To him, it was a no-brainer."

"That's not funny." Angie punched him in the ribs.

"Oooooffff!" Wolf crumpled over and leaned on his knees. "That's where Cleaver kicked me," he wheezed.

Angie gasped. "Oh, Wes, I'm so sorry."

Wolf straightened. "Just kidding. He kicked me on the other side."

Angie raised her hand to hit him but stopped. She held it steadily.

Wolf grinned, and her tight lips broke into a slight smile on the corners.

He tapped her chin gently with his finger. "That's what I wanted to see."

Freyja took a couple steps forward, bent over and picked up Wolf's handgun. "Don't forget your best friend."

Wolf walked to her, took the gun, lifted his shirt and inserted it into his holster. "Siggy wouldn't want to be left behind."

She drifted over to the railing and stared down into the entryway.

He strolled over to her, leaned and picked up his wallet, phone and keys. After stuffing them into his pockets, he looked over the railing. Margaret Winterstein's distorted body lay on the flagstone floor. Blood pooled around her acid-ravaged face. Her black dress added a macabre impression as if Alfred Hitchcock himself arranged the scene.

Wolf touched Freyja's shoulder. "I see you found your dress."

She raised her eyebrows. "It felt like one of those dreams where everyone is staring at you, and all you have on is your underwear. But it wasn't a dream."

"Last night I dreamed that Cleaver tossed me over this railing. I could actually feel myself falling."

"You're not a true prophet," she said.

"What do you mean?"

"If you were a genuine visionary, that would be your body down there instead of the body of that witch." She pointed to the scarred side of her face. "She's the one who did this to me."

"You told me an old man attacked you."

She wobbled her head. "I finally figured it out." She reached into her dress pocket and pulled out the key with the black triangular key ring. "We'll talk about it later. There're two sisters locked in a prison downstairs. It's time set them free."

Chapter 19

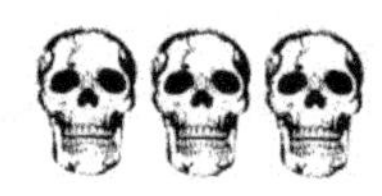

Freyja led the way down the steps and into the entryway. At the bottom she skirted around Margaret Winterstein's corpse and headed for a door to the left of the elevator. "The room is at the other end of the house." She opened the door, entered and pointed to the right. "The cook's and housekeeper's quarters are on that side of the house, but they usually don't stick around on the weekend."

She headed in the other direction and passed several doors. Wolf figured they opened into storage rooms that Mel had described over the phone. Freyja opened a door at the end of the hallway, reached around the doorframe and flipped on the light in the next room. It was a large garage. The florescent lights shining from a paneled ceiling illuminated a large garage with a dull yellow cast. A red Humvee, a white Mercedes Carvana and an ATV were parked in a row, just as Mel had reported. Bicycles hung on hooks screwed into the wall, and a slotted rack mounted on the adjacent wall held deep sea fishing rods and reels. A couple jet skis sat on trailers to the left of the fishing equipment. The three vehicles faced three garage doors.

Angie said, "Man, this place is expansive. I wonder how much Winterstein shelled out for this palace."

"A little over six million," Freyja said.

Wolf snorted. "That's more than I'll make in the next hundred years."

Freyja pointed to a door to the right of the fishing equipment. "The hidden room is that way."

They followed her through the door and into a room that seemed cramped. She flipped on the light, and a stainless-steel wall eight feet in front of them gleamed. A vertical seam scored the middle of the wall.

Freyja motioned toward the reflective steel. "This room used to be three times this big. Saul used it as a projector room to view auditions and watch movies."

"I guess he had other ideas for this space," Angie said.

"Yeah," Wolf grunted. "Ideas inspired by sleazy porno flicks."

Freyja walked to the steel wall and ran her finger down the seam. "The wall separates here. I bet there's a door on the other side. Where do we enter the combination code?"

"Over there." Angie pointed to the right corner of the room. On the adjacent wall a digital keypad was mounted a few inches from the steel wall.

Freyja stepped up to the keypad. "Oh no. It requires eight numbers." She focused on the triangular key chain. "There's only four numbers here."

"Let me see," Wolf said. He examined the key chain. "Look." He rubbed his finger below the four numbers. "Somebody sanded off the other four numbers."

Freyja frowned. "That's one way to add another layer of security."

"What're we going to do?" Angie said. "Break it down? We'll need a box of dynamite."

"Wait a minute," Freyja said. "What are the four numbers?"

Wolf checked the key chain. "Zero, three, one, nine."

Freyja grinned. "That's Saul's birthday, March nineteenth. All we have to do is add the next four numbers."

Wolf tilted his head. "1980."

Freyja quickly punched the eight numbers into the keypad. An electronic motor kicked on, sounding like the jarring hum of an elevator. The metal wall separated at the seam, leaving an opening slightly wider than two feet.

Wolf raised a finger. "There's a lesson to be learned here, kids. Never use the same password more than once."

As they neared the opening, they heard muffled sobs. A steel door about two inches back from the wall blocked their entry. Freyja turned the handle, but the door wouldn't budge. A dead bolt lock above the handle anchored it shut.

"Give me the key," Freyja ordered.

Wolf handed over the key, and she slotted it into the lock and turned it. She tried the handle again, and the door swung open. Two lamps cast faint light into the twelve-feet square room. Mel, sitting on a cot against the right wall, shot to her feet. Her eyes were wide and red-rimmed, her cheeks tear streaked. She rushed into Freyja's arms and wailed uncontrollably.

Her sister knelt at another cot on the opposite wall with her back to them. She wore a dingy dress. Wolf approached her. To the right of the cot, a door stood ajar. A dim light within cast a muted glow on a small sink and commode. To the left of the cot was another door with a similar deadbolt. As he neared Samantha, Wolf could hear her mumbling. Was it the Lord's prayer? He lowered his head and listened.

"Though I walk through the valley of the shadow of death, I will fear no evil. Thou art with me. Thy rod and thy staff, they comfort me . . ."

Wolf gently touched her shoulder. "Sammi."

She raised up and gazed at Wolf. Her face appeared gaunt and haggard.

Mel caught her breath and turned to Wolf. "That's not Sammi," she sobbed. "Sammi is dead!" She turned back to Freyja and planted her head against Freyja's chest, heaving and sniffling.

Wolf stared at the young woman with the brown hair, dark eyebrows and hollow eyes. "What's your name?"

"Jennifer . . . Jennifer Cobb."

Chapter 20

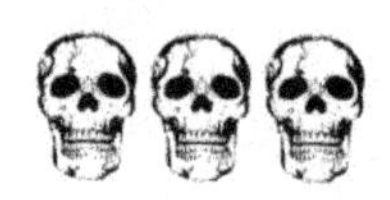

Her words startled Wolf. He took a calming breath and reached toward her. "Let me help you up." She grasped his hand, and he pulled her to her feet.

"What are you going to do with me?"

"Set you free. Don't worry, the people who lived here are gone for good." Wolf said.

Her dark eyes brightened. "I just want to go home."

"We'll take you home after you talk to the police."

"You'll take me home?"

"Yes. Your father hired us to find you."

"I want to go home and see my father. I don't live far from here."

Wolf nodded. "We know where you live. The police will be here soon."

Her eyes hardened, and her jaw became rigid. "Good. I want to tell the police what happened."

"Are you hungry?"

She bobbed her head slowly.

"We'll get you something to eat."

"I haven't showered in I don't know how many days."

"Angie and Freyja will take both of you up to one of the bedrooms. You can shower, and they'll get you something to eat." Wolf turned to Freyja. "Do you have to go through the entryway to get up to the second-floor bedrooms?"

"No," Freyja said. "There's a back stairway."

"Good. I don't want them walking past you know who."

Freyja nodded. "The Wicked Witch of the West."

"Exactly."

Angie crossed the room to the frail girl and took her hand. "Jennifer, my name's Angie. You can trust me. We're going to take care of you."

She sniffled and began to cry. Between halting breaths, she said, "I've been in this dark hole for days. I kept praying for God to get me out of here. It felt like the valley of the shadow of death." She steadied herself and took a deep breath. "Now I feel alive again, and I'm going home to my father."

Angie put her arm around her shoulders. "That'll be some reunion. C'mon. It's time for that shower and a good meal."

"Listen," Wolf said. "Don't call the sheriff's office until they've showered and ate. Winterstein and his mother aren't going anywhere. Cleaver will wash up sooner or later. Maxell is on a long beach walk. I want these girls to feel better before the authorities question them."

"Aren't you coming up?" Freyja asked.

"In a few minutes. I want to check out this other closet. It has a dead bolt on it like the entry door. Maybe that same key will open it."

"Here." Freyja tossed him the key, and he caught it.

"Thanks."

She took Mel's hand and led her out of the room. Jennifer and Angie followed.

Wolf glanced around the chamber. Besides the two cots, a couple lamps and nightstands, the place was bare, with dark gray walls. He walked to the door on the left side of the cot, inserted the key into the deadbolt and turned it. He grasped the handle and pulled the door open. On the inside wall he fumbled for a light switch, found it and clicked on the light. The closet was about six feet wide with shelves lining both sides. A large safe stood against the back wall. On top of the safe sat a small flatscreen TV with a DVD player in front of it.

He entered and examined the shelves. The boxes were labeled with titles of movies. Wolf recognized most of them: *Attack of the Piranhas, Ride into Hell, The Night of the Mist, Eight Who Hate, Penthouse South, Confessions of a Warped Mind.* Wolf chuckled to himself. *I've seen most of these. Got to give the guy credit. He could produce a good movie.*

He picked up a DVD case from one of the stacks and read the handwritten label: *Screentest – Marla Thompson.* He placed that one to the side and picked up the next one: *Screentest – Tammy Figaretti.* The next one was labeled: *Screentest: Rebekah Jones.* He stuck the DVDs back in order on the stack and eyed the multitude of stacks. *The guy conducted a lot of screentests over the years.*

He ambled to the safe, kneeled and tugged on the handle. *Locked. I wonder what's in there. Let's see, Winterstein's birthday was March 19, 1980.* He tried the eight numbers on the combination dial and pulled on the handle. *No luck.* Standing, he noticed an open DVD case next to the player. It was empty. After closing the case, he read the handwritten title: *Screentest – Samantha Bianco.* "Hmmmm. What do we have here?" He turned on the TV and hit the play button on the DVD player. On the screen a young girl crawled into bed with Winterstein. She looked a lot like Mel but slightly taller.

He caressed her face. "I'm glad you decided to visit me tonight."

"I know what you want," she said. "Do you know what I want?"

"Of course. You want to be a star."

"When're you going to take me to Hollywood?"

"Soon. Trust me. I love you. When I leave for California in a couple weeks, you'll be coming with me."

"If you don't give me that part, I'll just die."

"Stars never die. They shine forever. Make love to me." He began kissing her passionately.

"I can't watch this." Wolf hit the stop button and turned off the TV. He glanced at the shelves filled with DVD cases. *Those poor girls. Winterstein must have recorded all of his sexual encounters with them. The guy was a monster.* He hurried out of the closet, shut the door and locked it. He exited the room and stepped a few feet beyond the steel wall. Pivoting, he faced the prison chamber again. *I guess I'll leave the door unlocked and the wall open so the sheriff can check it out.* He about-faced and strode into the garage. As he approached the Humvee, he heard a horn beep twice.

Who could that be?

He cut between the Humvee and the Mercedes and walked to the middle garage door. Standing on his toes, he peeked out the window. An old white Chevy cargo van sat in front of the gate on the left. The vehicle was filthy with rust corroding the bottom edges. The engine sputtered unsteadily. "Well look who just showed up," he said. "That's pretty good timing."

Chapter 21

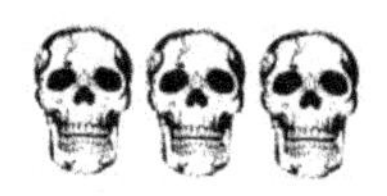

Wolf glanced to his right and noticed three buttons mounted on a panel next to an electric box. He hustled over and hit the center button. The middle garage door opened with the buzz of an electric motor, and sunlight flooded into the garage. He strode out onto the green paving stones and walked across the wide courtyard to the left gate. He squinted, his left eye still hurting, and saw two men through the glare on the windshield. A middle-aged guy stuck his head out the van window. His beat-up ballcap, pocked face and scraggly beard gave Wolf the notion that they had just driven from *Deliverance* country.

"Are you Cleaver?" the man called.

"Yeah, I'm Cleaver."

"We've come for the girl."

Okay. Now what do I do? Think! Think! "Did you bring the money?"

"Of course. Ten thousand, all in one-hundred-dollar bills."

"Great." Wolf smiled to himself. *I think I know how I'm going to handle this.* "Give me a couple minutes. I need to talk to the boss before I let you in."

"Hurry up, dammit! We ain't got all day."

Wolf trotted back into the garage, angled left and rushed into the hidden room antechamber. He pulled the door shut to the cell, whipped out the key and engaged the deadbolt. He zipped over to the keypad and punched in the eight numbers. The motor kicked on, and the steel wall closed. He checked his watch—3:15. *Hard to say when the calvary will get here.* He rushed back out into the garage and headed across the courtyard to the gate.

He approached the keypad mounted on a pole on the right side of the gate. *I hope 1980 is still a good year*. He poked the numbers into the keypad, and the gate cranked open. Wolf took a deep breath and blew it out slowly. *Jeeeesh. The luck of the Irish.* He pointed to the open garage door and said, "Pull up over there."

The van rattled past him, swerved to the right, and backed to the open garage door. As Wolf approached, the two rednecks got out, walked to the front of the van and faced him. The driver was a big guy wearing a wrinkled tan t-shirt and baggy jeans. His partner, short and squat with long arms, reminded Wolf of a chimpanzee. He wore a flannel shirt, had a flat nose and smoked a cigar.

Wolf stopped a few feet in front of them. "How was the drive?"

"Long and hot," the chimp piped.

The big one pointed at Wolf's face. "Looks like you tangled with a wildcat and lost."

"She's wild alright."

"Who?" the large man said. "The girl?"

Wolf nodded. "When I took breakfast to her this morning, she crowned me with a lamp."

Laughter burst through the short dolt's thick lips, and his cigar flipped up and down. "We like 'em wild. The wilder the better."

"I had to lock her in the closet."

"You didn't hurt her, did you?" the big guy grumbled.

"Naw. She's fine. Not a bruise on her. She's a beauty, too. Great body."

The little guy grinned. "Can't wait to see her."

"Hope you got something to tie her down, or she'll give you plenty of trouble."

"Don't worry." The bearded man knocked on the van's fender. "We're well equipped. Everything we need to cage a wildcat is in the back."

"Alright then, follow me."

Wolf led the way through the garage and made a left into the antechamber. The two rednecks stepped up to the stainless-steel wall and examined their contorted reflection.

"This is some setup," The big guy said.

"Your boss must be rolling in the clover," the short one grunted.

"That reminds me." Wolf patted his palm. "Before I let you in to get the girl, I want the Franklins right here."

The big guy straightened. "Don't we get to see the wares first?"

"Nope."

"No deal then."

"Wait a minute," the short one said. "He sent us pictures. She is an angel."

"That's true."

Wolf grinned. "She's a vision to behold, but it's up to you. Either give me the cash or go on your way."

The big guy clenched his jaw, reached into his baggy jeans and extracted a stack of bills. "We came too far to go home emptyhanded."

Wolf held out his hand, and he slapped the money into his palm. "Alright, alright, alright," Wolf drawled, offering his best Matthew McConaughey impression. "I don't have to count it, do I?"

"Go ahead if you want," the short one muttered.

"Naw. I trust you. We're good to go." He strolled to the keypad, punched in the numbers, and the metal wall hummed and separated. After returning to the door, he inserted the key into the dead bolt and unlocked it. He pulled the door open, leaving the key in the lock.

"Go on in, boys."

They entered.

"Where is she?" the short guy said.

Wolf pointed to the door on the left. "I told you I had to put her in the closet."

The big guy walked to the closet, turned the handle. "It's locked."

"Of course, it's locked. She's a wildcat. Wait here. I'll get the key. I'll only be a few minutes." Wolf pulled the door shut and turned the key to engage the deadbolt. He walked over to the keypad and punched in the code. The steel wall closed with a hmmmmmm and a thud. Wolf slapped his hands together several times like a carpenter shedding sawdust. "I think I just clipped the wings of a couple flying monkeys."

He exited the antechamber, walked into the garage, cut between the Humvee and Mercedes and stepped through the open garage door into the sunshine. In the distance he heard a siren. "Listen to that bugle blowing. The calvary is on its way, just in time."

Chapter 22

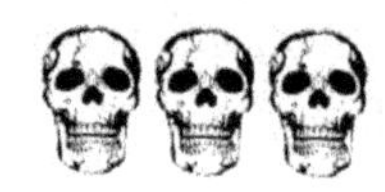

A white Ford sedan, lights whirling and sirens wailing, pulled through the open gateway, crossed the courtyard and skidded to a stop in front of the white van. Not far behind it, a white Ford Bronco with black trim and the Currituck County Sheriff's Department logo on the door, rumbled across the paving stones and parked to the left of the sedan. Wolf strolled around the van and gave a half salute.

A tall, young deputy in a gray and black uniform stepped out of the Bronco. Seeing his short black hair, muscular arms and cauliflower ear, Wolf recognized him. His partner, a solidly built burgundy brunette with a long ponytail, circled the Bronco and stood next to him. Two other officers skirted the vehicles and sidled up to them. They were older men but wore the same style uniforms, dark gray shirts and black pants. One of them had reddish hair and a big roman nose, and the other had a thick gray Sam Elliot mustache. They both wore black ballcaps with the law enforcement logo—the Currituck Beach Lighthouse with a duck flying over a pond.

"Good afternoon, Detective Wolf," the muscled deputy said.

"Nice to see you again so soon, Deputy Duncan. A lot has happened in three days."

"I guess so." The deputy examined Wolf's swollen eye. "Someone really tagged you good. You're going to end up with a shiner."

"No doubt."

"Your partner called us about five minutes ago."

"What did she tell you?"

He thumbed over his shoulder toward the house. "She said everything is under control, but there's a couple dead bodies on the premises. She also mentioned that two young girls had been held captive here, but they're okay."

"That's correct," Wolf said, "but that's not all."

"What else?"

"One of those girls is Jennifer Cobb."

"Shiiiiiit," the older redheaded deputy said. "We thought she drowned."

"So did I, but it wasn't her." Wolf eyed Deputy Duncan. "The body you pulled out of the sound was a girl by the name of Samantha Bianco. She traveled here from New Jersey, and Saul Winterstein offered her a screentest. She lived here for almost a month until she overdosed on alcohol and sleeping pills. To avoid a scandal, Winterstein and his cronies decided to dump her body into the Currituck Sound along with a kayak to make it look like an accident. We believe Jennifer was a witness to the overdose, so they locked her up in a secret room."

The gray mustached deputy took off his ballcap and ran his fingers through his thick salt and pepper hair. "Who's the other girl?"

"Samantha's sister, Melissa Bianco. That's her Malibu parked over by the entrance. She came here looking for Samantha. Winterstein gave her an audition, too, but his security man discovered her identity and locked her up with Jennifer."

"What were they going to do with them?" the brunette asked.

"Wolf pointed at the van. "Jake Cleaver, Winterstein's security man, had connections to people in the human trafficking business. They showed up about twenty minutes ago."

The young deputy knotted his brow. "Where are they now?"

"I've got them locked up in the same hidden room where they kept the girls."

"You've gotta be shittin' me," the redhead crowed.

Wolf reached into his shorts pocket and slid out the thick stack of one-hundred-dollar bills. "I shit you not. I made them give me the denaro before I opened the door to the room." He handed the cash to Deputy Duncan.

The mustached deputy grinned. "And they thought the girls were still in there."

"More or less. They didn't know about Mel. They came for Jennifer. If you check the back of their van, you'll find the tools of their trade—rope, duct tape, and other paraphernalia."

"I'll be damned," the redheaded deputy said. "You rolled a 300 game today. You pitched a no hitter."

"Not quite. Winterstein and his mother are dead. You'll find their bodies in the house. She fell off a balcony, and he shot himself. Two of his employees are unaccounted for. I'm almost sure that one of them drowned—Jake Cleaver. The other one, Elaine Maxell, should be walking along the shore a few miles north of here. I confronted her on the beach and forced her to tell me where the girls were hidden. I ordered her to keep walking until somebody from the sheriff's department picked her up."

The young deputy scratched his chin. "How secure is that room where you locked up the sex traffickers?"

"Oh, it's secure. They're locked behind two steel doors. No windows."

"Good." He turned to the older deputies. "Why don't you boys go check on the bodies and talk to the victims. Glenda and I will run up the beach in the Bronco and pick up Miss Maxell. When we get back, we'll arrest the sex traffickers."

"That'll work," The mustached deputy said.

"What's the description on Maxell?"

"She's about five six," Wolf said, "one hundred and twenty pounds, well built, black hair cut in a bob, and wearing a shiny green one-piece bathing suit."

"Shouldn't be hard to pick her out," the brunette said.

The young deputy and his partner climbed into the Bronco, backed out and drove away.

Wolf nodded to the two officers. "I'll show you where the bodies are, and then you can talk to the girls."

"We'll follow you," the redhead said.

Wolf led the two older officers into the garage. After cutting between the Humvee and Mercedes, Wolf pointed to the left and said, "I've got the two lowlifes locked up in that room."

The redhead laughed. "At least they got each other."

"Yeah," the other deputy said. "Let's hope they don't reproduce."

Wolf led them down the long hallway and through the door into the entryway. As soon as they saw Winterstein's mother crumpled on the flagstone floor, they gazed up at the balcony and back down to the body.

The gray mustached deputy grimaced. "That's what I call meeting your shadow head on."

"She must have forgot to put on her wings," the other one said.

Wolf shook his head. "No. She forgot her broom."

The redhead kneeled for a closer look. "What happened to her face?"

"I'd call it a case of acid reflex. She went to throw a bucket of acid on my partner, but Angie kicked it into her face. The witch went crazy and flipped over the railing."

"Shiiiiiiit," the redhead said. "With a face like that, she'd have to sneak up on a mirror."

Wolf took a step toward the stairway. "Her mirror-gazing days are over. Let's head up to the third floor. That's where her son did the Hara-kiri."

Wolf hustled up the steps, and the two deputies dawdled behind. Wolf kept his distance from the body as he waited for them. When they climbed the last few steps and drew near, Wolf gazed at the ceiling and said, "His brains are up there."

They raised their heads and examined the marred surface of the paneled oak and then lowered their focus to what was left of Winterstein's head.

"I wouldn't want to clean up that mess," the redhead said.

The gray mustached deputy searched the floor. "Where's the gun?"

Wolf patted his shirt where his Sig Sauer was holstered. "Right here."

A frown creased the gray mustached deputy's face. "He shot himself with your gun?"

Wolf raised his hands. "I've got two witnesses."

"That's fine, but we'll need your gun for forensic firearm tests."

"That's not a problem." Wolf lifted his shirt, unsnapped the strap on the holster, removed his gun and handed it to the deputy. "I've got plenty of guns."

The redhead cleared his throat. "How'd Mr. Winterstein get hold of your gun?"

"Now that's an embarrassing question. I had an altercation with his security guy." Wolf pointed to his eye. "Here's the evidence. Unfortunately, he got the better of me."

The gray-mustached deputy closed one eye. "And what happened to this security guy?"

Wolf thumbed over his shoulder. "He's swimming with the fishes. I'm sure he'll wash up sooner or later."

"You must have got even with him," the redhead said.

"I've got a friend named Karma."

The gray mustached deputy cracked his knuckles. "I'll let the forensic team know what's going on and call for a couple ambulances." He turned away and walked toward the middle of the room to make the call.

The redhead grinned. "Karma's a bitch, ain't she?"

"Nooooo. To me, she's a beautiful lady."

They walked down the stairs to the second floor. Wolf listened for voices and found the room where the girls had gathered. He knocked.

Freyja opened the door halfway.

"The Currituck County boys are here. They want to talk to Jennifer and Melissa."

She opened the door all the way. "Come in. I think they're ready to tell their stories."

They entered and stood next to a long oak dresser. Jennifer and Mel sat on a blue cushioned bench in front of a four-poster bed, its columns and tester elegantly carved. Angie sat in a blue cushioned wingback chair in the corner. Large blue rugs with Native American patterns on the edges covered most of the oak floor. Seascapes hung on the walls, and the front of the nightstands matched the same style of carvings on the bed.

"Officers," Wolf motioned toward the girls, "this is Jennifer Cobb and next to her is Melissa Bianco. Ladies, these deputies want to get as much information as you can recall about what happened here. Freyja, Angie and I are going to step out onto the deck while they question you. After they are finished, we'll make sure we get you out of here and on your way home."

The two girls nodded, their faces drained of color.

Angie stood. "I'll stay in here with the girls, if nobody minds. I might be able to help with a question or two."

"That's fine with us," the gray mustached deputy said.

Wolf faced the deputies. "Gentleman, I'm going to let you introduce yourselves." He pointed to the sliding glass door. "Freyja and I will be out on the deck. Come get us when you're done."

"We'll try not to keep them too long," the redheaded deputy said.

Wolf took Freyja's hand, led her to the door and slid it open. They stepped out into a refreshing ocean breeze, and he slid the door shut. They leaned on the railing and gazed out to sea.

"How are you hanging in there?" Wolf asked.

"I'm okay. Trying to stay strong for Mel."

"She took it pretty hard."

"She expected to see her sister when they opened that steel door."

"What did Jennifer tell her?"

"On Jennifer's first night here, there was a party. She auditioned a couple songs, and Winterstein was impressed. They scheduled a screentest for the next day, but she didn't want to stay the night. Sammi convinced her to stay and offered to share a bedroom with her. She said that Sammi had been drinking too much."

"Sammi wanted to be a star. I checked out the closet in the hidden room. There was a DVD labeled Samantha Bianco. I played it on a TV in the back of the closet. It showed her climbing into bed with Winterstein. He promised to take her to Hollywood, and then you know what happened."

Freyja bobbed her head slowly. "Yeah, I know: the lust-and-thrust session."

"Yeah. There were several stacks of those kinds of DVDs down there."

"Doesn't surprise me. Anyway, Sammi couldn't fall asleep because Saul promised to offer her a contract the next day for a part in *Somewhere in the Night*. Despite all the alcohol, she was still wired. Margaret had given her sleeping pills on a couple other occasions. She went up to get more pills. Jennifer said she came back down ten minutes later, crawled into bed and fell right to sleep."

"I'd like to know how many pills the witch gave her."

"Too many. The combination killed her."

"Do you think Margret did it on purpose?"

Freyja nodded. "Margaret had a jealous streak. When I saw her toting that bucket toward Angie, I recognized the way she walked. The old man who attacked me walked the same way."

Wolf straightened. "You told me she worked in the makeup department at MGM."

"That's right. After her acting career fizzled, she learned the tricks of the makeup trade and learned them well. Had me fooled for the last two years."

"Where did she attack you?"

"Out front by the entrance. I stepped out of my car, and she came around the corner of the house disguised as an old man. Once the acid hit me, I was in too much pain to do anything but scream. She disappeared, but I had no idea where she went."

"She wanted to eliminate you from her son's life."

"He was obsessed with me, and she couldn't stand it."

Wolf leaned his elbows on the railing and studied some cumulus clouds gathering above the horizon. The late afternoon beach crowd had thinned to about thirty or forty people spread out over the two-hundred-yard stretch of sand before them. A formation of pelicans glided just above the surface of the water.

Wolf grasped her hand. "What if I told you I'm obsessed with you?"

Freyja winked. "I'd ask you a few questions about your mother."

"Like what?"

"Does she live with you?"

"No. What else?"

"What would you do if you had to arrest your own mother?"

"Call for backup."

Freyja laughed. "I guess you pass."

"Jennifer Cobb's mom died a year ago."

"That's sad. She's had to face a lot of trauma lately. She said when she woke up the next morning and checked on Sammi, she knew she was dead—cold, gray, stiff, no pulse. She wanted out of there, but they wouldn't let her go."

"So they stuck her in the secret room until they could figure out what to do with her."

"They delivered food a couple times a day, but that's all the human contact she had. Little did she know that they were planning to sell her to human traffickers. I'm glad they didn't tell her."

"Those lowlifes showed up about an hour ago."

"Who?"

"The sex slave committee—two rednecks in a white van. Don't worry. I took care of them."

She squeezed his hand. "Are you serious?"

"Sent them into the secret room to find the girl and locked the door behind them."

"You're Batman."

"I am Batman. Does that mean your obsessed with me?"

"No. Obsession is a disease. Love is a cure."

"Does that mean you love me?"

She gave him a perturbed look. "Do you have to ask?"

Wolf shrugged. *I'd like to know.* A gathering crowd of people on the beach caught his attention. "Uh oh. Something's going on down there."

A young muscular man dragged a body up the slope to the dry sand. The crowd grew as the guy began pumping the victim's chest.

"Is that who I think it is?" Freyja asked.

"That would be my guess. Leave it to Cleaver to show up and cause a big scene."

"Let's go up on the tower and make sure."

Chapter 23

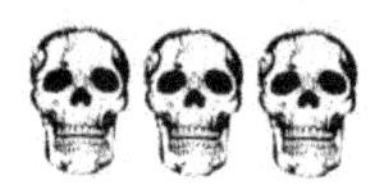

On top of the corkscrew tower, Freyja adjusted the focus wheel on the binoculars as she looked through the eye pieces. "That's him."

"Is the guy having any luck with the CPR?"

"I don't think he has what it takes to bring that ape back to life."

"Yeah. Not too many people can pass the walking-on-water test."

Freyja straightened and eyed Wolf. "I only know of one who did."

"And he caught the last train for the coast."

Freyja rolled her eyes. "Bye, bye Miss American Pie."

Wolf heard the short burst of a siren and turned to see the flashing lights of a white Bronco as it parked in front of Freyja's Renegade on the other side of the tall sea fence. "There's Deputy Duncan. I wonder if he managed to pick up Maxell."

"I hope so."

"I'm going to run down to the beach and find out."

"I'll check on the girls."

As they descended to the metal bridge at the second-floor level, Freyja turned and halted Wolf, pressing her hand to his chest. "What're you going to tell Deputy Duncan about my aquatic encounter with Cleaver?"

Wolf shrugged. "I don't know exactly what happened out there, and you don't need to give an explanation. I'll tell him Cleaver chased you into the water and didn't come back until a few minutes ago."

She took a deep breath and let it out. "That sounds about right."

Wolf hustled down the remaining steps of the spiral staircase, jogged along the edge of the pool to the gazebo and across the walkway. His ribs still hurt with every step, but his head felt better. He stopped at the gate, triggered the latch and opened it, reminding himself of the password to get back onto the property—1980, a year that opened doors for him. At the end of the walkway, he descended the steps and made a beeline for Deputy Duncan, who stood alongside his brunette partner a few feet from the body. The young guy had given up his CPR effort, and nobody else wanted to try.

Cleaver's corpse lay on its back in the dry sand, complexion as gray as a dolphin, black pants and shirt waterlogged.

Wolf stepped up to Deputy Duncan. "I see my buddy has come in from the sea."

"Yeah. Deader than Blackbeard."

"Except he still has his head."

A siren wailed in the distance.

"Someone already called an ambulance," the young lawman said.

"At least he'll get a free ride to the morgue."

Deputy Duncan chuckled. "Hope he doesn't mind a cold slab for a bed."

"The dead aren't that picky," the brunette said.

Wolf smiled at the brunette and then glanced at the Bronco's tinted windows. "Did you pick up Maxell?"

She shook her head. "No sir, we did not."

"We've got an APB out on her," Deputy Duncan said.

"She took off, huh? No doubt, she realizes she's in up to her eyeballs."

"She won't get that far in that green swimsuit," Deputy Duncan said. "Somebody will catch sight of her." He cleared his throat. "Got a question for you."

"Okay."

"How exactly did Cleaver die?"

"He drowned."

"No shit, Sherlock. What happened before he drowned?"

"He and I got into an altercation. My girlfriend, Freyja Beck, managed to get the key to the hidden room off him. He chased her out the door and into the ocean. She just kept swimming out to sea. I thought she was going to cross the Atlantic. He wouldn't give up the chase. I lost sight of them. A while later she made it back to shore, and he didn't."

"Until just now," the brunette said.

Deputy Duncan eyed the corpse. "I don't know. He looks like a strong, fit man. I don't see how he could have drowned out there."

Wolf raised his thick eyebrows. "Maybe a riptide got him."

"Maybe, but the ocean's not that rough today."

"You never know about these waters. A mermaid might've got a hold of him."

Deputy Duncan grinned. "Yeah, right. That's a good one."

Wolf thumbed toward Winterstein's palace. "I'm guessing they're about done talking to the girls. I promised Jennifer Cobb I'd take her home to see her daddy."

"Aren't you forgetting something?" the brunette said.

"What's that?"

"The two pervs you got locked up in that hidden room."

Wolf chuckled. "How could I forget those two chimps? I'll meet you in front of the open garage door."

Deputy Duncan turned to his partner. "You stay here with Michael Phelps and wait on the ambulance. I'll make the arrest."

Her eyes flashed resentment. "Why do you get to have all the fun?"

"Tell you what. My treat next time we go by a Duck Donuts."

Her mouth curved into a smile. "Deal."

* * *

Wolf and the Bronco arrived in front of the open garage door about the same time. As Deputy Duncan got out of the vehicle, the two older officers approached from the direction of the right entry.

Wolf eyed the two older guys. "Did you get the information you needed from the girls?"

The redheaded deputy said, "Sure did. They painted a pretty good picture of what went down here."

"Great."

Deputy Duncan said, "You boys ready to help us arrest the two desperados waiting in the hideout."

The deputy with the Sam Elliot mustache raised his hands as if they were pistols. "Giddyup."

Wolf led the way into the garage and made a left into the antechamber. When they had gathered with him in the small room, he said, "I don't know if these rednecks have guns on them or not. The big one wore a t-shirt. I didn't see any bulges, but he had on baggy pants. The short one wore a flannel shirt. You never know. He might be packing a rod underneath."

Deputy Duncan unsnapped his holster and withdrew his handgun. "There's only one way to find out."

Wolf raised his hand. "Wait a minute. Let me go in first. I might be able to say a few things to calm them down."

"That's up to you," Deputy Duncan said.

Wolf held his palm out toward the mustached deputy. "Can I have my gun back for two minutes."

"Sure. You might need it." He handed Wolf his Sig Sauer pistol.

Wolf walked to the keypad and punched in the code. The steel wall hummed open. He returned and knocked on the entry door. "You guys still in there?"

"Hell yes!" the big one yelled. "How could we get out? You locked the door."

"Sorry about that. I had to go get the key for the closet, and Mr. Winterstein didn't want you wandering around on the premises."

"What took you so long?" the short one snapped.

"Nature called."

"Must have been a long call," the big one groaned.

"I found the key. I'm coming in." Wolf turned the deadbolt and opened the door. His Sig Sauer led the way into the room. "Hands up!"

The short guy sat on the cot against the far wall, and the big one stood next to the closet. They slowly raised their hands in unison.

"What's going on?" the little one squeaked.

"Boys, I'd like to introduce you to the Currituck County Sheriff's Department." Wolf stepped to the side, and the three officers entered.

"We haven't done anything wrong," the big one complained.

"Yeah," the deputy with the Sam Elliot mustache said. "You're as innocent as a whore's smile."

Wolf put his hand on Deputy Duncan's shoulder. "If you've got this, I'm going to go check on the girls."

"We can handle it from here. Thanks for your help."

"No problem."

Wolf turned and headed out the door. As he walked through the garage, he lifted his shirt and slid his handgun back into his holster. He pulled his shirt down and patted the gun. *Home where you belong.*

As he entered the late afternoon sunlight, he saw two ambulances parked near the entrance of the house. *This place is really hopping today. Funny how death draws a crowd.*

The four women cut around the near ambulance and headed in Wolf's direction. Color had returned to Jennifer Cobb's face, and a smile tugged at the corners of her lips. Mel still looked downtrodden, pale with a tear-streaked face. Angie and Freyja bookended the girls as they walked toward him.

"Are we ready to get out of here?" Wolf said.

"More than ready," Freyja sighed.

Jennifer took a deep breath and let it out audibly. "I just want to go home."

"Mel and I will go get my Jeep. We'll stop back and get her car. Then she can follow me back to my cottage. She needs a good meal and some rest."

Mel nodded slowly. "I didn't get much sleep last night."

"Where are you parked, Angie?" Wolf asked.

"Across the road on the berm. Hopefully, I didn't get towed."

The five of them strolled across the courtyard, out the gate to the cul de sac and made a right onto the short lane that led to Route 12. There they split up. Freyja and Mel headed north to the end of the road and across the wide grate into the Wild Horse Sanctuary where Freyja had parked the Renegade. Wolf, Angie and Jennifer crossed the highway to Angie's Honda Civic.

"I only live a few hundred yards down the road," Jennifer said. "I can walk."

Wolf shook his head. "Your father hired us to find out what happened to you. We need to close the books on our investigation. Besides, I can't wait to see his face when you step out of the car." Wolf opened the front passenger side door. "Get in."

"No." Jennifer stepped away. "You're a lot taller than me. I'll sit in the back."

"Are you sure? You're the surprise guest of honor."

"I insist."

Wolf opened the back door, and Jennifer crawled in. Angie got in and started the car. After Wolf climbed in and shut the door, Angie made a U-turn on Route 12 and headed south. Jennifer hummed a familiar tune. Wolf racked his brain to remember the name of it. Finally, Wolf said, "I've heard that song somewhere before. Why don't you sing a verse for us?"

"Sure," Jennifer said. With a sweet, melodic voice, she sang:

"Amazing grace, how sweet the sound
That saved a wretch like me.
I once was lost, but now I am found,
Was blind, but now I see.
'Twas grace that taught my heart to fear,
And grace my fears relieved.
How precious did that grace appear
The hour I first believed.
Through many dangers, toils and snares
I have already come,
'Tis grace has brought me safe thus far
And grace will lead me home."

When she finished, Angie smiled, wiped a tear from her cheek, slowed the Honda and made a right turn onto Lost Lake Lane. "Is it possible, Wes, that you heard that tune in church?"

Wolf felt his face flush. "That's a possibility. Mom made me go to church when I was a kid. It was like trying to baptize a cat every Sunday morning."

They passed the graveyard of rusted cars and pickup trucks. The unpaved lane narrowed, and they entered the tunnel of overhanging trees and thick bushes. Wolf twisted in his seat and eyed Jennifer. She smiled at him from the shadows, quietly humming the song of grace.

"You're almost home," Wolf said.

They broke into the sunshine, and the beams lit her face. "My father's house isn't a mansion, but I call it home. There's always room for me there."

Angie circled the yard and parked in the middle of a patch of crabgrass.

Wolf popped open the door, sprung out of the car and yelled, "Mr. Cobb! Are you home!"

The big man opened the door and walked onto the sagging porch wearing bib overalls over a white t-shirt. "Detective Wolf, I didn't expect to see you today."

Angie got out of the car. "We stopped by to give you an update."

He stepped down onto the cement block and into the yard. His eyes were red-rimmed and puffy. "My heart's been heavy for days. I don't think there's anything you can tell me to raise my spirits, but I appreciate any new news."

"We did come across something new." Wolf reached and opened the back door of the Civic.

Jennifer extended her leg out, gripped the doorframe and arose from the confines of the back seat. Her dingy dress looked like graveclothes, but the sun set her face aglow with brilliant light. She walked toward her father and stopped a few feet away.

"Daddy."

His eyes grew wide, and his mouth dropped open, jaw trembling. He wobbled and fell to his knees. He raised his hands, and they shook like a wet cat on a cold Sunday morning. "It can't be! It can't be!"

"Daddy, I've come home."

"You've been resurrected! Holy God Almighty! Am I dreaming?"

She rushed into his arms, and he squeezed her tight, bawling like a newborn.

Angie leaned her head on Wolf's shoulder, and he clasped his hand around her waist.

After several minutes, Mr. Cobb's crying slowed to an occasional halting sniffle. Jennifer stepped back and helped him to his feet. He wiped his eyes with the backs of his hands and gently kissed his daughter on the forehead. Wolf and Angie approached, and the big man gathered them into a group hug.

After they separated, Jennifer said. "I want to go into my room and change. Freyja offered me some clothes that belonged to Elaine Maxell, but I didn't want to wear them."

"I don't blame you," Angie said.

She skipped up the steps and into the house.

Wolf smiled. "This case is closed, Mr. Cobb."

"How much to I owe you?"

"Don't worry about that now. We'll add up the hours and send you the bill."

His jaw muscles tightened, firming up his pudgy face. "Whatever it is, I'm going to double it."

"That's not necessary," Angie said.

"Maybe not, but that's what I want to do. My daughter was dead and gone. But now she's been raised from the grave. Tell me what happened."

For the next fifteen minutes, Wolf and Angie went over the details of the case. Mr. Cobb took it all in, listening carefully and nodding occasionally. After they finished, he sat down on the edge of the porch.

"This has been too much all at once." He placed his hand on his heart and took a deep breath.

"Are you going to be okay, Mr. Cobb?" Angie asked.

He bobbed his head slowly. "It can only get better from here. For the last few days, I felt like dying." A big smile brightened his demeanor. "I feel like living again."

Wolf said, "The sheriff will probably want to question Jennifer tomorrow. She may have to appear in court. Like I told you, Elaine Maxell took off. Once they catch her, they'll prosecute her. Jennifer may be the key witness."

"My daughter believes in justice. She'll stand up for what's right and tell the truth. It'll be the jury's responsibility to decide what to do with that woman."

"Jennifer is a strong girl," Angie said.

"That's my Jenny." Mr. Cobb struggled to his feet. "I appreciate everything you two have done."

Wolf held out his hand. "It's been a pleasure working for you, Mr. Cobb."

He shook hands with Wolf and then Angie. "Stop back and see us again sometime. You're welcome here like family."

Angie reached and touched his shoulder. "Tell Jennifer if she ever wants to talk to me, my cell phone number is on the card I gave her."

"I certainly will."

Wolf and Angie ambled back to the car, opened the doors and climbed in. Angie turned the key, and the motor grumbled and started. As they drove away, Mr. Cobb waved his big hand. They rumbled along the dirt lane into the shadowed cave of the overhanging trees and thick bushes.

Angie glanced at Wolf. "I'll never forget that scene as long as I live."

"We did good today." Wolf's eyes grew wide. "Watch out! Stop!"

Angie slammed on the brakes, and the Civic skidded to a halt.

A few feet in front of the bumper stood the darkened figure of a woman.

Chapter 24

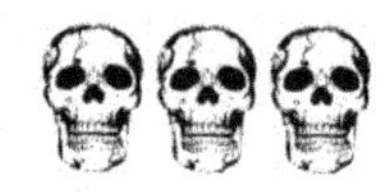

Angie gasped.

Wolf's heart thumped like a John Bonham drum solo.

Elaine Maxell placed her hands on the hood of the car, leaned and stared at Wolf. The umbrage desaturated color from her form, giving her the appearance of a leopard in the shadows, waiting to pounce. Her eyes bore into him. "I need to talk to you."

Wolf powered down the window. "Get in."

She edged around the car through the intrusive branches, managed to open the door and squeezed into the back seat.

"Where do you want to talk?" Wolf asked.

"Right here is fine."

Angie put the transmission in park and cut the engine. The silence and shadows gave the surroundings a creepy aura, interrupted by the occasional chirpings of a marsh wren.

Wolf turned in his seat and met Maxell's gaze. "You've been hiding out here, waiting for us."

"Yes. I knew you'd bring Jennifer back to her father's house. On the night of her audition, she told me she lived on Lost Lake Lane."

"Why do you want to talk to me?"

"Do you have the key to the hidden room?"

"Yeah."

"Did you use that key to look in the closet?"

"I checked it out. Lots of interesting DVDs in there."

"My future depends on one of those DVDs."

"How so?"

She didn't say anything for almost half a minute. "It's a bargaining chip."

"I see." Wolf rubbed his knuckles along his jawline, feeling the prickling of his five o'clock shadow. "You want to switch sides and become a witness for the prosecution."

"That's right."

"But who are we prosecuting? Your cohorts are all dead."

"Saul is dead?"

"Saul, Margaret, Cleaver, their final scene has ended. Lights out, projector off."

She swallowed. "There's a DVD inside the safe. Saul made secret videos of his important connections for . . . insurance purposes."

Wolf chuckled. "Just in case he needed to blackmail somebody."

"That's another way to put it."

"What was your involvement in all this?"

"I recruited talent."

"If you want me to help you, then be straight with me."

"I recruited young women who were desperate to break into the movie business."

"How desperate?"

"Desperate enough to offer their bodies up to the casting couch."

"So, this particular DVD doesn't feature Saul and these young wannabe starlets."

"No. These are covert recordings of sexual encounters between Saul's associates and these girls."

"Would I recognize any of these associates?"

"Probably most of them—actors, sports stars, millionaires, politicians."

"Hmmmmm." Wolf glanced at Angie. "What do you think about all of this, Angel?"

"Sounds like the circle of scandal is ever-widening."

He refocused on Maxell. "Were some of these young girls underage?"

"Yes."

"So this DVD could possibly send a slew of these privileged pigs to the slaughterhouse."

"Yes."

"And possibly cut your prison sentence in half."

"I'm hoping for better than half."

Wolf eyed Angie again. "Very interesting proposition. Should we help out this she-wolf who corrupted dozens of young girls for her own selfish gain?"

"I'd hate to hand Miss Maxell a get-out-of-jail-free card, but then again I'd love to see the balls of these bastards in a vice."

"Ooooooohhh." Wolf cringed. "I can imagine their pain."

Angie started the car. "Let's go get the DVD."

Wolf shifted his focus to Maxell. "Okay, but before I hand that DVD over to you, I want to see proof."

"Believe me," Maxell said. "You'll get an eyeful."

"Then I will personally escort you to the Currituck County Sheriff's Office."

"That's fine, but I want to call my lawyer. He'll meet us there."

Wolf pointed at the windshield. "Onward, driver."

Angie hit the accelerator, and they bumped along the dirt road through the cave of overhanging foliage and into the sunlight. She continued down the lane to the stop sign and then turned left onto Route 12. It didn't take long to get to the access road that led to Winterstein's beach palace.

When they approached the gate, Wolf noticed the same two ambulances parked near the right entrance. The same sheriff's vehicle, a white Ford sedan, was parked in front of the old white van by the open garage door. Mel's Malibu was gone, but another county vehicle took its place, a white Ford

Everest. He figured Deputy Duncan hauled the sex traffickers off to jail in the Bronco.

"Pull right up to the open garage door," Wolf said. "We can sneak her in from there."

Angie parked alongside the Ford sedan. "I have a raincoat in the back with a hood. It should come down to her knees and cover up that green swimsuit.

Maxell reached over the backseat, snatched the raincoat and slipped into it.

"I'll go scout out the danger zone." Wolf opened the door. "Stay here and lay low until I get back." He stepped out of the car, closed the door and panned the premises. Nobody in sight. He hurried into the garage and headed for the antechamber. The light had been left on, and the steel wall open. That made sense to Wolf because the lawmen didn't know the keypad combination. The second steel door was closed. Wolf tried it, and as he assumed, it was unlocked. He eyed the closet door across the cell. He remembered locking it before setting the trap for the two sex-slave lowlifes. *Everything's good. I've got the key in my pocket.*

He closed the steel door and turned to see Sam-Elliot-mustache deputy standing in the antechamber doorway.

"Detective Wolf, funny meeting you here."

Think fast. Wolf thumbed over his shoulder. "I can't find my Oakleys. I thought maybe I left them in here. Those things cost me over two-hundred bucks."

"I haven't seen them, but I am sure glad I ran into you."

"Why's that?"

He pointed at Wolf's ribs. "I need your gun back for those firearm forensic tests."

Wolf raised and lowered his head in an exaggerated motion. "I forgot all about giving my gun back to you." Wolf laid his hand over the bulge in his shirt. "I'm so used to Siggy hanging right here next to my heart."

"Isn't your heart on your left side like everybody else's? That gun's on your right."

Wolf laughed. "It's hard for me to find my heart. Many women have said I don't have one." Wolf lifted his shirt, unsnapped the holster and withdrew the pistol. He handed it to the deputy. "There you go."

"Thank you. We should have it back to you in a few days. Are you done in here?"

"Yeah. I'll hit the light on the way out. You don't mind if I run up to the third floor to look for my Oakleys, do you?"

"Not at all. A crime scene team is up there. Maybe they saw them."

"I hope so."

"I'll see you around, Detective Wolf. I'm heading back to the sheriff's office."

"Nice working with you."

"You, too." The deputy pivoted, walked through the garage and into the sunlight.

Dammit. He took my gun again.

As the lawman rounded the back of Angie's Honda Civic, Wolf watched to see if he noticed Maxell crouching in the back seat. The deputy walked right by without a hitch. Wolf waited in the shadows of the garage until the Ford sedan backed out and drove away.

He hustled to the car, opened the back door and helped Maxell get out. She pulled the hood of the raincoat over her head and straightened the rest of the coat to make sure it covered the one-piece swimming suit. Angie exited the car, and the three of them rushed into the garage. They hurried into the antechamber and through the door to the cell. Wolf shut the door behind them.

All three heaved in air, catching their breaths.

Maxell glanced around the austere room.

Wolf glowered at her. "Not the greatest ten-day accommodations for an innocent kid."

Maxell diverted her eyes to the floor. "No. Not at all."

"Better get used to it," Angie said. "Your cell will probably be smaller."

She gave Angie a poisonous glance and then faced the closet door. "Do you have the key on you?"

"Of course," Wolf said. "Nobody asked for it, so I didn't volunteer to hand it to them." He fished the key out of his pocket, stepped to the door, inserted it into the deadbolt and clanked the lock back. Opening the door, he swooped his hand like a doorman at a ritzy hotel.

Maxell entered and walked straight to the safe. She knelt and began working the combination. After a half minute of turning the wheel counterclockwise and clockwise, back and forth, back and forth, she pulled the heavy door open and stood. She leaned, reached in a pulled out a plastic DVD case.

"Stand back," Wolf commanded. "I want to see what else is in there.

"There's nothing else in there." She stepped up to the TV.

He grabbed her arm, yanked her out of the way, and checked the safe. Empty. Standing, he said, "Please don't let my lack of faith offend you. It's just that I don't trust snakes."

She glared at him. "Do you want to see the video or not?"

"I don't want to watch every athlete or movie star on there doing the four-legged Foxtrot with some teenager. Pick out a big name to impress me."

She turned on the TV, opened the case, and slid the DVD into the player. With the remote she brought up the index menu and scrolled to a video labeled King Tut. On the screen a young girl in a flimsy nightgown crawled into bed with an older man. He peeled the nightgown over her head and ran his hand down the slope of her bare back.

Wolf leaned closer to the screen. "Isn't that . . . Isn't . . . that . . ."

"Yes," Maxell said. "The former President of the United States."

Chapter 25

As Wolf and Angie exited the sheriff's office, Deputy Rob Duncan and his brunette partner stepped out of the white Bronco and shut the doors. The deputy stopped at the bottom of the steps and waited for Wolf and Angie to descend.

"What are you two doing here?" he asked.

"You'll never guess who we found," Wolf said.

"Elaine Maxell?"

Wolf nodded.

"Where did you find her?"

"Lost Lake Lane," Angie said, "near where Jennifer Cobb lives."

"What was she doing there?" the brunette asked.

"Hiding in the shadows," Wolf said.

Angie pointed to the office door. "She's in there with her lawyer trying to cut a deal."

"Don't they all?" Deputy Duncan sneered.

"She's got the cards to do it," Wolf said.

The brunette straightened. "Really."

"And a lot of those cards have familiar faces." Wolf slapped Angie's back. "C'mon partner, it's been a long day. Let's go home."

"I'm all for that."

"We'll see you two around." Deputy Duncan gave a half salute.

Wolf grinned. "If we don't see around, we'll see you square."

Angie shook her head. "You are one corny sonovabitch, but I love ya anyway."

* * *

The ride home was quiet until they passed the Farmer's Daughter in Duck. The same yellow sundress hung off the shoulders of a faceless mannequin outside the store.

Angie glanced out the side window as they passed. "She wore that same dress for ten days."

"Living in that cell had to be hell."

"And you're making a rhyme of it?"

"I'm serious," Wolf said. "It had to be a living hell, not knowing what was going to happen."

"It was a true test of faith."

"The valley of the shadow of death."

"She made it through, though. What a special young lady."

"You made it through the last few days, too," Wolf said. "I think you're a special young lady."

"I'd have to disagree. I had a difficult time facing those gory scenes. I don't think I'll ever get used to it. I don't know how the EMT people do it day after day."

"No sane person likes to see carnage, blood and death. You faced up to it and didn't run away. That takes courage."

"I felt like running away."

"We all feel like running away. Those who hang in there and do their job, despite their feelings, keep the foundations of society from crumbling."

Angie smiled. "I think that's the deepest thing I've ever heard you say."

"I'm no Pluto or Paristotle, but I have some deep thoughts."

"Oh, you're a Pluto alright."

When they passed the Jolly Rodger in Kill Devil Hills, Wolf said, "I really feel bad for Mel Bianco."

"It takes a long time to absorb the pain of losing someone you love."

"Yeah." Wolf inhaled and let it our audibly. "The pain of loss is like the ocean. It comes in waves. To get through it, you better learn how to swim."

"There you go," Angie said. "Two deep thoughts in one day."

"I better quit before my brain explodes."

After Angie dropped Wolf off in front of his bungalow, he noticed Mel's Malibu and Freyja's Renegade parked in her driveway. He decided to take a quick shower, freshen up and then stop over to see if Freyja wanted to grab something to eat. He checked his watch: 6:06. His stomach rumbled. He imagined a thick T-bone, baked potato and salad.

The shower renewed his energy. He looked forward to being with Freyja. He'd marry the woman if she'd say yes. *Am I crazy? I've known her for three days. Does love have a waiting period like purchasing a firearm? She probably thinks it does.*

He put on a pair of green cargo shorts and a black t-shirt with the Wolf-and-Stallone logo. He slipped into his sandals and grabbed his keys, phone and wallet off the dresser. Stepping out on the front porch, he glanced to his right. The Malibu was still there, but the Renegade was gone.

Maybe she went for some take out. I'm sure they're both hungry. He sat down on the steps. As the minutes slipped by, disappointment seeped into his gut. *Maybe I should go over and ask Mel where she went. Naw. Mel's probably sleeping.* He checked his watch: 7:03. *Crap! Another lonely Saturday night.*

He decided to get into his car and go for a drive. At the end of East Hunter Street, he turned left onto Old Oregon Inlet Road. He drove a couple miles and turned left onto Route 12. The sun lit the clouds above the western horizon with a brilliant array of yellows and oranges that faded into the dying blue dome of the sky.

After another mile, he made a right onto Bodie Island Lighthouse Road. He drove past the lighthouse. On the far turn he saw Freyja's olive-green Renegade parked on the berm. He pulled up behind it and cut the engine. *She left without me. Maybe she wanted to be alone. Maybe she's not in love with me.*

He walked toward the sound and saw her facing the sunset. He cut through the few bushes and tall grass to the clearing and stepped up beside her.

She gazed at the sun as its bottom edge kissed the horizon. "I've been waiting for you."

"Why didn't you stop by and get me."

"I wanted to see if you would come."

"I'm here."

She reached and grasped his hand. "I'm leaving tomorrow."

"What?"

"You heard me."

"You can't."

"Why not?"

"Because I . . . I . . ."

"Is it that hard to say?"

"I love you. There, I said it."

"I know you love me."

"Are you going to say it back to me?"

She kept her eyes on the horizon. "Do I have to?"

"No."

"Then I will. I love you."

Wolf felt suddenly elated. "It feels good to hear it."

She squeezed his hand. "You already knew that I loved you."

"Not really. I'm not that good at knowing what love is. I don't know if I've ever been in love. There've been lots of woman." He patted his chest. "But this spot right here has been empty."

She leaned her head against his chest. "Love warms us, fills us, gives us life and creates beauty."

"I wish I could lasso it and put it in my pocket."

"You can't capture it. Once you do, it's no longer free."

"Why do you have to leave tomorrow?"

"I'm following Mel back up to New Jersey. She's had a tough go of it. I want to spend some time with her."

"I guess that's what love is, huh?"

She pulled him closer. "That's what love does."

"When are you coming back?"

"Soon."

"Angie told me to treasure the times we've shared, focus on the now and keep low expectations for the future."

"Angie is a wise young lady."

"So let's focus on the now. What would you like to do right now?"

The sun, a blazing semi-circle on the horizon, sent yellow rays into the clouds, blending yellows into oranges into reds into crimsons. Above the splendid colors the dome of the sky faded from blue to violet.

She leaned and kissed his cheek. "Let's share the sunset."

THE END

I hope you enjoyed THE SINGER IN THE SOUND. If you did, please post a rating and review on Amazon.com.

Weston Wolf Outer Banks Detective Series

These are stand-alone novels and can be read in any order.

Book 1 – Roanoke Island Murders

Book 2 – The Singer in the Sound

Book 3 – Kitty Hawk Confidential (August 2021)

Outer Banks Murder Series

These are stand-alone novels and can be read in any order.

The Healing Place (Prequel to Murder at Whalehead)
Book 1 – Murder at Whalehead
Book 2 – Murder at Hatteras
Book 3 – Murder on the Outer Banks
Book 4 – Murder at Ocracoke
Book 5 – The Treasure of Portstmouth Island
Outer Banks Murder Series 5-Book Set

Other Books

The Old Man and the Marathon
A Running Novel

The First Shall Be Last
A World War II Novel

The Christmas Monkey
A Children's Book

About the Author

Joe C. Ellis, a big fan of the North Carolina's Outer Banks, grew up in the Ohio Valley. A native of Martins Ferry, Ohio, he attended West Liberty State College in West Virginia and went on to earn his Master's Degree in education from Muskingum College in New Concord, Ohio. After a thirty-six year career as an art teacher, he retired from the Martins Ferry City School District.

Currently, he is the pastor for the Scotch Ridge Presbyterian Church and the Colerain Presbyterian Church. His writing career began in 2001 with the publication of his first novel, *The Healing Place*. In 2007 he began the *Outer Banks Murder Series* with the publication of *Murder at Whalehead* (2010), *Murder at Hatteras* (2011), *Murder on the Outer Banks* (2012), *Murder at Ocracoke* (2017), and the latest installment, *The Treasure of Portsmouth Island* (2019).

Joe credits family vacations on the Outer Banks with the inspiration for his stories. Joe and his wife Judy have three children and eight grandchildren. Although the kids have flown the nest, they get together often and always make it a priority to vacation on the Outer Banks whenever possible. He comments, "It's a place on the edge of the world, a place of great beauty and sometimes danger—the ideal setting for murder mysteries.

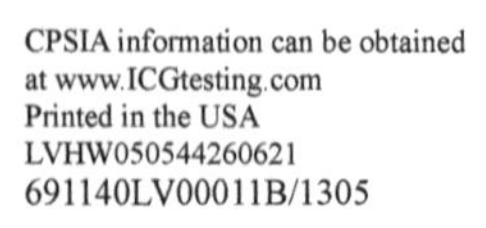

CPSIA information can be obtained
at www.ICGtesting.com
Printed in the USA
LVHW050544260621
691140LV00011B/1305

9 780979 665554